FIT THE CRIME

The Innocence Lie

CORINNE ARROWOOD

Published by Corinne Arrowood
United States of America
www.corinnearrowood.com

ISBN: 979-8-9873642-3-9 (eBook)
ISBN: 979-8-9873642-4-6 (Trade Paperback)
ISBN: 979-8-9873642-5-3 (Hardcover)

Cover and Interior Design by Cyrusfiction Productions.

TABLE OF CONTENTS

A Special Note

The statistics of PTSD are staggering. Many of our Marines and soldiers come home entrenched in the horrors they experienced and the nightmares they cannot escape. If you know one of our heroes that might be suffering from PTSD, contact Wounded Warrior Project, National Center for PTSD, VA Caregiver Support Line at 888-823-7458.

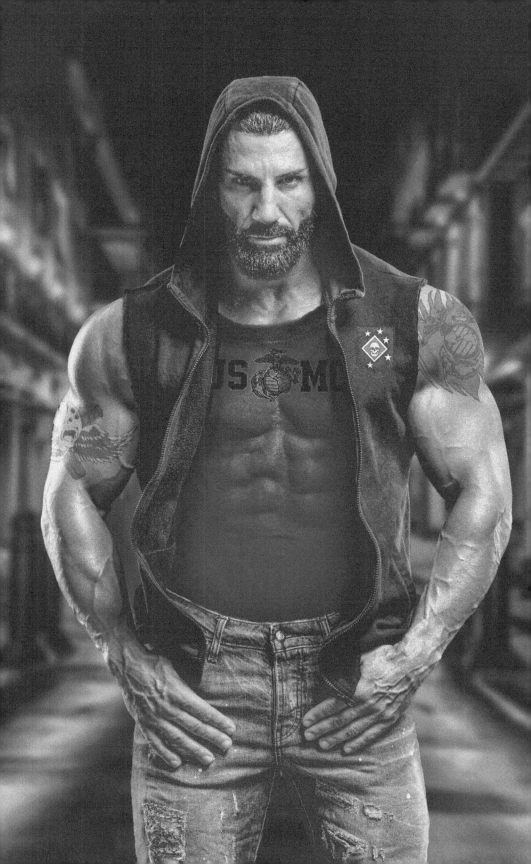

PROLOGUE

The room had the same plain eggshell walls he'd seen in all the other offices. Centrally located on the far end of the room was the military-issue nondescript brown wooden desk; behind it, a picture of the President, a Marine flag in one corner, and an American flag in the other. Behind the desk on the credenza were a few personal photos; otherwise, it was spotless, Marine standard. Indeed. He stood in front of the desk at attention, waiting for instructions.

Commander Deary, a spry fifty-something with dashing silver hair and steel-colored eyes, looked up at his Marine and spoke, "We go back too far; I'm not going to mince words. Are you sure about your decision, son? You've got, what, ten-eleven years? Civilian life isn't meant for everyone, Vicarelli. You've been a model officer, a true Corps leader, and a force to be reckoned with for your country. Take a load off, Marine." The Commander pointed to one of two chairs before his desk.

As ordered, he sat, cleared his throat, and spoke, "I've completed all the requirements for separation, sir." The Commander put up his hand and stopped him.

"I'm aware you've crossed all your t's and dotted your i's. I wouldn't have expected anything less from you. It concerns me that life outside the Corps may not be as fulfilling as you think." He set his jaw with a slight jut, squared his eyes, and looked deeply concerned. "Think twice."

The Marine drew a deep breath making his chest swell and rise, letting the air out slowly. "All due respect, Commander, I've given my best to the

1

Corps; now I'm all out of my best, and I won't serve as mediocre. I'm sure you understand, sir." Their conversation concluded with the Commander wishing his Marine the best of life.

It was time; he knew it was. He remembered the operation that took the edge off his best. The day after completing the assignment, upon returning to base camp, he began the more than-year-long separation process. His heart was heavy with the thought of all the mundane but required steps his departure from the Corps demanded. As quickly as possible, he applied for the Complete Individualized Counseling Session and Pre-Separation Counseling Brief. As suspected, it would be a full year plus before steps to leave would gain any traction. He'd never been a social or chatty individual; he was more private to himself than most and knew it, which others sometimes found unsettling, especially the psych community.

There were many nights he stewed on his decision weighing the pros and cons. Truth be told, he knew very little about being an adult in a civilian world. In one of his thoughtful moments, he imagined a civilian life, but this montage of ideology had a dark cast filled with odd-man-out and loneliness. He erased the bleakness and concentrated on the good which lightened his heart. There had been fun times before the Corps; it wasn't all bad. A smile came to his face remembering his high school days, then his mind set on graduation. The only people that ever showed interest were his grandfather, his mom when able, and Coach Kennedy, his wrestling coach.

Jack Kennedy was a Marine veteran and the big inspiration behind the decision to join the Marines. They kept in touch throughout his college days and through law school. The man was a hero, and still, at his age, maybe in his late fifties, could put anyone down. He was a powerhouse, and though only five-nine, he had brute strength like a grizzly bear with the agility of a cheetah; with that came earned respect or an ass beating.

Then there was his mother, Anna. She was not only movie star beautiful and striking with naturally platinum blonde hair and pool-blue eyes, but statuesque at five-eleven. For such a solidly built person, she allowed his son-of-a-bitch father to reduce her to a shadow of herself. On occasion, she would attend his wrestling competitions, but usually not. Farfar, the Norwegian term for grandfather, was his mom's dad, who almost always occupied a seat. Thinking of his grandfather brought a sense of warmth to his heart. Being the closest male, he was the go-to person regarding life, and all that came with it, including the unfair hands dealt.

The relationship with Coach was different, and while an influential factor in his life, the young man didn't speak much, sharing an acknowledgment or nod of the head. But, he listened intently to Coach, taking in all the minute details and nuances—like eye contact, posturing, and careful word selection. All were qualities he assumed of a Marine, something he might be one day.

His tenth grade year was the first time he remembered crying since being ten. His grandmother, a tender, caring, and loving woman, passed. Being quiet by nature, he didn't often speak with her, and perhaps he now had regrets about that, but his heart fluttered, and he felt a decisive lump choke his throat whenever he thought about her. She was one for pearls of wisdom, whether sought or not like she read what was on his mind. He'd politely accept her advice with a one-sided smile and slight nod and then store the thought away for use as needed.

On a wrestling scholarship, he attended college and went on to Law School, as suggested by his grandfather, but once all schooling was said and done, his longing remained to join the Marines, like Coach Kennedy. He wanted to be part of something greater than himself with purpose. The Corps was where he belonged, and he served with excellence. After ten and some years, he felt he'd given his best and began the arduous year-plus task of separating. While it tore at his heart, and he was conflicted, he knew it was the best thing; it was time to hand it off to someone younger.

Once discharged from the Marines, he returned to New Orleans. The first stop was his grandfather's; he strolled up to the home on Chestnut Street, duffle in hand. Many a night, he'd slept with his mother in the stately old home. Rune Johansen, his mother's father, opened the beveled glass door before his grandson stepped to the front porch. Age had crept up on the man, which was alarming. Like most people, when he was younger, he never thought about his grandfather aging as the years passed. The older man was still with a tall, straight back and powerful embrace. "Come in, come in, my Sonnesonn. Look at you, such a handsome specimen." The Marine couldn't help but chuckle with a slight rumble in his throat.

"Farfar, I look like pictures of you when you were my age, just with darker hair," his grandson replied while squinting and tapping the side of his head. "I still remember," and he winked.

The homecoming was all he hoped it would be, with a fine meal and a few beverages. "I sent word to your great uncle Bjorn in Trondelag that I needed something reminiscent of home for when you returned from war. Arrived just in time." His grandfather went into the kitchen and came back with four bottles, two in each hand. He passed one to him, an amber-colored bottle with a bright green label and red band emblazoned with STJORDAL boldly across the front. "Let us drink to your well-being, and we must talk. I want to hear about your adventures; I know the darkness of war and am not prying into those blistered parts of your heart. It's been two years since our last brief meeting, I believe, and still, I see the silence festers in you. Maybe one day you will find the right woman, like my Astrid, rest her soul, and your heart will melt freeing your words."

They sat across from one another, feeling the time lost and aching for more time together. "I'm sorry, Farfar, that I couldn't come for my mother's funeral, but she and I had a few moments on my last leave here. She didn't look well, and I knew her day was coming sooner than later. At least she doesn't have to see G—"

4

"Don't mention that name, ever." His face turned crimson, and the deep grooves on his face soured even more. "I should have killed that man for what he did to my precious Anna, but she begged me not to interfere. No more talk of him." With an abrupt movement of his hand, he sliced the air.

The younger man took a few full swigs from his bottle. "And you? Are you well?"

"Tch." He beat a fist on his chest. "Do I look well?" He looked the younger man directly in his eyes as he took a long draw on his beverage, then let out an impressive belch. "I still belch like a young man but fart like an old codger," and laughed. "I can go in peace now that I've laid my aging eyes on you."

"Nothing to dampen the atmosphere, Far." The younger man relaxed back in the chair with a melancholy smile.

"Nonsense, death is just the next landing on the journey. Now let's eat before the meal loses its temperature, and Ruthie will have to put it to heat. Now that you are here, maybe she will leave." He put a finger to his lips and whispered, "She helps with the cleaning and cooking but is a pain in my arse. I long for the time each night that she departs. Nice woman, and she has been a benefit, but you are here now." The older guy beamed with pride.

They sat at the ten-foot dining table. "Ruthie, is it? What happened to June?" The older man rolled his eyes.

"Too much to tell. I think June expected more than to be my housekeeper." He raised his wiry white eyebrows. "Good riddance, I say. But on a serious note, everything I have is yours when I go, says so in my Living Revocable Trust, a document my financial advisor suggested instead of the usual Last Will. But until then," he chuckled with a gravelly rumble, "you can live here with me."

The younger closed his eyes, settling his voice for what he knew would be a dispute. Looking directly ahead, he took a few mouthfuls of food and swigs of his bottle while the older man concentrated on cutting his meat and looking at the plate as though willing the food to move into his mouth. "I'll stay until I can get a place and buy a vehicle, probably a truck. My benefits are good enough to rent something small in the French Quarter. That way, I'll be around people, and maybe it will be easier to acclimate to civilian life. From what the counselors told me, solitude isn't good, nor is having someone assume my bills and real-world responsibilities. No offense and I appreciate the offer. At least I know I have a place I can go to get away from all the noise. We can plan on a meal once a week if that's alright?" He watched as the elder struggled to cut his meat. "Here, let me help."

His grandfather showed signs of agitation. He looked up from his plate, eyes wide open as if in shock. "Am I seeing things, or is it truly you, Sonnesonn? Where did you come from?" He slightly bowed his head with his eyes cast downward with sadness. "Sonnesonn, I have hard news to tell you." A tear came to his eyes, and he sniffled. "Your mother has passed, darling boy." The need for a busybody housekeeper became evident; she was his caretaker. He swallowed hard as he looked at the older man.

"I know, Farfar. It is sad, and I'm sorry I missed the funeral, but she and I spoke on my last leave."

The night's veil drew closer; the darker it became, the more abstract his grandfather's thoughts were. They turned in for the night, and the question was, which version would he face in the morning? Perhaps if his grandfather were lucid, he'd take him on an outing. The Marine had only a few changes of clothing, a cell phone, some photos, and toiletries, so he set his agenda for the following day—purchasing a truck and finding an apartment while perusing the French Quarter. He bet it had been some time since his grandfather had been out of the house, and an adventure as such might spark the neurons. Just as he needed interaction with civilians, so too did his grandfather.

Morning came, and when he went down to the kitchen, his grandfather was up and dressed. It was five, and the sun was breaking for a new day. The old guy seemed chipper and full of life, hardly the man he'd put to bed the night before. "Good morning, young man. How about some coffee, and then when Ruthie gets here, she can fix us a breakfast meant for royalty. Don't ever think you're too old to hug me." The two were of equal size, although the younger had audaciously defined and well-developed musculature.

Patting his grandfather on the back, "I'd like coffee, thank you, black. How would you like to go with me to buy a truck and then go on a quest in the French Quarter? You can help me find a place to lease; how about it?" His grandfather perked up with a spark on his face and a spring in his step.

"Wonderful. I hope you get one of those big trucks with some umph. Large fellas like ourselves need a well-built vehicle. Sonnesonn, you are a strapping specimen. You know there was a time when rarely a man would buck up to me." He had a sparkle in his eyes. "I need to read my paper and take my constitutional after this cup of coffee."

"Very well then. I hope you don't mind if I do some exercise and take a run." He looked at his watch. "By that time, your housekeeper will be here."

Donning his running shoes and togs, he headed out the front door and took to the street with a fast-paced jog. Rolling in his mind, he could hear the Commander's voice. *Vicarelli, civilian life isn't meant for everyone.* He'd heard the horror stories of vets lacking coping mechanisms, not accustomed to a no-schedule kind of existence. He'd have to establish a routine; the sooner, the better. Not that he didn't love his grandfather, but he couldn't be a caretaker, and he didn't want to interrupt the routine of the house; he knew that wasn't good for older people, either. The planned activities for the day may even be too much; he'd check with Ruthie when she arrived.

He'd nail down as much as he could. First: the truck; Second: an apartment; Third: hopefully a job. It would be a whirlwind kind of day.

All set, with Ruthie's blessing, they called an Uber and went to a Ford dealership. The first truck on the lot was a slightly used year-old Ford two fifty with low mileage. *Perfect.* He checked off the first thing on his mental list marking it as accomplished. He loaded his grandfather in the truck; the smile on the older man's face was priceless. "We look like kings in this giant wooly mammoth. Well done." The younger man shook his head and sniffed out a soft laugh.

As they turned onto Dauphine in the French Quarter, plain as day was a FOR LEASE sign. They found a parking spot and called the phone number on the sign. The woman who answered was pleased to meet them at a moment's notice. The place was small, having one bedroom and living space with a matchbox kitchen, but the bathroom had recently been renovated and had a massive shower made of marble and glass—most importantly, it was tall enough for him. Item number two on the list, check. He signed a year lease which she would prorate so he could move in anytime. He said it would be at least a week. She commented that she was more than happy to assist him in finding furniture and showing him around the city.

Judging from the flirtatious glances from Denise, the real estate agent, he knew she'd be helpful in more ways than one. She was probably ten years older than him, with a head full of curly dark hair and green eyes. The body could've used some work, but it looked like some had already been updated. It might be nice to have female company, especially getting into his new digs. He casually mentioned looking for work, and low and behold, it just so happened she knew someone that worked for a construction company, and he hired vets. She wrote down the address on her business card.

After arranging a date with her later that week, they headed out of the Quarter and crossed Esplanade into the Faubourg Marigny. Sure enough, the super on the site had an affinity for vets, and he was offered a job on the spot. *This is too good to be true, beware!*

GIVEN NAME

The air was heavy, like a damp blanket in a musty old attic. It wasn't just the humidity on the hot New Orleans night. No, that merely served to exaggerate the worn atmosphere inside Louie's Tap. The centuries-old mahogany bar stretched more than halfway down the side of the establishment, giving plenty of elbow room for the nightly visitors looking for a strong drink and maybe some company for the night, preferably not the ones working for cash. The French doors along the front wrapped around the side street and were propped open in hopes of catching a slight but unlikely breeze. The stagnant air slowly lingered in, with the occasional waft of ripened piss and vomit piercing the pungent stench of stale booze and decades of bar grunge.

The redeeming factor that brought him in night after night was Trinity. His body longed for hers even though they had barely shared a word. Quiet and always unobtrusive, he took his nightly seat at the end of the bar, where he could observe the interaction of people. There was a constant stream of stories if one were to take notice. Wedding band or not, it was easy to detect who was tiptoeing along the tightrope of infidelity. Young studs would strut like peacocks trying to allure naïve girls eating up the attention but unaware of the intention at heart, and then the working girls, they were not as obvious as one might suspect. Everyone had a story, and with his years in Marine special ops, he could size up situations and people a bit better than the next guy. Still, his ever-present awareness was always on Trinity.

She was tiny but fit, with a glow to her glistening roped arms, perfectly cut back, and tight round ass—just watching her lean into the voices to hear a drink order compensating for the louder-than-background music heightened his pulse. Her caramel-colored skin and jet-black locks, usually braided to the side, lightly brushed along her waist, exaggerating her intense raw sex appeal. Now and then, he'd catch a flash of her almond-shaped ebony eyes, which roused his soul. As the night progressed and the music picked up pace, she'd swing and sway to the tunes. It was enough to raise his temperature and create an uncomfortable tightness in his jeans that required the occasional adjustment; nonetheless, he watched over the top of his tumbler of scotch. The two-finger pour was enough to last him hours. He sat observing every detail like a lion stalking in wait for his prey—statue still, the only movement was his eyes.

Either he had a neon sign over his head that said do not approach, or he didn't have the look of someone wishing to be bothered. Either way, it was just as well. If it was action he desired, the assortment was ripe for the picking; all he had to do was lend one of his coy smiles, and it was as though he'd snapped his fingers or waved a hundred-dollar bill. In a blink, there would be someone to satisfy his every desire.

When the bar was down a cocktail waitress or two, Trinity would walk the drinks to the tables, sometimes passing next to him, close enough to catch the fragrance of her perfume combined with her delicious natural scent. He nursed his drink the entire night, watching, desiring, hoping for an organic conversation to develop, but other than ordering his beverage, she was consumed with pouring concoctions for the other guests. His mind began to wander as he watched her work.

Before learning about the offerings of plate dinners at Louie's, he'd pick up a muffuletta or grab dinner at a cheap café. Nearly a month into civilian life, the Marine stopped by the café for grub. As he unwrapped his sandwich, sitting at a table outside the hole-in-the-wall eatery, a disheveled man with a dirty dog started walking in his direction, stopping everyone he passed for a hand-out. The big guy knew what it was to feel hungry, so as the man approached him, he gave him half his sandwich. The man looked at him with disgust. "I don't want no fucking sandwich; how 'bout a fiver?" The ungrateful S.O.B. dropped the sandwich on the ground, and the dog, undoubtedly starving, started to chow down. The man kicked the dog in the gut, making it yelp. Then he hit him on the side of his head, "Shut up."

"Five dollars, you say? Follow me; I got it in the garage." The big guy stood, looked down at the pathetic excuse for a man, and walked toward an open but vacant building. The man followed him in. The big man began to put his hand in his pocket but came back with a roundhouse to the wretched man's jaw and then kicked him in the gut. Although enormous and built, he was still agile, flexible, and trained in combat fighting of every kind. "How'd that feel, tough guy? Treat your dog better." The man pulled a knife from his pocket and slashed through the air. "Nice try, asshole," he said with a sarcastic chuckle, then kicked the weapon out of the man's hand and, in a split second, had the man's arm behind his back as he cranked it toward his neck. The crack was unmistakable as the derelict bum let out a yelp similar to his dog's when kicked.

"You broke my fuckin' arm." He whined.

"Mister, you're lucky that's all I broke. Now get the fuck outta here with your nasty pitiful self. Don't come 'round here again. Next time I'll break a lot more than your arm."

The Marine drew in a deep breath, and inside he felt a sense of pride. He controlled himself; the docs would call it progress. His instinct was to snap the guy's neck and do a favor to the world, but he could make a point without taking a life. Next time, if the man showed his face, the game would be on, and he'd show no mercy. Picking up the leash, he walked back to where he'd been eating, let the dog finish the pieces left on the ground, and walked toward Louie's. Maybe someone there might want the mutt.

The memory of that encounter ended, and his mind was back to watching the sweet Creole blossom. She moved to the music, making the customers smile. She teased back and forth with some of the old-timers. It was all in good taste and fun; then, the lively, enjoyable times turned into loud, obnoxious noise from a group of people that entered. Their presence sullied the atmosphere.

His eyes focused on the collective, obviously college kids with little to no self-control. As usual, the kids were boisterous and drippy with outlandish trolling. He rolled his eyes at the ridiculous behavior. The boys were eager to say anything to get inside the pants of the young girls. They would have been better served to cough up a hundred bucks and get a guaranteed ride of a lifetime. It didn't take long for one of the boys to venture where he wasn't welcome, and that was Trinity.

"Hey, sweet cheeks, pour me a Maker's n'coke, and don't skimp on the Maker's, darlin'." She smiled, and as she turned, the boy had the rakish audacity to swat her on the rear. She struck lightning fast like a cobra with squinted eyes and a look that screamed to back off. The young man put up his hands in surrender, "Sorry, I didn't mean to offend. Thought you might take it as a compliment." The look of disgust on her face said it all. "I see; I was mistaken. Too bad, you have no idea what you're missing," and he grabbed his crotch. The boy handed her a fifty to pay for his fourteen-dollar drink.

Trinity pocketed the money. "Thanks for the tip," and she grinned with a look of satisfaction.

"Um, where's my change?" She smiled. He turned up his hands, hunching his shoulders in question. "Bitch."

She scoffed with a hand on her hip, "You touched, you pay. That's the way it works around here, boy." It was a moment that brought on an inward chuckle for the observer. She got her revenge, although he would've liked to kick the boy's ass. It would only take the slightest effort—a solid strike on the jaw, and he'd be out like a light. People with audacity didn't deserve even a smile from her luscious full lips. The boy made the right decision; he licked his wounds and walked away. The Marine stared into the amber Glenlivet, giving it a gentle swirl.

Now that the amusement was over, his mind started with monologues from past training, rambling and consuming his present thought as a dream with flickering images. They said he might have PTSD, but he was stronger than some cheap alphabet diagnosis. He was quiet and didn't pour out feelings, which the counselors didn't like, so they had to conjure some malady. He had seen and subdued others struggling in combat; he knew what the diagnosis meant, and it didn't apply in his case. *Once a Marine, always a Marine.*

The deep bark of his no-nonsense drill instructor began in his head. *When it comes down to it, it's you or them. You must stay laser-focused at all times; one wrong move and you or someone on the unit gets erased. You are a deadly weapon deployed on command. There is no time for doubt. Kill or be killed, fight or die, we chose you, the best of the best, to carry out the impossible. It is yours to execute to perfection; nothing else will do. Do you understand me? A pause indicated instruction over. Ooh-rah!* He forcefully growled.

"*Ooh-rah!*" the company of Marines answered with purpose.

The orders echoed in the hollows of his mind, almost reminding him every day and, depending on his stress level, multiple times a day. He was at the top of his game, which gave him the ability to fight for those too weak to fight, punish those that needed punishment, and kill those unworthy of life. Although his special op days had ended, he felt obligated to continue the mission until he drew his last breath. There were just as many, if not more, enemies on the streets of New Orleans, invisible to the untrained eye.

A hand snapped in front of his face. He looked over at the smile that sparked his way. "Hey, Cutie, want another drink?" Her smile melted his heart.

"No, ma'am, I'm good, thank you." He could feel his cheeks warm as he returned the smile with a shy upturn on one side of his lips. He had a hard time grasping these new feelings. He wasn't supposed to feel; they trained him to be stoic, with no time for emotion, but her smile reduced him to putty.

"You been comin' up to my bar for a few months, and you've never said anything but," she altered her voice with a deep male resonance, "two fingers Glenlivet, ma'am." He tilted his head to the side, raised his glass, toasting the air, and drew a sip, staring at her from atop the rim. "You got a name, sweetheart?" she asked with one hand on her cocked hip in a sassy, playful manner.

"Babe." His mouth upturned on one side again, waiting for the usual remark, 'Like the pig?' *Fucking ridiculous name for a pig.*

"Seriously, Babe? That's your given name or nickname, cuz I can see why women might call you babe." She arched an eyebrow, pursing her lips while rocking her head. He felt his cheeks flush even brighter, and he chuckled slightly.

"Yes, ma'am. My name given at birth was Babe."

"Well, it's nice to meet you, Babe; I'm Trinity." Her eyes twinkled beneath a fringe of lashes.

"Yes, ma'am. Nice to officially meet you. By the way, do you want a dog? " His furry friend remained at his feet as though commanded. He'd trained the pooch well, and they'd been companions of sorts since the departure of his owner a couple of months before, but the dog needed a real home.

One of the rowdy spring breakers banged his empty beer mug on the bar. She turned, then looked back at Babe and winked. "That's my cue," and off she went. The guy was a friend of the fifty-dollar jackass. Looking in that direction, he noticed the jackass hitting on one of the girls. She pushed him away, turned her back, walked to her friend, a dark-haired girl, and whispered something. The two girls were obviously in disagreement, but the quiet blonde reluctantly nodded and succumbed with a forced smile. *Cute girl,* he thought. Then another of the boys whispered in her ear. This time she slapped him and headed to the restroom, thoroughly disgusted, almost running into the busser, who contorted himself to avoid smacking into her.

Babe doubted anybody else noticed the interaction except the busser, who was still reeling, trying to maintain his balance. Mr. Fifty-Dollar Fool raised suspicions for the Marine. He'd been around enough pompous assholes, but something didn't ring true with this sack of shit. He wreaked entitlement and misguided intentions. Somebody needed to put him down like a rabid dog. The too-full-of-themselves usually got their comeuppance, and sometimes he was the one to help it along.

Slowly the crowd dissipated with young couples peeling off two by two. All that was left was the fifty-dollar jerk and seemingly sweet girl with the dirty-blonde hair and deep, perfectly symmetrical dimples accompanying her warm smile. She briefly spoke to the busser as he took her empty glass, and she turned to walk out. Babe noticed the busser quickly clocked out, grabbed a top shirt, and ran behind her.

Another night in Louie's Tap had come to an end, so Babe got up and left with his four-legged friend, leaving ten dollars on the bar for sweet Trinity.

THE BUSSER

"*G*otcha pepperoni and six-pack." Tiny squeaks betrayed the nervous excitement in his already quaked voice as he juggled a six-pack of beer, extra-large pizza, and a thirty-two-ounce Sprite. He'd never been the guy who attracted the pretty girl, and yet, here he was, invited to her hotel room. She'd already delivered a helluva kiss when she sent him out for pizza and beer. He reveled in the thought she chose him, a busser from the Irish Channel.

She hid beneath the covers as he entered the room. Setting everything on the table, he tiptoed to the side of the bed and pulled lightly on the sheets, fully expecting a high-pitched squeal. Nothing could've prepared him for the paled face and empty clouded eyes. "Jessica!" He shook her body which rocked from his shake but nothing more. He shook her a couple more times. Putting his hand beneath her nose, he hoped for a slight breath of life, then felt for a pulse, but nothing. He backed away from her, completely bewildered. He'd been gone thirty minutes at the most.

The way the covers draped her body made it look like she had intended to startle him by surprise or play some flirty game, but she was dead. His heart pounded like a sledgehammer against the pavement. He did the only thing he knew to do; he pulled the covers back over her face like he'd seen in movies and called his mother. It was late, and he knew a call from him at a late hour would send her into a panic, but she was the only one he knew to call.

On the third ring, she picked up. "Finn, what's the matter?" He had woken her up, and indeed she sounded panicked. This time she had every reason.

"Ma, I don't know what to do. I met a girl at the bar, and she invited me to her room—"

"Sean Finnegan, how many times I—"

"Ma, she's dead!" The pause was deafening. "Ma?" He could feel his pulse storming his body in a rage from the tips of his toes, up to his legs, to his heart, and any minute it felt like his head would explode jack-o-lantern-M80 style.

"Jesus, Mary, and Joseph. Sean, who's there b'sides you?"

"Nobody."

"Nobody? What y'all doin' in that hotel room that she should die? What happened?"

"I dunno. She asked me to go for a pizza and beer and come straight back, so I went. I come back, and she's dead. I was only gone a half-hour."

"Where you at?"

"Hotel Noelle."

"I'm on my way, but you gotta call the police. Sean, nothing else you gotta tell me? Y'all using drugs? You had intercourse with her?"

"No, Ma. What do I say to the police?"

"Exactly what you told me. You sure you ain't done nothin' wrong?"

"No, nothing. I swear." Beads of sweat formed along his upper lip, and his wringing wet armpits left huge circles on his shirt.

"Let the hotel people know, too. This is a sorry state of affairs. Poor girl. I'm on my way, baby." She hung up the phone.

His mind rambled. Thoughts zinging through his mind. *Who to call first? The hotel? The police?* He debated back and forth. Finally, he picked up the hotel phone and asked for the manager. The front desk seemed put out and took their time. Meanwhile, he used his cell and called the police.

"911 operator. What's your emergency?"

"I'm in a hotel room with a dead girl."

"Excuse me? Did you say you have a dead girl in your room?" The operator's voice seemed to go up an octave.

"It's not my room. I'm in her room. I went to get pizza, and when I got back, she was dead."

"Who am I speaking with?" The operator calmly asked.

"Finn. Look, I dunno what happened. I didn't do anything."

"Finn, the police are on the way. You're at Hotel Noelle? What room?"

"Yes, room two-o-six—" His voice felt shaky and hesitant.

With the other phone to his ear, an irritated voice came on the line. "This is the Manager. How can I be of assistance?" He could tell the guy on the phone was probably rolling his eyes; he had that tone in his voice—an all-too-familiar condescending whine. He'd seen the rolled eyes and pursed lips many times in Louie's, although never at him; he was just a busser.

"Um, I'm in two-o-six, and there's a dead girl in here." Suddenly the game was on. The jerky manager was at attention. "I've already called the police."

"I'll be right there, sir." *Sir? From nuisance to sir just that fast.*

Within minutes the small hotel room was buzzing with official-police-type people. The big question was what had happened. He had no answers. He pointed to the untouched pizza, six-pack, and thirty-two-ounce Sprite attesting to his whereabouts.

The Medical Examiner arrived and pulled at the sheet—it was the first time the covers had been drawn all the way down, and the discovery was alarming. Jess was naked from the waist down. Some bruising had started to form on her body, legs, and arms. Accusatory faces turned to him. *What the hell*, he thought.

A commotion started at the door, and he recognized the voice instantly. "No, you move out the way. That's my boy you got in there." She barreled her way through. She saw the bottomless girl and shot a look his way.

"I dunno, Ma." Finn shrugged his shoulders with upturned hands. "I swear." The police escorted him from the room.

She bustled behind them. "Where you taking him? Where you taking my boy?" She scurried around them and stood in front, blocking the way. "Where?"

"To the stationhouse. Then probably OPP." The officer was none too kind.

The other officer compassionately commented, "Ma'am, only a few blocks over."

Finn's legs felt like spaghetti, as though he'd run a marathon, and the hall looked like something from a funhouse. Everything seemed distorted. Curious faces gathered and gawked as the police led him out. His mother was on the phone hysterically talking with what he figured was his Parran, Liam Finnegan, his late dad's brother.

They loaded him in the back of a squad car. Patti, his mother, grabbed a cab and followed them to the station house.

Once at the station, they put him in a room with a table and three chairs.

A youngish-looking man, maybe early thirties, stepped into the room with a file and a pad. "Finn, is it?"

"Sean Finnegan, but everyone calls me Finn. Where's my mother?" He felt fidgety, his fingers twitching uncontrollably as though there was a keyboard in front of him.

"Finn, I'm Detective Trey Kimble, and I'm the detective on this case. I'm sure you've told your story a few times, but you'll need to explain it to me, okay?" He was trying to be friendly, probably thinking he could loosen him up and the truth would come spilling out, like on TV. There was but one truth, and he'd told it over and over. It wasn't going to change. He went through the story. The whole time the detective nodded and took notes.

"Okay, Finn. I want to start back before going to the hotel room. Paint a picture for me so I can understand."

Finn took in a deep breath and hung his head. A heaviness weighed him down, almost crushing the breath within him like being in a vice grip as it got tighter and tighter. "I work at Louie's as a busser. Jessica, Sloane, and a couple of girls from their sorority came here for spring break. There were some dudes from the same school with them but not with them. I guess wanting to be with them. I was bussing like usual, and I could feel someone lookin' at me, like watching me. I look over, and I see one of the prettiest girls I've ever seen smiling at me. I smiled back but kept working. The eye contact happened a few times during the night. It was getting close to the end of my shift; most everyone had gone. Some of the girls had gone with some of the guys, where I don't know. This one dude keeps bugging the girl named Jessica. She slaps him in the face, runs into the restroom for a few minutes, then comes out and starts to walk off by herself. I punched out quickly and ran to catch up with her. She shouldn't have been by herself. She says, hey, I say hey. I told her I'd walk her to her hotel to make sure she stayed safe. We talked along the way. She told me her name and her friend's names. The only one I remember is Sloane because of Ferris Bueller's Day Off. I know, stupid but true." He laced his hands through his hair and clasped them together in exasperation. A pounding sense of fear and befuddlement grew in his chest.

"Okay, Finn, did you feel like you needed to make sure she was safe all the way to her room?" The detective had a serious expression even though he was being a smart ass.

The walls felt like they were closing in on him, and he was finding it hard to breathe. "Where's my mother?"

"Son, you're over twenty-one. You, my friend, are a grown-ass man and don't get momma. So, who made the move for you to go to her room?" He flipped his pen, going back and forth in a nervous and most aggravating manner.

"She asked me. We'd been playing eye games kinda, but it blew me away when she asked me to her room." He cocked his head to the right like he was done. "Can I get some water or something?"

"Sure. In a minute. Wow, you musta felt like you won the lottery to have this pretty girl invite you to her room. I guess you were looking forward to a roll in the sack." The detective smiled as he tapped his pen on the pad. "What a great piece of ass that was gonna be."

"It wasn't like that. I think she was lonely because everybody else was hookin' up and kinda left her. I think she just wanted to go to her room and figured I'd be company. She invited me in, ordered a pizza, and asked me to get it and a six-pack. I also got my Sprite. And you know the rest of the story."

The detective got up. "I'll get you some water and a Sprite." Back in the interrogation room, he sat staring at Finn, sizing him up but still toying with the pen. Tilting his head to the side, a wry smile formed on his face. "So, Finn." He put the pen to his lips. "When is it that you took her pants off? Before or after she ordered the pizza?" He leaned on the table and looked the boy straight in the eyes. "And did she fight you at first, or was it because she called it quits before the main attraction?"

Finn leaned back in his chair with his hands balled. "Everything you just said is bullshit. I've told you the truth." He thumped his fists on the table, not hard, but it made a thud. "She kissed me when I left to go get the pizza. She was alive when I left." He slugged down some water. Heat began building in his body, surging to his throat. He could taste the acid coming up with the water, and his anger was to the point where he was shaking inside. He felt like the bottle of Sprite sitting on the table. If shaken too much, it would explode, and he felt like this guy was shaking him as hard and fast as he could. He took a deep breath. "Detective Kimble, I don't know who pulled Jessica's pants down. All I can think is somebody went into her room between the time I left and came back. She was a nice girl, and if anything would've happened between us will remain a mystery. She kissed me. That's it."

"With tongue or no tongue?" The detective taunted.

"What? Are you kidding me?" Finn stared him eye to eye with contempt in his voice. "Parted mouth. No tongue. A nice kiss. Enough details about the kiss?" His gut had a steady rolling boil going.

"For now. But I just don't see the attraction. You're what, five-ten, a buck seventy at most? You're decent-looking but nothing to write home about, and this girl invites you into her hotel room? Boy, it was your lucky night. I'd even go as far as to say, a miracle night." He laid his hands flat on the table. "Now, why didn't you ask the girl to go with you for the pizza?"

"Cuz she asked me to go. I dunno why I didn't ask her to go. I thought I was being a good guy doing what she asked."

"Uh-huh." He nodded his head, but he didn't appear to care about an answer. Whatever was swirling around in his mind made him like a dog with a bone; he wasn't letting go. "Make me understand. Tell me again from when you arrived on your shift. Better yet, what about yesterday? Let's start with yesterday. By the way, you date anyone? How's your sex life? You gettin' some?"

Finn felt beaten. He'd answered every question. Now the guy was trying to piss him off. He threw his arms in the air. "I'm done. My life is my business and has nothing to do with this."

Detective Kimble patted the table. "Settle down, settle down." Like a dual personality, the detective switched back to the guy who gave a damn. With a velvet voice, he began again. "I need to get to know you better, Finn. Like, are you a football, basketball, or baseball guy? Are you a Saints fan? Any plans for the future? Do you have a special girl? See, I need to know about you so I can fit all the pieces into the puzzle. You say you didn't do anything to this girl. I want to believe you, but it's hard to figure someone coming in, raping her, and killing her all in the time it took you to pick up a pizza and a six-pack. Finn, I want to believe you. These are some serious charges you could be looking at and a lot of jail time."

The questions seemed endless.

Finn was at this guy's mercy. It was obvious he wasn't letting him go any time soon. "A'right, I'll play. I'm a Saints fan, but who isn't around here? I watch b-ball some; I played some rec baseball. I went to Ben Franklin, yeah, the brainiac school. Maybe I don't sound it, but I'm good at school, what can I say? Looks can fool ya. I go to UNO and work at

Louie's at night, oh, and I go out with a few girls, and to answer your last crude question, I get plenty. Any more?"

"Homelife? Is it good?" Was this guy trying to piss him off, or what was his deal? Hot, then cold, then hot again.

"Look, Detective, I don't got a beef with anyone. I'm a basic guy. I go to work; I go to school; I live at home to help out my ma. Dad died three years ago. My family is Irish-Catholic; we live on Constance, next door to my aunt and uncle, my dad's brother. There's just me. I don't got brothers or sisters. My parents didn't drink too much, beat me, or mistreat me; what can I say? I'm just some boy from the Irish Channel who happens to work in a bar and grille in the French Quarter and got lucky to catch a smile from a pretty girl. I wish I had answers to your question of who done this, believe me. If I had been there, one thing I can promise, she would still be alive."

Detective Kimble got up, pushed his chair to the table, picked up his pad and bottle of water, and headed out the door. He turned back, "That's all I got for now."

"Great. Now, where's my mother?"

"Probably trying to find you a lawyer is my guess."

"Hey, can I call her?"

"I'll see what I can do." The detective looked tired. His eyes were bloodshot and bleary, and while Finn was exhausted, the angst had every nerve on edge and doing a stress dance. Sleep was nowhere near his radar.

A good twenty minutes passed, and a young female police officer handed him his cell phone. "Reception is crap."

He called. "Ma?"

"Sean!" She began to sob.

"Please, Ma, don't cry. I didn't do anything wrong, so I don't know how they can keep me here, but I'm doing whatever they tell me."

"Sean, they told me to leave and find you a lawyer. They wouldn't let me see you, but you do what they say and be polite, don't let your temper flare, you hear me? Liam has a friend, who has a friend, that's a good attorney. Saul Jacobs or some name like that may be Jacobson. Oh, Sean, I don't know. I gotta ask, you do anything with the girl?"

"Chri'sake, no. She kissed me, that's it. Like I told ya. She invited me in, ordered a pizza, and asked me to get it and a six-pack. I feel like a freakin' loop. I've said this over and over, what the—"

"Sean Murphy Finnegan, you watch that mouth. Liam just walked in the door." He could hear them talking. The attorney was coming down to the jail; his name was Saul Jacobson. "You heard Liam?"

"Thanks, Ma."

ROAD HOME

*B*etween the constant ringing of phones, the static of never-ending talking, and the frequently raised voices, the young detective was well into his case, a crazy and horrifying story, every inch of it sludging along as it coursed through his veins. All he wanted was peace and quiet to mull over the situation.

Getting called out for a murder on a Saturday night was commonplace. He had made it past midnight, a good sign; perhaps he'd escaped a call out, but no, and it was a doozy. He'd left Steph snuggled in bed, sound asleep. Thoughts of his quiet home in Tremé, a neighborhood outside the French Quarter, helped take the edge off some of the calls that beckoned him all too frequently. It was his sanctuary, his retreat from the madness of the job and the barrage of violence, day after day, twenty-four-seven, three-sixty-five.

As a detective, he came in after a crime had been committed rather than perhaps shutting it down, preventing it from happening, the hero kind of stuff. No, he was the accusatory son-of-a-bitch, who browbeat suspects with his torrent of questions—the puzzle master. He felt like there was a death grip on his brain. This fresh case was going to be a beast.

The obvious conclusion, he knew in his heart, was way beyond reality. He knew the kid in interrogation wasn't the perp, even though every arrow pointed in his direction. Reaching into his top desk drawer, he grabbed the aspirin bottle, popped it open, tapped out four, and slugged them down.

The men's room was down the hall; perhaps he could escape the noise while taking a most needed piss. Relaxing his bladder, his mind rolled back to the kid. Finn was his kind of people. Maybe Trey wasn't from the Irish Channel, but Mid-City was much the same, at least his street. Raised by blue-collared parents, he, too, was an only child and worked his way through college working the bar scene. He remembered those long nights of one drunk after another, knowing he'd have a paper to write or studying to do after a shower to get rid of the nasty funk of the bar he carried home. The muscles in his neck were so tight they felt like strained cords pulling his shoulders up toward his ears. A few shoulder rolls and neck stretches provided a brief reprieve. Rubbing his eyes, he drew a deep breath and walked back to the squad room.

Standing at his desk was an older guy who had a look on his face that seemed permanently chiseled with an expression as though he had smelled something foul. The sides of his mouth drew downward, and his nostrils flared just enough to create little pointy peaks. This guy looked as bad as Trey felt. "Can I help you?" He asked.

"You're holding Sean Finnegan, I believe? I'd like to see my client and sonny; what's the charge?" Saul handed him his card. "Saul Jacobson, attorney-at-law. My client, if you please."

"Right this way. No charges yet." Trey showed him to the interrogation room. He knew the kid would be going home within minutes. At best, there was nothing but circumstantial evidence, and actually, the kid did the righteous thing and called it in. In all actuality, he could've slipped out of the room with the pizza, beer, and Sprite, and no one would've been the wiser.

He could see Finn telling the story to his attorney, and then the older man patted him on the back. Trey opened the door; Saul smiled, "Detective, you have bupkis. Now, if you don't mind, Sean and I are leaving."

Trey watched as the young man walked out with his lawyer. While the case was just beginning and a young girl's life had been snatched before its time, he felt lighter knowing the kid was going home. A calm had come over his heart as they disappeared from sight. Had it been him at Finn's age, there would've been no way that he could've held it together without losing his temper.

He felt a small chuckle deep inside. While Finn's attorney looked archaic, he was sharp as a tack. *Good,* he thought, *the kid's got somebody with teeth in his corner.* The fact that he wasn't the one delivering the news to the girl's parents was a blessing.

Although only a ten-minute drive, the way home gave Trey a few moments to plot out his next steps—the hotel, any witnesses to the traffic coming in and out their door, and was there any other exits for guests? Did someone share the room with Jessica, and if so, where were they? He turned his car around and headed to the hotel. Crime lab techs were probably still there or leaving. He got his second wind, his stomach churning with possibilities. Too many times, he felt like a hamster running on the perpetual wheel to nowhere. His gut told him this was not going to be one of those times. He may have to go through a couple of rabbit holes, but like Alice, he was most curious.

Thump. Thump-thump. Trey's heart rate picked up in cadence with the marching band of possibilities parading through his mind. Placing his parking permit inside the windshield, he hopped out. While greeted by the front desk, he blazed past, and hopped in the elevator to the second floor. As speculated, the techs were in the process of packing up.

"How's it going?" He learned after many encounters the value of innocent information gathered at the crime scene from lab techs. The head honchos were gone; the dirty, tedious work was always left to the grunts. "How many suitcases y'all find?"

With a head full of black wavy hair pulled into a man bun, one of the techs looked up as he jotted down a few notes. The name tag identified the tech as Tony Luca. He flipped through the forms. "Two suitcases, a duffle, and the vic's purse."

"Tony, you happen to remember the name on the cases and duffle?"

The tech touched his thumb to his tongue, quickly scanning each page. "Suitcase one, pink-flowered, belonged to the victim, Jessica Lambert. The second one was purple and tagged Sloane Liberto, along with the duffle."

Trey carefully walked around the room, looking from different angles. The damn pizza, beer, and drink were labeled. He heard a screeching female voice coming from the hall like fingernails on a chalkboard.

"What the hell are you people doing in my room?" Her voice pierced the nerves running through his cervical vertebrae, causing a wince on his face. With quizzical, analyzing eyes, he studied her face. She was a pretty girl, maybe twenty, with shoulder-length dark brown hair, olive skin, and brown eyes so dark her pupils blended. She was more angry than confused. Pointing at him, "And who are you? Are you the head of this circus? I need to get into my room." She was with a young man, probably the same twenty-ish age, that stood utterly silent and bamboozled. His eyes looked like saucers, almost making him look like a cartoon character. Silently, Trey dubbed him Mr. No Personality and evidently no balls. The guy should've taken charge, maybe said something, but Miss Sloane Liberto was the one with the stones. "Well, are you going to let me in my room or not?"

Trey looked up with a totally deadpan face, "Not. Ma'am, aren't you the least bit curious why we're here in your room?" He didn't blink as he stared directly into her eyes.

She rolled her eyes and copped an attitude. "What? Somebody broke into our room, probably stole our bags. This is, after all, New Orleans!" She tugged on the shoulder strap of her purse.

Either the girl was intoxicated or a total bitch. There wasn't a trace of civility in her tone. "Actually, Ms. Liberto, my name is Trey Kimble, a detective with the NOPD. I need you to go down to the police station." He radioed for a unit to retrieve Ms. Liberto and Mr. No Personality. "I have questions regarding last night." He addressed the guy, "And you are?"

"Uh, uh?" The guy looked like a squirrel or some kind of rodent with a speedy metabolism making their movements twitch and jerk. Clueless, useless.

"It's a pretty simple question. Your name?" Trey moved closer to the couple.

"Scott Duplantis, sir. Um, I'm a junior at Ole Miss. We came for spring break." Beads of sweat formed on the kid's brow, and he had a tremor in his voice.

"I'm going to need to talk with you as well."

"Yes, sir. Where's Jess?" He looked around, trying to peer into the room.

"Not here." Trey succinctly answered. He heard the ding of the elevator and looked up. Two patrol officers stepped off the elevator. Trey nodded. "These two. I'll be there shortly."

The girl sputtered, her face twisted in an angry, shocked, and appalled contortion. "Excuse me, but I am not going anywhere."

No balls spoke up, "Sloane, shut up and do as they say. Don't make a scene, and stop being a bitch." *Well*, Trey thought, *maybe he does have a set.*

He slyly grinned at the boy in approval, "Well said, and Ms. Liberto, I'd listen to your friend."

Again she rolled her eyes and scowled like a spoiled brat being sent to their room for being mouthy. She turned with a huff, and the two went with the officers.

Trey sized up the room; there wasn't anything to suggest a struggle. She must've known her visitor. The mattress was just off-center, but he knew sitting on the bed could jostle it a smidge. Everything in the room was in place and unremarkable. He wondered what the toxicology report would show.

Satisfied that he got the information he wanted, he decided to wrap up his time in the hotel room. Yes, there had been a roommate, and she was now in custody. He wouldn't have to run that particular bit of information down. He'd caught a break and was thankful. With long strides, he made his way to the elevator. He looked around for the eye in the sky. He spied it, but it also looked dusty, old, and dull, suggesting dysfunction, certainly grainy images, if any.

He walked out of the hotel to an almost rising sun and a buzz of his phone. "Steph, you're up early."

"When you gonna be home?" the pleading voice asked from the other side of the conversation.

"Everything okay?" he queried.

"Yes," followed by a heavy sigh. "I'm just asking. It doesn't mean anything's wrong. So?"

"Maybe an hour or two."

"Never mind, then." The disappointment was more than apparent. Heaviness grew inside his chest like a hundred-and-ten-pound weight was sitting on it. Silence mounted the tension.

"I got up early because I wanted to watch the sunrise over the river with you and maybe, just maybe, have some beignets or coffee or not even anything, just you. You and me time. I hate your job." The disappointment in the voice stabbed at his very soul.

"Steph—"

"As I said, never mind. Gotta go. Ciao!" Then the dreaded disconnect.

Her words rang in his ears, tugging each time at his heart. He felt deflated. Sometimes he hated his job, but he and the job were connected. It was part of who he was. Slowly he pulled up to the station.

"What you doin' back here?" a voice echoed behind him. Startled, he turned to find Max Sledge, the other side of his tag team. "What, you don't trust me to handle the friend?" Max was five-six, with a thirty-eight girth, not the specimen Trey was, but then, Trey worked and ate for his physique. "Boy, this case ain't going nowhere anytime soon. Do everyone a favor; go get y'self some rest. I'll see you Monday morning. You stay much longer, and your alter-ego, Captain Trey-hole, will emerge, and I don't need that shit. Trust me; this ain't going nowhere."

His mind weighed the cautionary advice. The thought of seeing their expressions when they found out Jessica Lambert was dead was too enticing to leave. It would speak volumes. He felt his heart begin to race, increasing his respirations which pushed him all the more to be in the first round of questions with the roommate. Sloane was the one that could answer most of the questions, like how many and who were the kids with them on spring break? Were they all staying at Hotel Noelle? Like the old adage, "Curiosity killed the cat, but satisfaction brought him back." He needed some answers to truly rest.

"Max, I promise no Captain Trey-hole emerging. Man, I need some answers. I promise to stay only a few. Steph is already mad at me; all I need is you up my butt."

Sloane was in Interrogation 1, and the Duplantis boy in 3. The two detectives entered room 1. Trey had a new box of tissues that he tossed on the table. He knew it wasn't gonna be pretty. While Sloane was bitchy, he was pretty sure she had never received news like he was about to deliver. In his mind's eye, he imagined Stephanie in the chair across from him. His demeanor, his face, and his body language softened. His shoulders dropped, and his eyes took on a look of sadness and empathy. "Ms. Liberto, I'm sorry you came to your room as we were processing it. I'm sure it was shocking, but you need to listen carefully to what I'm about to say. Okay? Your friend, Jessica Lambert, was found dead in the hotel room. Her body is—"

"You're wrong. I was just with Jess, and she was fine. In fact, I left her with Stevie. He would've never let anyone hurt her, and I mean anyone. You're wrong." She set her jaw, crossed her arms, and turned her head. "Wrong. Way wrong. I bet she stayed with Stevie. Jess doesn't like being alone, so I know she wouldn't have been in the room by herself. She's my best friend. I know her better than anyone, and I know she's fine."

Trey tucked his lips over his teeth, then relaxed, "I'll try this again. There was a dead girl in your room. When we looked through her purse, we found her driver's license, and the girl was most definitely Jessica Lambert—no doubt about it. I'm very sorry for your loss. Maybe you could help by shedding some light on Saturday night." He kept his voice calm and steady.

Sloane blankly stared at him, and it was as though a light switch had turned on. Her body heaved with outbursts. She was beyond comforting. Max called for an EMT. She hyperventilated and looked like she was about to pass out. The tears flowed like rivers. "Her mom, somebody has to tell her mom and dad. Oh my God, they didn't want her to come anyway. I told them I'd take care of her. This is my fault. All my fault. Oh my God. No. No. No." She laid her head on the table and wept.

The EMT entered the room. "Sloane, I'm Tracy. I'm an EMT. Is it okay if I take your vitals?"

After comparing notes, Max and Trey deduced that Sloane, while a raving spoiled bitch, knew nothing, and the drip, Scott Duplantis, was like the president of Sloane's fan club. What they were able to gather was the names of all the people in the spring break group, so they'd pick them off one by one.

Max put his hand on Trey's shoulder. "Okay, Trey, get home to Stephanie. Try to make nice with her; if ya not careful ya gonna lose the best thing that eva happened to you. By the way, ain't y'all got an anniversary coming up? Don't fuck that up, ma man."

Trey grinned as he started walking off, "I've had the whole thing planned for at least a month."

5 A.M. TOO SOON

*T*he alarm went off with the usual wake-up announcement so cleverly programmed in the squawk box. "There you are, snuggled in bed, but it was your idea. You said you wanted to wake up, so WAKE UP, WAKE UP, W-A-A-K-E UP—"

"Alexa, shut the fuck up." He grunted. "Alexa, STOP." He rolled over and looked up at the ceiling.

Babe's mind strolled back to Saturday night. The inconvenience from that night was just that, an inconvenience. He expected even more childish behavior from the asinine moneybags and was prepared to give him a stern warning but ended up being drawn off point by a creep. While he knew it was true, and the deed was necessary, his capabilities were a scary proposition probably to some, but it was his mission to protect the weak, even if this weakling was a pompous asshole. He watched Mr. Fifty Bucks tail the girl and the busser down the street. Then he observed a degenerate from the bar following the flashy wallet. While he had no love lost for the arrogant little prick, he wasn't about to let the kid get rolled, so he followed undetected in the shadows, watching and waiting.

He saw the ne'er-do-well bring out his shiv, preparing to slice the boy for the bucks in his wallet; Babe stole behind silently; Fifty Bucks moved at a quick clip and had the degenerate run after him; there would be no element of surprise. The big man moved undetected and pulled the degenerate into a darkened doorway. The man attempted to fight back, but Babe quickly torsioned his neck with the crunching sound of death. He dumped the body on the doorstep like the day's garbage, with moneybags, none the wiser. Babe completed the mission in a blink. Fifty Bucks must have felt a presence behind because he turned to look but saw nothing as Babe had slotted into another darkened doorway.

A block ahead of the near attack, the young busser practically skipped backward as he led the cute girl to her hotel. The look of surprise when she invited him in, was priceless. Luck like that didn't happen for guys like the busser, blue collars, that is. They were two ordinary kids filled with promise and carefree happiness. Whether they were bed-bound or just flirty petting made no difference to him. All of the girl's friends had abandoned her, and whoever the lad was at the bar seeking her attention seemed to piss her off enough for a stinging slap in the face—well done for the young busser gallantly stepping up. He would reap the reward for seeing her back to the room safely.

Pushy and rude, the punk with the big bankroll had pissed him off when he dared to touch Trinity. While not his woman, he wished something would develop in time. She made him sweat with just the thought of caressing her. He imagined her muscular thighs wrapped around his body. He'd hold out, making the burning passion perfect for her. Trinity wasn't like all the other chicks he'd encountered in the New Orleans bars. He couldn't count the number of times he'd gone into a side alley for a quick fuck or the number of girls who gladly got on their knees in the restroom. Trinity was different—it wouldn't be a quick tumble. He'd please her beyond her wildest dream. If possible, for him to love, perhaps, he loved her.

Babe made the perfect Marine. He had no home life, raised by an abusive alcoholic father and a submissive sheep of a mother; he'd always been on his own. He'd learned to defend himself by the age of twelve when his father, while drunk, began the abusive name-calling and hit his mother. A powerfully built tall boy, even for twelve, he stood between his parents, grabbed the wooden kitchen chair, and proceeded to pummel his father to near death. As he saw it then and now, it was the only way to protect his mother. He didn't understand and was void of compassion for his father. Following the incident with his father, the system forced him into counseling with social workers, psychologists, and even a psychiatrist. Intense questioning and digging into the boy's possible disorder turned into the main attraction instead of the deranged behavior of his abusive father. The medical team seemed more interested in his rage.

As far as he was concerned, his actions were rational and that of a sane person, not someone with a mental disorder—it was clear-cut. The violence had to end, and without emotion, he ended it. The beating he gave his father injured the man to the point where he could no longer raise his arm and was left weak as a kitten. Babe had completed his objective. A knife across the throat would have done the trick if he wanted to kill the man. The social worker and psychiatrist were perplexed by the boy's unemotional or unaffectedness by the incident. *What was there to understand?*

Babe was a Marine's Marine. He was given orders and followed them to a tee with no emotional overload. It wasn't that he was Billy Badass or mean; he was cut and dry, with no room for question. He did what needed doing without worry. Some may have deemed him a psychopath, but that was their problem. He was fine with who he was. He was strapping at six foot five of pure muscle; his body was perfect, defined, and cut in all the right places.

Rolling out of bed, he cracked a few raw eggs, swallowed them with a quart of orange juice, and proceeded to do his morning workout, starting with pull-ups on the bar bolted into the doorframe and a routine of free weights, lifting to fatigue. He followed this with push-ups, sit-ups, and a half-hour on the heavy bag. He took a quick shower and was out the door on foot to the local construction site, where he worked until knock-off at 5 P.M. The day seemed to fly by.

After over a half-dozen bottles of water and a brisk wash down, he headed to Louie's as part of his daily routine. It was Monday, so he knew Trinity wouldn't be there, and he'd have to deal with Samantha's non-stop querying, heavy flirting, and aggravation. On more than one occasion, he thought he should just fuck her and satisfy her interest. He'd be a box checked, a one-and-done, and it'd be game over then, but he never wanted that to interfere with possibilities with Trinity.

Samantha coyly waved to him, standing behind the bar as she took an order from another patron. He nodded her way, then stretched his neck and shoulders as he sat down. She brought him his drink before he had time to order. She flipped her long bleached curls over her shoulder, tilted her head flirtatiously, and smiled while batting her eyes. Crinkling her brow, she cupped her mouth, "You heard about the dead girl? She was here Saturday night with her college friends." He tilted his head like he hadn't a clue. She looked around to make sure no one was listening. "Yeah, they think Finn, ya know, the young busboy had something to do with it. He was down at the station all night. Ya aks me; I don't think Finn would do something like that; he's a sweet kid, just putting himself through college." She winked at him as she moved toward a beckoning customer. He watched as she leaned in, pressing her elbows against her breasts to give an eyeful of cleavage, which the patron gladly observed. *Tips for tits, hm.*

Thoughts rolled thickly through his mind like an early morning fog. For once, he agreed with the bimbo; no way the busser did the deed. He was on top of the world to talk to the girl. Even if things had gotten steamy between them and the girl backed down, the kid would've been stuck with a stiffy but never forced himself on her, let alone kill her. It wasn't in the boy's demeanor. His mind swiftly jetted to the face of Mr. Flashy wallet and to think he'd saved his ass. Maybe he'd be the kind to get rough if he didn't get his way. Then again, the girl had slapped some other guy at the bar, but dollars to donuts, the slap broke any spirit of possibility for that kid. No, his bet was on Moneybags or someone he hadn't encountered yet; but then again, he hadn't spoken to any of them other than the fifty-dollar poser. Babe looked around for the busser; he was nowhere in sight.

He motioned for Samantha with his finger. Not that he was one for gossip, he'd found the only way to get answers was to distract. He smiled as the barmaid came over. "I'd like a dozen wings if you don't mind." He tried his hand at charming, not that he was astute at the flirting game, then furrowed his brow. "You said some girl got killed last night? She was here?"

"No, Saturday, well it was after midnight, so technically, it was yesterday. Can you believe it? A group of college kids in for Spring Break were at the bar, and one of the girls left and invited Finn, our Finn," she giggled. "He's a cute kid, but handsome Harry; he ain't. Anyway, she invited him to her room. I guess checking out the local talent." She shrugged a shoulder. "Whatever. The story is he left the room to get some beer, and when he came back, the girl was raped and dead." She raised her eyebrows. "Of course, the police think he did it, but I know Finn, and he's not the type to force himself on no one. He's a good Catholic boy. I'm not sayin' he wouldn't be up for a li'l somethin'- somethin'," she waggled her head from side to side like a springy figurine on a dashboard, "but he's not the violent kind. I'm guessing you were here last night, um, no, I mean, Saturday night?"

Babe nodded. "Tragic for the girl. The police think your boy here did the deed?"

"Well, they haven't come in asking about him, but if they do, I'll let them know what I think." She put her hand on her hip with attitude. "Course, I wasn't here. I hope the group comes back tonight; then, I'll give them the once over. I can spot a bad seed from a mile away. Be back in a jiff."

Babe slowly sipped his scotch, watching as the bar began to fill up. She quickly placed the order and headed back to drink orders. Mr. Fifty-

Dollars made his way into the bar. He had a couple of his buddies, but none of the girls were with them. He bellied up to the bar. It was apparent he had already established a rapport with Samantha.

"Hey, sweet cheeks." He winked at her and tapped the bar as if to say, bring me my drink. Babe couldn't help but think the boy was a wannabe player, just the kind that deserved a boot up the ass. She giggled and did the cleavage show for him. He tucked a bill into her top and winked at her. "Lookin' to make some extra money? See, I got my bud here with me, and well, let's just say he hasn't gotten very lucky on Spring Break."

She gave him a look of saddened disgust. Babe picked up on the bad vibes immediately. She took the money from her bosom and handed it back to him. "I ain't no whore. What happened between you and me I thought was fun, but that was between us and in the moment."

Tipping his head to the side with a look that screamed imposter, "I'm sorry for the confusion. No harm or insult meant, truly. Friends?" He took her hand and returned the money. Babe made his way toward the place where the boy was standing.

"Samantha, I might just have that second drink, ma'am." He shouldered his way, knocking the spoiled brat out of the way. "Everything okay over here?" He asked her, looking down at the kid.

Taken out of left field, she hemmed. "Uh, yeah, it's cool. No big."

The punk, maybe all of five-six, looked up at the towering hulk of a man and knew better than to push his luck. Turning his head to the side and scanning the room, Babe saw two men enter with the distinct look of law enforcement. The timing couldn't have been better—he had suspicions that Fifty-bucks was somehow mixed up in the mishaps of the night of misfortune, but maybe he just didn't like the arrogance of the little prick.

The younger of the men approached the bar. "Is the manager in?" She flagged one of the bussers and told them to get Shep. A balding, gray-haired man with a pot belly and dirty apron came to the front within a few minutes.

The younger man spoke, "You the manager?"

"Owner. And you?" He puffed out his chest with hands on his hips and a stance that screamed superiority.

Trey flashed his badge. "Detective Trey Kimble, NOPD, and this is my partner Detective Max Sledge. We have a few questions to ask you regarding Saturday night. Is there somewhere we can speak privately?"

"Sure." He led the detectives toward the kitchen. "I'm guessing it's about the young girl from the other night. If y'all are thinking Sean Finnegan had anything to do with the death of that young girl, I can tell y'all ya barking up the wrong tree. The kid's a good kid; he works hard, doesn't miss a shift, is never inappropriate with any of the guests, and believe me, we got some assholes." He wiped his hands on his apron. "We had a full house with Spring Break. Surprisingly, nobody was acting a fool since the place was crawling with joe college; I figured we might have one or two imbeciles. Look, Finn ain't here tonight; he works Tuesday through Saturday five to close unless it gets slow, and then I cut him loose. Actually, ain't no one here that worked Saturday. We got some of our regulars that's here every dang night; I can point them out for ya, if'n ya want. They'd probably see more, anyway; all the workers are, well, workin'. In fact, we got one who's ex-military here every day like clockwork. Neva drunk, minds to hisself. You can't miss him; he's at the end of the bar; he's a walking wall." He scrunched his face to the side. "Boys, I gotta get back to the grill."

Trey handed him a card. "And you're Louie; I take it."

"Nah, that was my great grandpaps, but I'm the owner now, and Shep's the name, Nathan Shephard, but everyone calls me Shep. Come back tomorrow, and the Saturday crew will be on." Max and Trey shook his hand and headed back to the front.

Trey looked toward the end of the bar, and just as the man had said, the big guy was there. Babe watched as the two officers meandered through the crowd. He gave a half-cocked grin and stood. Trey couldn't help but think the guy was indeed a specimen and screamed military.

Babe put his hand out. "Good evening, officers. I'd offer to buy you one, but I suspect you're still on duty, so how about a Coke or Seltzer? I'm Babe Vicarelli."

Max was the first to speak. "Babe?"

"Yes, sir. My Gramps was a Babe Ruth fan; what can I say? One thing for sure, it made me tough." He gave a light chuckle.

"What branch?" Trey asked.

"Marines."

"No one to mess around with, right? Tough to the core." Trey sat on the stool next to him while Max and Babe stood. "Y'all, please sit."

"Yes, sir. You sure I can't buy you a Coke or something?"

"Marine, I should be buying you a drink." Trey grinned. "God, I tried to join." Trey grabbed his right knee. "Bad knee from football, and they wouldn't take me, so the next best thing was cop, and even then, they questioned my physicality. Shit. Last game of the season, one play with one wrong plant of the foot and a tackle on my ass, and that's all she wrote, but it's strong as can be now." He nodded as though confirming.

Max interjected. "I gotta listen to your whiny ass story again and again?" Looking at the big man, he asked, "So I understand you come here often?"

"Yes, sir. Just about every night for one scotch and somethin' to eat. I work construction now that I'm out of the Corps."

"You know the busser, Finn?"

"No, sir, but I've seen him; he seems like a good kid." He took a sip of his drink.

Trey questioned, "You here Saturday night?"

Babe smiled. "Yes, sir, and I watched the drama as it unfolded. There were a ton of college kids, most of the guys trying to get laid," he coughed a laugh, "but there was this one young lady. Cute girl with a great smile. She had them lined up, hitting on her. Hey, I don't blame them; she was pretty and seemed refreshingly nice. Some guy came on strong, and she slapped him and then went into the restroom. Her friends must not have noticed because they all went their separate ways. When she came out of

42

the restroom and started to leave, the young man that works here stopped her. I have to say it made me curious, so I followed them out. They were just a couple of kids. She was laughing, and he could hardly keep still. So innocent, sir. He walked her to her hotel, and they seemed happy. I started to walk home, but my dog, Gunner, had to lift his leg and then spent ten minutes sniffing all the other marked areas. I noticed the busser sprint out of the hotel; it roused my curiosity, so I watched. Baby Don Juan ran across the street, picked up a pizza from the corner, some beer, and a soda or something, and ran back to the hotel. Maybe took him twenty minutes, Gunner and I stood for a bit, and that's about all I can tell you."

"You see anyone else go into the hotel behind them?"

"There was this one boy, but I think they all stayed at the same hotel. I gave him the name of Mr. Fifty Bucks. Spoiled kid, you know the kind, entitled." He put his head down and smirked.

Trey ordered a Coke. "Why Fifty Bucks?"

"I watch people and read their body language—something I've always done. Anyway, smart ass kid flirts with the bartender, a sassy small Creole girl, Trinity. Pretty girl, beautiful actually, but doesn't take shit off anyone. The kid orders his drink; when she turns to grab the bottle, he smacks her on the ass. She turned back around with a spicy little smile and mixes his drink. He hands her a fifty-dollar bill, and she stuffs it in her pocket and says thanks for the tip. The boy comes a little unglued, but she says something about him touching her; I thought it was funny, sir, that's all."

"He here tonight?" Max asked.

"Yes, sir." He closed one eye and lifted his glass in the direction of the boy. "Sandy blond with the cocky attitude."

"Got him." Trey took a sip of his Coke. "You've been a big help. Oh, and by the way, it took only a minute in the interview, and I knew the kid, Finn, wasn't the doer. Just an unlucky kid—wrong place, wrong time. It's a shame, and I plan to catch the bastard." Trey started to get up, and in mid-stance, he mentioned, "It was a night for murder. Beat cops found a

John Doe with a broken neck in the doorway. They said it looked like he was sleeping a binge off, but he was dead. You pass him or see anything?"

"Can't help, there, sir." The voice echoed; *no, I should have said, won't help. The douchebag got what he deserved.* They parted ways, and Babe watched as the cops approached the snot-nose.

ROSY PALM

7he night dragged on without Trinity. Samantha was okay, but he wouldn't tap that and ruin a chance at the real prize.

"Hey, big guy, whacha doin' later tonight? Buy a girl a drink when I get off." She leaned forward, her breasts just about tumbling onto the bar.

" 'fraid I'm gonna have to pass, ma'am. Work comes too fast, and I gotta get some shut-eye. Maybe some other time?" He warmly smiled. That was the only thing warm on his body; as far as he was concerned, he didn't even register a pulse below his belt pertaining to her. He was holding out for Trinity. The thought of her tight little body moved him, and yet he had no idea of her story. She didn't wear a wedding ring, but for all he knew, there was a Mister and a houseful of kids. *Nah, not with that tight perky ass,* he thought; *no kids, but maybe a Mister.* Now that was enough to bring him to full salute. He laid a couple of dollars on the bar and headed home.

Babe's mind flickered with thoughts of Trinity the whole way home. As far as he could tell, the streets were quiet; of course, it was Monday; nonetheless, sickos didn't care what day they raped, murdered, or molested. The closer he got to his apartment, the more vivid the frames in his mind depicted an interlude with Trinity.

One more block, and he'd be home free. He heard the whine of a screen just in front of him. "You ungrateful little bastard. You live in my house, eat my groceries; you could show some appreciation." He heard the smack of a slap. It hadn't been the first time he'd experienced commotion from the apartment, but it wasn't his business, just the man and his woman quarreling again.

"Get your hands off me, you perve." The higher-pitched voice rang from inside the door: Smack, another slap. "Get off me. Help! Someone, help!" The heavy door slammed but cracked open with a bounce.

Why can't the animals behave one night? He turned toward the door and pushed the door open. Inside, he found a drunk middle-aged slob pulling the pants down of a thirteen, maybe fourteen-year-old boy he'd seen a few times walking the streets. The degenerate's pants were already off, with his johnson at the ready to abuse the kid. "Who the hell are you? Get out my house." Sights like the one before him made him angry beyond comprehension. This kind of creep was habitual, not a one-time abuser drunk; he had the look. The abuse would continue if someone didn't step in. He grabbed the man by the collar and held him at a distance.

He looked at the kid, who stood with his mouth gaping and shock in his eyes. "Who's here, kid?"

"Me and him," in a frightened whisper, "my mother's boyfriend," pointing at the sack of shit Babe held by the neck. The boy kept his head turned away from the big guy. The more the perve struggled, the tighter the grasp became.

The boyfriend thrashed, trying to kick Babe. "You got anyone else?"

"Grandparents uptown." He intently stared into space, completely freaked out and making a point not to look at Babe.

"Go!" He threw ten dollars at the kid and kicked the door closed behind him as the boy ran out.

The man windmilled his arms while Babe looked at him. "What to do with you?" He commented in a monotone drone. "We both know you're not gonna stop. The boy's right; you're a pervert. Neva gonna change." Babe jutted his jaw forward with a pan look, void of inflection in his voice or expression in his eyes. He rocked his head like he was making a decision, weighing the facts. "How 'bout I stick something up your ass?" The man struggled, his eyes bulging in fear. "The world will be a better place without you." In one swift move, he pulled a blade, cut the man from ear to ear without hesitation, wiped the shaft, put the knife back in his pocket, and left. Leaving the door closed but not locked. Someone would find him, and judging from the size of the boy's pupils, he was already moving into shock. Case closed—one more piece of shit off the street. Maybe the grandparents would take the boy in, but it wasn't his problem. He'd eliminated the threat.

Finally home, he removed his boots, placed them perfectly in his closet, stripped off his clothes, tossed them in the washer, and jumped in the shower. He leaned against the wall absorbing the spray pelting his neck and back. The same recurring thought traversed his mind. *I hope you had a good day, Trinity. Relax in the shower with me.* As always in the script, she looked up; *I love you, Babe.* In the coils of his imagination, he responded, *Let's take this to the bed. No? You want me right here?* He imagined his body rocking into her as his grip tightened. *Girl, you feel so good; I can't hold back.* The spoils of his labor plastered the tiles as his knees weakened, and he shook the thought pattern from his mind.

After drying off, he wiped the fog off the mirror above the sink and looked deep into his eyes. "One day, Trinity, I will be the man you need and want, but until then, my fantasy does the deed."

The morning dawned, and he went through his ritual of raw eggs, juice, pull-ups, weights, sit-ups, push-ups, and heavy bag, then off to work with his four-legged partner.

"9-1-1, what's your emergency? Slow down, ma'am; I can't understand you. You say you found your boyfriend dead, and your son is missing? I have a unit dispatched to you. Please stay on the line with me until they get there. Don't touch a thing. Ma'am, perhaps you should stand outside your door until the police arrive. I'm right here with you. You say you came home from work a few minutes ago, and the door was open? They'll be there in minutes, dawlin'." The dispatch could hear the car as it pulled up. "The officers are there? You take care, ma'am."

The officers radioed in, asking for a detective. Max called Trey, "Where y'at? Still at home? You sick? We got a hot one. Tell Steph you gotta go to work. Fuck it; Happy Anniversary. I got this one. I'll catch you up to speed when I see you. Have one for me, ya hear?" Max hung up.

Stephanie smiled at him with one of her naughty girl grins. "I can't believe you told Max no. I'm proud of you. C'mere, you." She threw her arms around him and kissed him softly.

"Stay, just like that. Don't move." Trey rushed from the bed and ran to the kitchen—she could hear him open the fridge and clank around the room. He returned with a tray presenting a vase of roses, a plate with powdered Bavarian cream donuts and chocolate-covered strawberries, and a small gift-wrapped box with a card. He had a broad smile. "Well, open it."

"You are so sweet. Flowers, powdered creams, chocolate strawberries, and a present, too? The gift I got you is pretty lame compared to this."

He lay on the bed. "Steph, shhh, just open it."

She untied the bow, slowly opening the tiny velvet box. Her eyes sparkled with glistening tears while she quickly slid the ring onto her right hand. "Opal, my birthstone, you remembered. Trey, it is so beautiful; look how fiery it is. It must've cost you a fortune. Are you sure?"

He held her hand up, admiring the ring on her finger. She told him years before that she always wanted a beautiful opal one day, unlike the plastic or glass ones her parents had given her as a child for her October birthday. She still had them in her jewelry case, but now, the one on her finger was the real deal. "I've had an estate appraiser on the lookout since you first mentioned it. Sexy lady, it's been a great five years. Thank you for putting up with me, my work, and my crazy mood swings. I love you, Stephanie. You have no idea how much." He picked up the tray from the bed and placed it on the chest of drawers.

"My donuts." She reached, almost pouting.

"They'll wait." He seductively smiled at her, glancing at her lips. His kiss explored her mouth, then he kissed her chin, neck, breasts and kept going. Sex with her was a spiritual experience taking his mind into some distant heaven. Sated, he rolled over, still holding her. "You are an amazing woman. The way you make me feel is indescribable."

She pulled from his embrace. "Now for your present." She sat up and reached into the drawer of her bedside table.

"Oh, I thought I'd already gotten it." He blushed. She laughed, commenting on his cherry-red cheeks.

They'd known each other since they were kids, although she was from the lakefront, a different neighborhood than his. One of her cousins lived down his street, near the bayou in Mid-City, and he suspected the neighbor girl had a fascination with him. In the afternoons, he and a bunch of other neighborhood boys would ride their skateboards up and down the street, sometimes walking the few blocks to Bayou St. John. Before the city repaved, it was like an obstacle course, and he found himself sailing through the air on more than one occasion—nothing ever broken, just scraped to all hell. He was a plain old kid, he thought. Nothing special.

Trey remembered seeing her for the first time. It was one of those days that Steph hung out with her cousin and went to watch the goofy skateboard riders. Their eyes locked as they searched each other's expressions, trying to get a read. At that time, he was all legs standing at six feet; the filling out started sometime later. His hair was dark, almost black, contrasted by greenish-blue eyes and a medium olive complexion.

The picture of Stephanie imprinted on his memory from that very first meeting. They were polar opposites, she being blonde with brown eyes and lily-white skin. She had a small turned-up nose, full pink lips, and a great smile even with a mouth full of braces—her body was already in full bloom. They didn't start dating until the summer after his third year in college; the rest was history. They were in love and inseparable. After college, he joined the NOPD, and she worked from home as a graphic artist. They were and had been in that forever kind of love.

Trey went in later that day. "Well, looky, who decided to come into work after all, but boy, am I glad to see you. We gotta interview some of the kids from the other night; besides, some guy got his throat slit while standing in his fuckin' kitchen. There's some strangeness to it, not just ya easy home invasion.

"This guy had his pants down like he was about to hose someone. The girlfriend was at work. Her kid, a teenage boy, is staying by his grandparents. I spoke briefly to him, and all he could say was the guy was a piece of shit." Max wriggled his eyebrows. "Grandparents said the kid came over like usual and then went to school. Mommy dearest works a pole on Bourbon, according to the grandparents. Evidently, the boy's dad split, and the mother has taken up with this P.O.S., says the kid. The grandparents are the parents of the flown-the-coop dad. The slit throat and kid are all local, but we only got the rest of the week for the Spring breakers without all kinds of red tape. Also, the dead girl, Jessica Lambert—her parents have been here for a couple of hours. Cap's been talking with them, but they wanted to talk with you since you were the first investigator to see the scene." Max stayed silent for a moment but then smirked at Trey. "I saw that bounce in your step. Musta been quite a morning." With hands on his fat-hidden hips, he pistoned his body with a snorting laugh.

Trey shook his head in disapproval. "Just cuz you're not getting any doesn't mean I need to give you all the details so you can live vicariously through Steph and me. Can you even see yours still?" Trey laughed.

"Very funny." He cleared his throat. "Talk to Jessica's parents or round up the Spring Break kids first?"

Trey picked up a stack of papers. "I'll call the Captain about Jessica's parents and get the thumbs up on the round-up of breakers. It might help the parents to see we're doing what we can. I don't know how easy or even if it's possible to pick up the whacko that did the girl. He's probably long gone. Right now, I don't give a hearty shit about the home invasion if that's what it was, besides we have cases out the wazoo."

HARD TIME

7he Captain told them to come to the office pronto. As they went through the door, there was no doubt these were the Lamberts—they looked broken and dazed. The dad grimaced, holding his lips rigidly still, making them almost form a perfect line. His eyes continually blinked as he fought back the tears.

"Mr. and Mrs. Lambert, these are Detectives Kimble and Sledge; they're working diligently on your daughter's investigation."

They both nodded. The pain on their faces ripped his soul, but Trey cleared his throat. "I am very sorry for your loss, Mr. and Mrs. Lambert. Everyone I've spoken to has remarked on what a sweet girl—um, I'm sorry."

The mom sat wringing a tissue in her hands. "We were out of the country; that's why it took so long to get here. We didn't get Sloane's call—you know Sloane is much more worldly than our Jess. Jess is naïve and wants to see the best in everyone. She's younger. We would've preferred her going to the beach, but not that New Orleans isn't a lovely place—uh," her breath hitched. "I still can't believe it."

Trey looked her in the eyes with compassion, "You're here now." He closed his eyes and nodded slightly. "Being here any sooner wouldn't have made a difference, Mrs. Lambert. We are preparing to speak with the young people in their group. We've already spoken to a couple." He looked to the Captain for confirmation and got the official nod.

The mom spoke again. "We'd like to speak to the kids on the trip if that's okay."

The Captain interjected, "Let us talk with them first, ma'am. Not until we finish with them." Her eyes looked downward. Trey detected a slight shudder.

For the first time, the father spoke. "I see no reason why we can't talk to Sloane. She was the reason our daughter even came to this city. Surely, Sloane could use some comforting at this time." His fists were balled, and his body tense almost in an authoritarian demonstrative manner.

Max sputtered, "I believe Trey already interviewed Sloane Liberto."

Trey nodded, "I did. We have to get this done thoroughly yet quickly. I'm sure you understand."

The dad was piping mad, "Do you really think one of these kids could have done this to our daughter, their friend? It was probably some degenerate from your city." His body trembled, Trey could tell he wanted to hurt someone, and he didn't blame him. If it had been his wife or a daughter, somebody would pay and pay dearly.

His wife interjected, "Dear, they have to do their job. We need patience. Getting outraged will not bring her back to us. We must let them do what's necessary." She looked directly at Trey, "You will find out who did this, won't you?"

Trey looked back, wanting to say no guarantees, but responded, "We will do our utmost, and, Mrs. Lambert, we are good at what we do. Take comfort in that." The Captain dismissed them.

Once out the door and out of earshot, Max commented, "You sounded like a real cheesedick, 'we are good at what we do,' really? These people have just lost their daughter, who, by the way, was brutally raped, as well. All they want is their kid back, and dumb-fuck, we can't do that."

Trey sarcastically responded, "But we can find the bastard that did this. Now that you've beaten me down, have we gotten anything from forensics, like info on fluids, hair, skin under the nails?"

Max exhaled loudly. "If Forensics had anything, they would've called. We can touch base tomorrow or give a call, but I'm heading back to the bar. I want to talk to the kid, Finn. I know he's not the doer, but he might be able to remember anything about who was left behind. Remember, The Hulk said Fifty Bucks followed them to the hotel, and that was after she'd slapped one of the other boys. I got sweat rings, look?" He was holding his arms out. It was hot, especially for April; no denying it. "I don't see rings under your arms, Trey."

Trey smiled at his partner. "You, also, don't work out and run." He wasn't going to mention the extra sixty-odd pounds Max carried around his gut and jowls. Chuckling, he said, "I guess I got all my sweating out this morning."

"Rub it in, rub it in. Some partner you are."

They arrived at the bar around 4:30. There were a few businessmen that had gotten out of work early and Trinity, the bartender Babe had mentioned. She was busy wiping things down. The Hulk had been right; she was attractive, and when she smiled, her eyes glistened.

"Good afternoon, guys; what's your fancy today, beer, wine, Old-Fashion, or you still on the job?" When she said on the job, Trey snapped his wrist and pointed, signaling still on the clock—she smiled, looking down at their shields on their belts and the guns on their hips. "Gotcha; how about a Coke or water since you're still on?"

Trey spoke first. "Water with a lime?" She nodded.

"I'll have a Diet Coke." He heard Trey snicker under his breath.

"And that's gonna make all the difference, eh?" Trey playfully questioned.

"Fuck you." Max faked a solemn expression.

She hustled the two beverages to them. Trey pulled out a five.

"On the house, guys." She smiled. "What brings you in this afternoon?

I guess still working on the murder of the college girl?" They nodded.

Trey took a long sip of his water, wiped his mouth, then started the questioning. He hitched a hip onto one of the bar stools like he planned on being there a minute. "Is there anything you can tell me about that night? Anything odd? Describe the night as you saw it." He pulled out his pad and pencil. "First, your name?" The detective had a friendly upturn to his mouth as he spoke. "I'm Trey Kimble, and this is my partner Max 'Diet Coke' Sledge." Max rubbed his middle finger along his cheek.

"Hey, now, I'm a Diet Coke girl, myself. And the name's Trinity, Trinity Noelle, and before you ask, yes, those Noelles." She sighed and became serious. "We had a pretty full house, everybody here scrambling with spring break in addition to our heavy list of regulars. I pour some damn good drinks if I don't say so myself. Anyway, we had a couple of college groups in, normal shit, ya know. Loud, too much beer, and singing at the top of their lungs way off-key." She giggled. "One of the groups was more intense, like the name of the game was pairing up and getting laid. The drinking, music, and joking around were B team material."

Max chugged a few swallows of the diet and muffled a burp, " S'cuse, I got the impression spring break was all about getting hot under the sheets, no?"

She put her finger up to say stop as a customer bellied up to the bar. After taking care of the order, she continued. "Getting laid is the deal, but everyone's doing everyone. The days of winin' and dinin' are over, my friend, and fidelity, forget about it, at least down here." She changed the subject oddly. "How long y'all been with NOPD?"

Max answered after a gulp, holding up both hands flicking them twice. "Twenty for me and ten for the kid," pointing at Trey. "It's his fifth anniversary today. Me, divorced two times; I'm just not the marrying kind, I guess."

"Yeah, I hear ya," she mused. "I was married to the blue line for, um, three years. Given my background, Joey had a hard time dealing with me working. He figured I didn't need to work because of my family, yet here I was night after night. The man would stop in sometimes five times a night and, ooh, let him hear anyone flirt with me. Hence, he's no longer with the department, and we're not married." She shook her head. "A shame, too. He was basically a good guy, and I was head over heels for him, but that's ancient history now." Another customer required her attention, thus a break in conversation.

"She's a chatty one, Max, just your type, maybe twenty years ago. You know who has the hots for her, I think?" He swirled the lime around his glass with a thin black cocktail straw and gazed across the bar. "The Hulk. She doesn't seem to be looking for Mr. Right, so he may be barking up the wrong tree. Wonder what he'd think of Miss Trinity being from the Noelle family. I wonder if she lives there; convenient to work." He chuckled, then plucked and bit into the lime, puckering his face.

Things started to get busier; she ran back to them. "I'm —"

"No problem," Trey smiled, "We can see. Any of the weird breakers here?" She pointed to the far end of the room. Three tables were pushed together, with nine people sitting quietly, whispering to themselves. Four girls and five guys. Sloane was missing. *No Sloane. Hm.*

The duo walked over. Trey spoke, "Hi-ya, Scott. Where's Sloane? She not out with y'all?"

The boy looked up with a sad sack downward turn of his lips and furrowed brows. "No. She stayed in the room. She hasn't left the room since—" and took a slug of his beer.

As though he understood, Trey nodded with an attempt at sympathy. In reality, nothing about the case was understandable. Things had not even come close to adding up. "I see. Y'all might want to head down to the station. You know where it is. We have a few units on the way to pick y'all up. Better get some go cups or down them. Just sayin."

Fifty-bucks pushed his chair from the table with a half-cocked smirk. "I'm not going anywhere and certainly won't speak with anyone regarding Jess' death. I know my rights."

Max had heard enough and leaned on the back of Fifty Bucks' chair.

"Do ya now? What, first or second-year law or maybe just Pre-Law?" Max rocked the chair backward, startling the boy, but quickly set it back on all four legs.

The kid was disagreeable and a smart ass, provoking instant dislike by the two detectives. Trey jotted a note in his trusty pad. "None of the above. Just not a dumb-fuck." The boy smirked and was way over his head in confidence. The air of conceit was disturbing. "My father's an attorney, and I know. None of us are saying a thing."

Trey held up his hands in a surrender fashion. "Whoa, everybody, calm down. We just need to talk, maybe y'all might remember something that didn't seem like anything, but we could possibly glean vital information. We're not trying to be jerks or rain on your NOLA parade; we only need a minute of your time. Scott can tell you we're easy and reasonable." The boy nodded, and his shoulder dropped. "We want to find out who murdered your friend. Don't y'all?"

Scott pushed from the table and stood as though commanding others to follow suit. "I'm going; y'all can do what you want, but the quicker they get the information, the more chance they can find something out. Besides, I know my liver can use a rest tonight." Everyone got up to wait for their ride, but Fifty Bucks, who sat rigid with a puss registering contempt and defiance. "Trev, you *really* gonna act like an asshole? W-T-F?"

Trey patted the lone sitting boy on the shoulder. "I been callin' you Fifty Bucks, you big tipper. What's your name? I want to keep it real; you feel me?"

He slowly rose. "Trevor Lennox and I guess I'll head down with everyone else." The arrogance turned to defeat in one fell swoop. The kid was going to go one way or another—voluntarily made things easier.

Trey winked at him and patted his shoulder again. "I'll try to be quick."

As they were all walking out the door, Babe strolled in. He glanced at the boy, then at Trey. "Good evening, detective."

"Heya, Babe. What time you leaving tonight?" He quickly stopped. "Eleven, sir."

"See ya later." Trey continued walking.

"You got some big ones, callin' that massive dude babe, or, uh, never mind."

Trey chuckled. "Nothin' like that. Babe's his name."

Trevor let out a whistle. "That's messed up. Poor guy, bet he got hassled when he was a little dude." He walked by Trey's side and had become a bit more cordial.

"I don't think he was ever truly a little dude. You? The man's owed respect—Marine and obviously a warrior." Trey tried to get as friendly as possible to Trevor; something about him set off warning bells. Maybe it was his cocky spoiled attitude or the fact that he thought he was God's gift to humanity, but he smacked of something else. Perhaps the kid had a thing for Jessica, and it wasn't reciprocated; whatever the case, Trey knew there was a story somewhere, and one of the kids was blazing to tell; he just had that feeling. Maybe he was wrong, and it was a creep off the streets, but there was no sign of forcible entry; it had to be someone she knew or someone posing as hotel staff. At least everyone was agreeable to interviews. Something had to give. The pain in Jessica's mother's voice and desperation to discover what had happened pounded in his head, setting a fast course through his body.

"Two fingers—" Trinity began, already turning toward the back bar.

He interrupted, "No, ma'am, three fingers and a hamburger, please."

"Let me get the order in, and I'll be back in a jiff with your drink." She smiled and winked at him. *What is this? Is she flirting? Shit, control, control, control.*

"Thank you, ma'am." He took in a slow deep breath, silently exhaling.

She was exhilarating, and any of his fantasies would push him too far. He'd have to leave, but more than anything, he wanted to spend time with her, even if it was only a quick word here or there.

He waited, drumming his fingers on the bar, wondering who the cops liked for the murder. If they could give him two minutes with each of the young men, he'd have their answer. Case closed. Of course, his interrogation method was completely different from law enforcement rules. No, he'd been interrogator, judge, jury, and executioner more than he could count, and Uncle Sam was happy with the results and welcomed being blind to the how.

Trinity walked back with his drink and a full-on smile. She *had* been flirting with him. *Why? To what end?* "Here you go, Babe, and I put your order in. It won't be but ten minutes. Three fingers, hm, had a rough day? Tending bar, I hear it all, so while you got the chance, get it off your chest." She stood with a hand on her hip. "I promise, nothing you say will shock me. I've heard it all. Problems with the wife? Boss?" She cocked her head to the side.

"No, ma'am. Decided to shake it up a little tonight." He took a slow sip from his drink, looking into her eyes over the rim of his glass. He could feel the heat rising in his body, unable to control the lustful glimmer in his eyes, and she saw it, sure as day, and she liked it. Her eyes twinkled back, and in a momentary pause in the universe, their intensity was like a sensual duet. "You got a Mister at home?"

With a sultry smirk, her teeth barely grazed part of her bottom lip with a fleeting tease of her tongue. With a deep sigh, she answered, "No Mister and no kids. Babe, I'm my own woman beholden to no one, just the way I like it." She slowly batted her eyes. He could feel his pulse rev, sending lightning bolts through his body. She could most definitely handle him, maybe even tame his inner demons. Perhaps the doctors had been wrong, and he *could* feel genuine emotion because what his body said was that he was closing in on love with Trinity. What pounded in his heart was a brand-new feeling.

The moment was interrupted by a patron clearing his throat for attention. She winked at Babe. "Do what ya gotta do, ma'am. I'm here for a while." The young busser placed Babe's hamburger and a host of condiments on the bar. "Thanks, Finn."

Finn turned back with a questioning look. "Welcome. I know I seen ya here, but have we met?" The busser looked puzzled, making eye contact as though searching his mind for interaction he'd forgotten.

"We haven't been introduced, if that's what you mean. I'm Babe Vicarelli. I come here a lot." He grinned at the boy, who nodded in affirmation. "Samantha mentioned your name."

Finn nodded, "Yeah, everyone here knows The Hulk, no disrespect," and smiled. "Dude, I mean, you're freakin' huge. I bet you work out a lot, yeah? Babe, like in Babe Ruth?" He rested his elbow on the counter next to Babe.

"You got it, Babe Ruth, not the cartoon pig." He coughed out a chuckle. "Working out is part of my morning ritual, but I bet you have some strong guns carrying all the trays you do. You work your ass off." Babe did the guy nod with a twitch of his brows.

Finn laughed, "I guess. Neva thought about it that way. Thanks." He turned and returned to bussing.

Since the teen mob had left, there were only a few people in the place, so he hoped he might have more time to talk to Trinity, but then a tour group entered, and that idea flushed down the drain. So, he sat and marveled at her energy and created other dreams of interaction with her as he observed all her body parts.

He loved the tautness and definition in her arms. She had an engraved silver band that settled in the contour of her bicep; it was sexy and matched the ring on her right thumb. Other than a few earrings in each ear, that was the extent of her jewelry. Her black Louie's tank with its purposefully ragged edges was tied at the waist just above her short denim skirt. His mind drifted—he wondered what kind of panties she wore. It was more than obvious she wasn't wearing a bra, as he could see her well-defined bead-like nipples. The torrent of thoughts washed a continual reel of pictures in his mind, and if he didn't stop the loop, things would become even more uncomfortable. Babe adjusted himself, scarfed down his burger, and drained his drink with a few large gulps. He needed to get out of there.

When he stood to leave, he noticed Trinity look in his direction. Her dimpled smile vanished, and the starry sparkles in her eyes dulled. She was disappointed, which made leaving even harder. She stopped what she was doing and quickly skirted around the bar. "You leaving so soon?" She was tiny. The top of her head barely reached his sternum.

"I'm paid up." He commented.

"Yeah, I know; it was just—never mind." She gave a half-hearted smile.

"It was just what?" He had to hear her say she wanted to spend time with him, even if it was only to talk. What could he say? Something like, 'I want to hold you, kiss you, feel you?' No, he couldn't and wouldn't say any of that. "What?" His gaze cast down into her eyes, and the warmth she emanated pierced his heart.

She nervously shuffled her feet and rocked from side to side, almost like a bashful young girl. "I was hoping to talk; I'd like to get to know you better. I don't want to sound cheap; it's just that you intrigue me and have from the first time I saw you. Please don't leave yet." She smiled, his soul exploded like a blast of dynamite, and his heart fluttered. *What is wrong with my body?* It was all so confusing.

The twinkle was back in her eyes, and her smile was perfect. Babe couldn't deny her; he'd have to control his impulses and mind trips through rabbit holes; they always posed an issue.

"Put that way, how can I do anything but stay?" He lightly touched the small of her back as she turned to go behind the bar. Like a weak electrical current, tingles ran from his fingertips up his arm.

She turned back and smiled. "You shocked me. Did you feel it, too?" He just smiled.

Trinity brought him a two-finger pour. "That's on the house since you doing this girl a favor." He gave her a half-cocked smile.

Watching her was no good, so he concentrated on the silent images on the television. There was a picture of the dead douchebag who tried to rape the boy and then an interview with the woman he suspected to be the mother. At first glance, she appeared torn up, but her expression and body language screamed liar from the point of view of his trained eye. The screen changed to a reporter interviewing what he assumed was the grandparents. They looked upset but relieved at the same time. The caption read. "Boy saved from a brutal attack by mystery hero." Babe wondered what the boy remembered. He was pretty sure, not much.

He and Trinity had broken conversations throughout the night that didn't amount to much but a moment of each other's attention. It was a start.

THE HEAT IS ON

*B*ack at the police station, the group of college kids sat in chairs lining the wall. The first two had been taken to the Interrogation Rooms.

Max took Becca Straus, one of the girls; her room was down the hall from Jessica and Sloane. As promised, Trey took Trevor in first. Given the boy's arrogance and entitlement, which triggered instant dislike on the detective's part, he couldn't help but feel Trevor wasn't the doer, even though his gut told him at first he was.

"Hey, Trevor, I promised you'd be first so you could be out faster and back to NOLA partying. I know this isn't what you expected from Spring Break. Before we get started, I'm going to read you your rights, so I know you understand them, not that I'm implying you did anything, just protocol." Trevor said he understood his rights and to proceed, Trey continued. "I understand you were in Louie's with the group for most of the night—that we have established. How well did you know Jessica Lambert?" Trey toyed with the pen, ready to start making notes.

Trevor clasped his hands, then placed them flat on the table, fingers spread. "Look, Jess and I dated at the beginning of the year, but here's the thing, she's one of those girls that plan to wait until she's married to have sex." He put both his hands up, flaring his fingers. "Okay, I get it. If it were my kid sister, I'd want her to be like Jess. Sweet, cute, and, well, not easy, but dude, I'm in college. I want to get as much play as possible before I graduate, find a wife, blah, blah, blah. Jess understood, and we parted friends. While cute and fun, Jess wasn't the girl for me, if you catch my drift."

Trey pursed his lips, raised his eyebrows, and nodded. " I hear ya. So, who were you looking for a good time with that night? Which one of the girls?"

Trevor leaned back in the chair. "I wasn't. I was looking for a pro. On our second night in town, Sunday, I hooked up with the girl tending bar. Gotta say they make some killer drinks, really. If you haven't had one there, it's a must." *Arrogant prick* was Trey's involuntary thought.

"Trinity?" Trey knew that had to be bogus. Trinity didn't come across as someone to entertain the customers that way; besides, the owner had said the Saturday crew didn't work on Sundays.

"Nah, the bleach blonde, Samantha. She actually did me in the bathroom. I thought she was a pro. My dad shared a piece of advice with me. He said, rather than tangle up with girls from school— this is after Jess and I parted ways— to get my jollies with pros. The sex would be far better; they'd do anything you wanted and didn't have the hassle of," he raised his voice to a higher pitch like a girl, " 'Call me.' Pros know the score and are a sure bet. Does that surprise you?" He postured with a cocky tilt of his head.

Trey watched him with little to no expression."Trevor, not much surprises me, sorry to say. I think it's a bold move on your dad's part, but his information is correct. I've never been with a pro, but it certainly makes things a lot simpler unless, of course, you get busted, but then I guess your dad can get you out of it. Just make sure to wrap it up. If I were a betting man, I think your dad was referring to call girls, not street hookers." Trey looked down at his pad and made a few notes.

"Um, no kidding. Look, I had too much to drink, and Samantha is cute. So, what're a hundred bucks? She knew what she was doing and was damn good. I really thought she was a pro and made the huge mistake of trying to get her to do Adam; he's still a virgin. Can you believe it? A guy in college and still, oh well. Samantha got pretty pissed."

Trey's body slightly bounced as he nodded with raised eyebrows and a wicked grin. "Oh, I bet she did. Okay, so tell me about when everyone left."

Trevor leaned on his elbows toward Trey. "I think, not a hundred percent sure—Sloane headed off with Scott; they're a couple or friends with a twist. Sometimes it's hard to tell; Sloane flirts pretty hard." He shook his head back and forth slightly, ear to shoulder. "Stevie had already tried to hit on Jess, who slapped the shit out of him. I think he asked her to either fuck or blow him. Stupid. Everyone knows the deal with Jess. He ended up leaving with Jasmine, who'll pretty much do anybody; she's like a nympho or something. Oh, Desondra, Becca, and Adam left to go dance. I think maybe that's where Sloane and Scott went; I don't really know or care. I didn't realize Jess was still in the bathroom, but when she came out and started to leave, the busser guy from Louie's escorted her back to the hotel. I was alone and followed them. I don't know this guy, and well, I wanted to make sure Jess was okay. They seemed to like each other; they joked and laughed. So I called it a night, went to my room, and made a call. I can give you that number if you need it. The chick's name was Barbie." He rolled his eyes. "I said, 'well, I guess I'm Ken, haha.' I did my deed, and she left. Stevie came in about an hour later, maybe 3. That was my Saturday night." Like it or not, Trevor wasn't the perpetrator, Trey surmised.

"Okay, stud. I have your cell number. You are free to go. See, simple, right? I'm not the dick you thought I was; admit it." Trey pushed down on the table, leaning forward as he started to rise.

"I stand corrected; you are not the dick I thought you were. I'm out of here. Good night, detective." He had a glib tone.

"Trevor, seriously, be careful. This city can get dangerous late at night. Don't go walking about alone and stay on the main streets." Trey advised.

The boy turned at the door as they were walking out. "Gotcha."

Max had already interrogated Becca and had Desondra in Interrogation 3. Trey called Stevie into the room; he was nervous; beads of sweat formed on his top lip, and he visibly trembled.

"Want some water?" The boy nodded, and Trey got up and grabbed a bottle. "Now, Stevie, or is it Steve? Just for protocol; you have the right to remain silent—" Trey continued reading him his rights.

"I got it, sir. Stevie is what everyone calls me." The boy couldn't sit still for more than ten seconds.

"Okay, Stevie, it is. Let's talk about Saturday night at Louie's. I know y'all were all there having a good time. Start from mid-evening. First, how well did you know Jess?"

"Uh, um, I m-met J-Jess after the semester break in Jan-January. I didn't know her well."

His hands were trembling, making it hard for him to hold the bottle.

"Stevie, what're you so nervous about, son? Did you do something wrong?" With that, the boy burst into tears, sobbing. "Did you hurt Jessica, Stevie?" He nodded. "What did you do to her? Get control and take your time."

Several minutes passed, the crying and sobbing had stopped, and he could hold his bottle of water without fear of spilling it all over the place. He seemed in control; thus, the interview continued.

Trey nodded to the boy to proceed. "Hookin' up is a big deal on Spring Break. Everyone had been making fun of Adam because he's still a virgin. I've had sex, but not a lot like Trevor and Scott." He looked downward, his chin nearly touching his chest. "When it looked like everyone was leaving, I asked Jess if she wanted to, you know," he looked up and whispered, "Um-f."

"Fuck?" Trey filled in the blanks, which was against how he'd usually conducted an interview. He didn't make a practice of filling in the blanks; that was up to the person in the hot seat, but the boy was beyond a mess.

"Y-yes. She slapped me hard in the face and stormed off. I hurt her feelings. I had too much to drink, and I'm sorry I hurt her feelings, and I can't make it right because she's dead." The boy's face was red as berries, and he was sweating profusely, gripping handfuls of his hair.

"Ah, I see. So what did you do then?" Trey tilted his head to the side while making marks on the pad, waiting for an answer. Getting anything from the kid was like pulling teeth.

With a sheepish tone to his voice, he answered. "I hooked up with Jasmine."

"Did you see Jessica after that?" Trey watched the body movements, and the answer was clear, no, he had no idea what happened after he left with Jasmine. He was getting his rocks off, and the last thing on his mind was Jessica or the slap in the face. It wasn't long before he dismissed the boy, giving the same warning he had given Trevor.

By the time Trey's second interview was over, all the girls and Gage had spoken with Max. He shrugged his shoulders as if to ask Trey what was taking so long. "Max, that last boy was a mess. Trevor isn't the doer, and this boy Stevie, the one that got slapped, was a trip and a half. You want Scott, and I'll take Adam? We still have to speak to Sloane."

"Trey, the Duplantis boy was with Sloane, and you already talked to him, right?"

"Yeah, but I gotta interview him like I did the other boys. And, by the way, how'd you get all the girls and I got stuck with the boys. Girls are so much easier to communicate with than guys." Trey theorized.

Max put his hand on Trey's shoulder. "You stick with the boys; I will run down Sloane; besides, partner, I spoke with Gage."

"Good luck getting Sloane, ya hear? Max, you gotta be delicate with her; I know she comes off at first like a class-A bitch, but there's more to her than spoiled brat." He knew how Max could be. He'd grown up rough, completed high school, and joined the force. Max's parents' house rules were clear; once he and his siblings turned eighteen, they were on their own; it was merely a fact, and they all knew it.

"Hey, if she doesn't answer the door, I'm gonna get the hotel to open it for me. The girl coulda gone off the deep end." He grabbed his Diet Coke before leaving.

Trey chucked Max on the shoulder. "You get the girl; bring her here. I'll do the Duplantis boy last. He seems calm, cool, and collected. We pretty much know he didn't do it. This kid Adam, from all accounts, I don't see as the attacker, but we'll see. He comes across as quiet and not like the others—maybe studious and kinda nerdy." Trey walked toward the kid named Adam. "Follow me." He walked Adam to Interrogation Room 1.

Adam was five-ten, had a decent build, and looked like an ordinary kid, but looks were often deceiving. He was composed for being a kid getting interrogated. The boy strolled into interrogation and sat entirely unemotional. Zero nerves. Trey read him his rights. The boy said yeah, he understood.

"Adam, this is how it goes. I ask you questions, and you answer. The sooner you respond, the quicker we get out, and you return to your Spring Break fun. Got it?" Trey asked.

"Got it." The boy had a blank expression, utterly deadpan.

"How well did you know Jessica Lambert?" Trey's notepad was open to a blank page, ready to scratch a few notes.

"I didn't. Scott, my friend, dates Sloane, Jessica's best friend. I met her at the hotel for the first time." The boy droned an answer.

"Did you know anything about her?" Trey looked him directly in the eyes.

"Nope. Just that she and Sloane were BFFs, if not lesbian lovers; Scott told me they were always together, and Jessica was possessive over Sloane." Trey thought, *a new angle to the picture. Interesting.*

"Describe the night of Jessica's murder to me." Adam had piqued his interest.

"Nothing much to tell," still, the kid was void of expression. "We all drank a lot; I got a little hassle because I didn't talk about wanting to get laid all the time. I figure either you do it or talk about doing it. Desondra and Becca wanted to dance, and it sounded good to me, so we went to a club. As soon as we entered, it was pretty easy to see it was a gay club, and, well, I have nothing against gays, but I didn't stay. Desondra and Becca stayed and promised to Uber it back to the hotel. That was my night." Something about the kid got under Trey's skin.

Trey frowned, "So you just went back to the room, nowhere else?" It sounded sketchy like he was hiding something.

"Nope, straight back to my room. Any more questions?" Blasé wasn't even close to the boy's demeanor, clearly a flat affect.

"Tell me about your home life. Mom, Dad, Siblings, dog? You know, what's it like at home, and then I'll ask you about life at school."

"What the fuck?" In a flash, it ran through Trey's mind; *really, kid, got some balls, don't know about brains, but balls.* "I have an older sister, a younger sister, a bitch of a mom, and a workaholic dad. The man has no choice with the three gimme, gimme, gimme bitches in the house. No pets. Mom doesn't want the hair." *Wow, Houston, we have a problem.*

"Okay, I get the picture. How about dorm life? You room with Scott?" Trey had already penned a few words.

"No. I live at home. My older sister wanted to live in the sorority house. Princess got her way, and I live at home. Are we finished yet?" The boy was impatient, so far, the only human quality Trey had seen.

"You have a girlfriend back home?" Trey tapped his pen on the pad.

"Yeah, why? Like everyone else, I bet you think I might be a virgin and have some pent-up angst. Olivia and I have been together for a while, like years. We have a great sex life because that'll be the next question. I don't need to get pussy anywhere else. Satisfied?"

Trey had seen almost everything, but this kid was a different kind of special. "You friends with the other boys, or just Scott?"

The boy turned his hands up. "What does it matter? They're okay, I guess. This whole trip was Sloane's idea, and because Scott's whipped, he put the guys together, and Sloane handled the girls."

"Why didn't your girl come?" Things were getting more and more curious.

"Because she's got a fuckin job."

"I've let you slide, but what's with the attitude? I've questioned almost all of you guys so far, and you're the only one to give me grief. Check your language, dude." Trey was getting pissed. Adam had no respect for the situation or the police.

"Or what? If you got anything on me, arrest me, or let me get the fuck

71

out of here. Y'all got nothing. You're wasting my time, and I paid a lot to come on this trip."

Adam was one of those kids; Trey wished he could pop in the mouth and muscle some respect, but a cooler head would prevail. "Sorry to take your time, but Jessica has no more time, and any light you could share might help."

The kid shifted in his chair, looking like he wanted to say something but was entertaining an internal debate. He turned and said with a soulless stare, "What, there's no evidence? You know, like DNA shit? Or was the killer too smart to leave anything behind?" That sealed it in Trey's mind. Adam was at the top of his suspect list. Now, he truly wanted to talk with Scott and get a read on Adam.

"Seems you're on top of forensics. It doesn't work like on TV; it takes longer to process everything, and we have a backlog of cases. New Orleans has the best forensics, and if there is even," he squinted his eyes while pressing his forefinger and thumb together, "the most minute irregularity, they are on it like white on rice." He sat silent for a minute, letting his parting words sink in. The boy didn't have the slightest flinch, pupils stable and non-responsive, same deadpan look—smug and defiant. Trey would make the asshole sit it out for a few just for grins. "I'll be right back; gotta check something." After twenty minutes, Trey returned, and the boy was decidedly pissed. Mission accomplished. "That's it, Mr. Decker. Be careful; New Orleans can be a dangerous place." Trey sarcastically smiled.

"Whatever, dude, I can take care of myself."

As the kid walked out the door, Trey said, "I bet you can."

He watched as the boy walked away, assuming the same quiet, nerdy persona, a total contrast to his attitude in interrogation. It was downright creepy. Trey had seen soulless eyes before; it always made his skin crawl. He shuddered.

Scott was the last on his list. "Buddy, you ready? I saved the best for last. Since we already spoke to you, I figured there was little else to ask you, but, my bad, I didn't read you your rights before, so—" Trey smiled and Mirandized him.

Scott nodded, "Sure, I understand them. No problem. I'm really not in the partying mood anymore, I guess." Trey could see the sadness in the boy's eyes.

"You want a bottle of water or a Coke? I know you've been sitting here for some time. My partner is at Hotel Noelle, hoping to talk to Sloane." Scott had no bounce in his step and cast his eyes toward the floor.

"I wish him luck. Sloane won't answer the door, my calls, even my texts. At first, I was scared something might have happened to her, but I could hear her moving around when I put my ear to the door. A Coke sounds good; you have anything else?" He asked as they walked toward the interrogation room.

"You like root beer? We have the best here, Barq's. You had it before?" The boy smiled briefly. "Ah, so you have." Trey led him into interrogation and popped out to grab the drinks.

Trey took on a caring, gentle look. "How're you doing?"

Tears formed in the boy's eyes. "Not good, but what makes it worse is that Sloane won't talk to me. I mean, I know she's hurting, but we could at least console each other."

Pen in hand, Trey asked, "Y'all haven't talked at all?"

"No." He shook his head. "I think you were the last person she talked to; wait, no, she did speak with Jess' mom. She's feeling so guilty—talking Jess into coming here and then," he put his head down, "not that this is important to the case, but the night before leaving for the trip, everybody got trashed." He put his hands over his face and then moved them, looking at Trey intensely. "I passed out, but I woke up," he cleared his throat, "she was making out with Adam. Everyone else was passed out, and I acted like I was still out. The next day everyone was busy getting the cars loaded. She barely spoke a word to me but hugged me right before we took off and told me she loved me."

Scott looked down again, shaking his head, "I know we were all drunk, but shit, he's my friend, and she's my girlfriend. Come on. I had to act like I didn't know anything. The girls were in one car and the guys in the other. I know, so high school, but when we got to the hotel and settled, I asked her to walk with me. I told her what I saw, and she totally denied it—even 'how dare'd me.' Man, I saw it. Adam was on top of her, and they were at it." He rubbed his eyes. "I apologized and said maybe I dreamed it; I know I didn't, but I forgave her, even though it was a dream, which it wasn't." The boy was animated, and there was no doubt in Trey's mind that Adam had boned the girl. The thought crossed his mind that maybe Sloane was passed out, Adam raped her without her knowledge, or perhaps a rufie. *Nah*, he thought, *total drunk.*

Trey knew that scenario was possible because there had been several times when he came home from being called out, and Steph was sound asleep. They'd made love, and she hadn't any memory of it. Steph always seemed aggravated that she hadn't woken up for the fun ride, even though she appeared to be awake. There was never any doubt when she woke up in the morning, and she'd laugh, saying she'd missed the main event. His wife was always up for a good bonking and seemed pissed at herself for missing out on the good time.

"Wow, Scott, I bet that pissed you off. How'd you deal with Adam? Did you ask him or just pound his face? That woulda been my gut reaction." Trey leaned into the conversation, both elbows on the table, eyebrows furrowed, and intent on every facial expression and body movement made by the boy. Sometimes just the slightest twitch or wayward glance of the eye could indicate the truth of the matter. He felt for the kid.

The tears started filling Scott's eyes. Trey passed the box of Kleenex. "Yeah, I'm still pissed with Adam. I thought he was my friend, but the more I look back on our friendship, the more I see it was one-sided." He shook his head slowly, tucking his lips tightly around his teeth, making the dimple in his right cheek more profound. "I didn't want the confrontation. I didn't have proof, and it's not like Sloane said anything. She totally denied it."

Still in the same position leaning into the conversation, Trey tilted his head to the side in curiosity. "How long have y'all, you and Adam, been friends? He's not living on campus; is he a neighbor or something?"

Scott twisted a tissue in obvious deep thought. His nerves were raw, and he was exhausted. "I've known Adam for four, maybe five years. He was the lifeguard at the club pool. He was like a chick magnet, but the thing is, the dude never spoke. He'd just sit in his chair with dark sunglasses on and occasionally blow his whistle if some of the younger kids were running or people were getting too rough in water fights. I guess he was mysterious to the girls." He closed his eyes and slowly shook his head. "He used me; he uses everyone, and I bought it."

"Okay and?"

Scott sighed. "I'm the guy girls want to be friends with, you know, *that guy*. I'm, to quote them, 'sweet, cute, and funny.' Everyone wanted to be my friend, not their boyfriend. So, one day when the girls were in the locker room, probably smoking, gossiping, or putting on make-up, I sat on a lounge chair near Adam. I told him hi; he told me hi; I asked where he went to school, how old he was, how he got the lifeguarding gig, etcetera. Before long, I ordered him a burger when I ordered mine, and then on Mondays when the club was closed, he'd come hang at my house after he'd done whatever maintenance was needed."

He turned his hands up with an embarrassed look on his face. "I come from a wealthy family, and we're all close-knit. I guess he didn't have that at home. Later I found out he hated his mom and sisters. Who hates their mom?" Scott skewed his face with confusion. "Anyway, we started hanging out together, but then he met Olivia, a girl in his neighborhood. She's hot, smokin' hot, and I know this sounds snotty, but in a trampy kind of way. The club pool closed when summer ended, like Labor Day weekend, and school was back in session. I was in my senior year, and my dad bought a Corvette for me as a senior present. It was for graduation, but Dad got it at the beginning of my senior year."

Trey's eyes opened wide, and he smiled from ear to ear. "What color, don't tell me red?" Scott nodded. "No way, my dream car, always. Now that had to be a chick magnet and not just cause you're a nice person, but, friend, it's good that you're who you are; you'll go much farther in life than a mute lifeguard." With that, Scott laughed.

"Yeah, I know." Scott sat silent for a moment with his eyes closed. Then, with a look of embarrassment, he began to speak again. "I missed, and I don't want to sound gay, our dude time. I told him everything, but I did all the talking," he changed his voice, "I guess cuz he was a mute," and laughed again. "Anyway, he knew I was going to Ole Miss; my family has been Ole Miss all the way for generations. He wanted to go," he flicked his hands open, "so my dad got him in. He was able to get a way-reduced tuition, but not dorm, fraternity, or anything else, but he seemed appreciative of what my dad did for him. We started hanging out again. Olivia set me up with some of her friends." He blushed a brilliant shade of red.

"I'm guessing from your Corvette red face that you were experiencing many of the pleasures of life, am I right? Guess you got some of that nice guy shine dulled a bit?"

"Uh, yeah. Olivia has some hot, uh, slu, um, easy friends." He grinned. "We both ended up at Ole Miss, and even though I lived close, I did the dorm fraternity thing. I was the story of two lives—Frat college boy and, well, not-so-frat boy. God, my dad would've been so ashamed. I was acting like some kind of street punk, m-f-ing this-m-f-ing that.

There was this one girl I dated a few times, not Olivia's friend; the chick was in my poly-sci; she gave all the signals that she wanted to, you know, but when I pulled out the packet to wrap it up, she was like, 'uh, I don't think so.' Okay, my bad." He put both his hands up like an apology. "Anyway, I'm telling Adam about the date. I told him everything; when I got to the part where she tells me no, he says, 'And did you tell her that's not the way the game is played?' I said, 'No, cuz that *is* the way the game is played.' His response to that freaked me. He said, 'You tell her she got you this way, and one way or the other, she was gonna take care of it. She had her choice, hand, mouth, or, well, you know.' I was like, 'No way, dude.' He shook his head and said, 'Whatever, lame, Scott. What, you had to jerk yourself off? Hell no, I woulda pinned her down and hard fucked the hell out of her prick-teasing self. I guarantee it woulda been the last time she toyed with a guy about sex.'"

By this time, Trey had his hands holding his head. "Wow. What a punk, and you're right, no is no, and anything else is punishable by law. I would nail your ass for sure. So, how does he end up on the trip?"

There was a tap on the window. Trey stepped out for a few minutes, came back in with a pale in his complexion, and saw the panic in Scott's eyes. "She's okay; Max got inside the room, and she is on the way to the hospital. She'll be okay, just way drunk."

The boy stood, his hands trembling. "Can we finish this tomorrow? Please. I promise not to run off anywhere. Can y'all call me a cab? What hospital? I was scared she'd do something to herself."

Trey felt bad for him, and while he wanted the rest of the story, he knew the kid was stand-up. His only worry was that Adam, out of anger or sheer crazy, would attack someone else. The sooner he got the kid arrested, the better. He had no evidence, and not liking someone's attitude or thinking they were a piece of shit wouldn't be cause for an arrest warrant.

DOES IT MATTER?

*A*fter a night of abbreviated conversation with Trinity, Babe delighted in the walk home. The pop of a car's backfire triggered his reflexes, and he dove between two parked vehicles. His heart leapt, driving his pulse to a maxed-out fury. Quickly realizing it hadn't been gunfire, merely a car in need of a tune-up, he righted himself taking note of the stripe of grunge from his hip to his knee from sliding on the pavement. He thought, *probably layers of old piss and vomit, maybe even dog crap*—the jeans were going in the wash anyway, just sooner than later. The rest of the way home was uneventful.

Once home, he put his jeans in the wash and jumped in the shower. It had been a good night. Trinity had asked him to stay at Louie's; she wanted to be with him and learn more about him. Her voice alone aroused him; it wasn't just the body, the eyes, or the smile; she was the whole package, and until he could get himself straight in the head, he couldn't chance to stay a night with her. His thoughts churned as the water beat upon his back—the fact that he could kill without feeling or remorse should have been unsettling, yet his years as a Marine Raider removed the connection between mind and heart. It was life or death, them or him. The voice of his staff sergeant resounded in his head. They always yelled everything with a passion that made him come alive.

The flashback began: *"What's my name?"*

He answered with the same velocity, *"Staff Sergeant Wilcox, sir."*

My mission is to train each of you to be a United States Marine. The best, the brightest, with the highest purpose. What do we need? Discipline and spirit. Never give up—a Marine never gives up. Even if you give up on yourself, we will never give up. We will push you to be the best. I will lead you 100% all the time. A Marine does not lie, cheat, or steal and must be trained in what, Vicarelli?

Barking back, Discipline and spirit, sir!

You control your mind. A Marine never quits.

Babe shook his head, splashing the wall as he shook the speech from his mind. Could Trinity deal with his intensity? Perhaps he needed to stop his nightly indulgence at Louie's and turn away from the temptation knowing he would never be able to fulfill her needs. There was a reason he had never had a relationship with anyone. It complicated things; it was much easier to be alone. There was no one to disappoint, hurt or surrender to—what if he couldn't control his desires—what were his desires? Did he want strictly carnal interaction; he could have that easily, but Trinity was different. Did she have enough soul for the two of them, enough goodness for two?

His mind buzzed with flashes of random thoughts. Sleep beckoned. It was not like he would make any big decision that night or like there was even a decision to make. Babe's mind drifted to her glistening eyes and full puckers. The morning was but a dream away.

Trey's day had ended, yet he never made it by Louie's. It was late, and there was no need; what he needed was time with Steph.

As he pulled up, he saw the TV screen and an episode of Friends playing. Typical Steph; it's part of why he loved her so much; she knew how to dial out the craziness of the world and relax.

She opened the front door and stood at the screen, watching him gather his things to come inside. "You're early," as she opened the screen door, "welcomed surprise." She stripped his arms and put his satchel on the entrance table for a proper welcome home hug and kiss.

"Good day today for you, Steph; any complaining clients? You're a far better person than I am; I think I'd have to shoot some of yours." He looked into her eyes, holding her with his hands on the small of her back. "I love you. Thanks for being so supportive; I promise we'll take a weekend soon and go to the coast."

"Sounds like a plan," she pulled him close. "Until then, I'll take what I can get. How's it going with the dead college girl? Progress?" They walked into the kitchen, and she started making a salad as his dinner heated. "Her poor parents; it's heartbreaking," she sympathized.

"Yeah. Jessica, that was her name, was a good kid from all accounts. The whole group, save one asshole, are pretty good kids, but the one; you'd never call it if you saw him. I sure didn't. I figured him to be quiet, maybe the nerd of the group; that's how he presents until you get him in interrogation. He's a punk, and I mean punk, a real piece of work. I think he may even be the doer. I don't have a scrap of evidence yet, but I feel it in my bones. The kid is soulless, like nothing behind his eyes. Sicko." He watched as she carefully sliced the tomato. "I think he is truly a psychopath or sociopath. I always have a hard time telling which is which, but I'd like to get our psychiatrist to talk with him; however, I have to have more than my thinking the kid's crazy. I have nothing to go on but my gut." After passing him the salad, she sat at the counter with him, munching on a small bowl with her favorite salad fixings.

"Does he move his arms when he walks?" She asked between bites.

"What?" He gave her a cock-eyed smile. "I don't know. Why?"

"I think I heard on TV that true psychopaths don't move their arms when they walk." He could feel his stomach bubble with the thought that she was just so damn into him. It was one hell of a case of butterflies that landed below his belt. "See, didn't know I was a plethora of information." Stephanie giggled. His heart filled watching her; she was vibrant with life, candid in her laughter, and dedicated to him.

He ravenously ate his dinner, rinsed his plate, and then the two showered. Naked hugs were the best, and kisses beneath the spray of the shower were magical. She warmed him to his very core.

TV off and lights out, they headed for bed. "We need to put some shutters on the den windows. I could see you watching TV, even that you were watching Friends. The curtains only create minimal privacy. What if I were walkin' around in my drawers?" She laughed; he always walked around in his boxers.

"Okay, Trey, we'll go pick them out this weekend." She happily agreed.

Quiet. "Steph, that was too easy. You usually put up a fight when I want to spend money on the house. Something spooked you?" In the darkness, he couldn't see her face to weigh the reaction.

"No, Trey," she placated. "But I've thought the same thing a few times, ya know, what if. Besides, I just got paid for all the work I did for Kelly's Klosets. It was an expensive job; unlike others who want everything for nothing, they were lovely to deal with. We made out good, babe." She rolled close to him. "Smooches? My eyes are getting heavy. Sleep, Trey; morning will come too soon."

He laughed, "You can't call me babe anymore."

"What? Sleep, Trey."

He held her hand. "There's this guy that hangs out at Louie's. He's enormous, a brick shithouse like you wouldn't want to get on his wrong side. His honest-to-goodness name is Babe. The word or term 'babe' has taken on a new meaning. We gotta go to Louie's one night so you can see this guy. He was in the Marines, and I'm betting on one of the special ops teams, like with Terminator intensity."

They were in total darkness; she spooned next to him. "Trey, either go to sleep or—"

"Game on." He chuckled and pulled her on top of him.

Max drove Scott to University Hospital following his time with Trey. The kid's voice cracked from nerves and fear. "What was Sloane like when you saw her? Did she take pills or try to cut her wrist? Where would she even get pills to take?" The boy was jittery and babbled incessantly from nerves.

"Son, I have no idea. She didn't cut herself; she was out of it, and I had to get the hotel to open the door. The hospital will run tests. I think she might have alcohol poisoning, but I ain't no doc. All's I can tell ya is she kept sayin' it was all her fault. Jessica was dead because of her."

For a few minutes, there was utter silence. Max figured Scott was hashing and re-hashing the situation. "How could she say she was responsible for Jess being dead? What about that boy from the bar? Wasn't he the last one with her?" Silence again for a few moments.

They pulled up to the hospital. Max grabbed the boy's shoulder. "Scott, you gotta stay calm; you got me? Getting yourself all in a tizz won't do her no good, and I'm not even sure they'll let you see her." Scott maintained control and walked with Max into the E.R. The detective spoke with the person in charge, and they agreed to let Scott see her for a few minutes. He returned to the boy and quietly said, " Here's the deal, kid; they'll let you in for a few minutes. They have her controlled for the time being. No pressuring her or asking too much. Hold her hand, give her a kiss on the cheek, or pet her hair, you hear me?"

Eyes wide, he nodded and responded, "Yes, I understand." He cautiously walked into the assessment room.

Sloane sat in the bed, her head hung into her chest.

"A-hem," he cleared his throat. "Hi, Sloane. I've been worried about you; we all have."

She continued to look down or away from him. "Sorry."

"No need to apologize." He walked to the side of the bed, put his hand on hers, moved to her chin, and steadily lifted her head. "I'm sorry about Jess, Sloane. It wasn't supposed to –" Sloane was in her own thoughts and didn't hear Scott's words.

Tears began to tumble from her eyes as her shoulders flinched. "It's my fault. I shouldn't have ever said—" Sloane drew her hands to her face.

He stroked her hair. "Sh. No, it's not. We all wanted to come to New Orleans. She wanted to come."

"I know, but—"

She started to cry again, which triggered the nurse to check on her. "Sir, maybe tonight isn't the best time to visit."

"No!" She cried. "I want Scott here."

The nurse shook her head and told Scott to keep her calm.

"Sloane, I'm here. Everything's going to be okay." He tried to speak as calmly as possible.

"No, Scott, it isn't. All I know is I wanted to stay with you Saturday night since we weren't getting along. Remember what we discussed because you said you saw me with Adam?"

Scott's eyes teared up, "Maybe I was wrong; it doesn't matter."

She hung her head again, "but you see, it does." She barely whispered, looking at him pleadingly, "I think I gave Adam my room key. I'm not sure; I don't remember, but I couldn't find it anywhere in my room." The nurse returned and shushed him again, telling him he had to leave. It was time for everyone to tuck in for the night.

Babe's phone buzzed just before his five o'clock Alexa harassment. Wiping the grog from his eyes, he grabbed his phone, "Vicarelli."

"Sir, this is Ruthie from your grandad's house."

"Yes, ma'am. Is everything okay?" he asked, guessing the reason behind the call.

"I'm sorry, honey, Mister Rune, passed. He was peaceful. You got a key to his house?" she asked in a motherly, caring manner.

"Yes, ma'am." He got a strange tightness in his chest and swallowed the lump forming in his throat.

"You need help setting up the arrangements? I know he didn't want nothing special; he left instructions. Should I call his brother Bjorn or do you want to?" *What is the right answer?*

"No, ma'am, I'll call when I come by his house." The thought of going through his grandad's things was less than appealing, but someone had to do it, and unless Bjorn wanted to do the honors, Babe would be the only other option. "If you want anything in particular, Ruthie, help yourself." Whatever she took would be one less thing he'd have to contend with in the house.

"Thank you, sir. Maybe I'll take one of his handkerchiefs. Oh, and dawlin' don't put his passing in the newspaper right away, or the place will be easy pickings for thieves. Wait until you move in, suga." *Move in?* He had to think the whole thing through. Babe knew he didn't want to live in the house uptown and didn't want to hassle with renters. He remembered Denise. *All in due time.* "If you need any help, give me a holler. Mr. Rune had all the burial information in a file he'd given me some time ago, so I'll call them to pick up—um, suga, he sure loved you, talked about you all the time. I'm glad y'all had these past few months to spend together. I'll leave all the paperwork on the kitchen counter. He has everything spelled out."

"Yes, ma'am. I'll be there shortly."

Ruthie was still at the house waiting for the funeral home when he arrived, and indeed the old codger had everything in detail. "He passed in his sleep, honey. The way we'd all like to have our departure. It's interesting how much you look like him. I've seen photographs of your mother; she was a beautiful lady; she favored your grandmother. I never saw your father, but you're the spittin'-image of your grandfather, except for your coloring; you musta gotten your darkness from him." Babe couldn't help but think *yes, not just the hair, but the bleak inside his soul.*

She offered to fix coffee and breakfast while they waited, but he declined the offer with a one-sided smile. He glanced over the pages of instruction as they waited. As conveyed in bold bullet points, he jogged up to his grandfather's bedroom. The old guy did look quite peaceful. "I read your instructions and will execute them as outlined." He held the man's hand, leaned over, and kissed him on his forehead. He wished he could be half the man his grandfather had been. In the top bureau drawer was a brown leather box containing what little jewelry he had, a signet ring, and his two watches, both expensive. Also in the box were his grandmother's and mother's wedding rings, pendants, and bracelets. It was all sparkling with a high-quality heft.

The money clip he described, a handsome piece in itself, held a couple hundred dollars comprised of twenties, tens, and fives. He quickly scanned the room and sat on the side of the bed. "I'll miss our weekly visits. I had planned on introducing you to Trinity; we ran out of time. She's spunky, you would've liked her, but Jeez, she's a tiny thing." He looked down at his hands. "Farfar, I'm not going to live in your house, and I hope you don't mind, but I'm going to sell it. Having a home such as this is way beyond my scope. I'm used to living the life of a Marine, ready to bugout at a moment's notice. I don't have room for all your furniture, but I'll figure something out. I know you said it's all mine, but I think I'll settle for your bedside photos; that way, I'll always have y'all near."

The chimes of the front doorbell interrupted him. He heard Ruthie as she directed them upstairs. The men were properly attired in dark pants and a polo shirt with the name of the funeral home. They nodded with somber faces expressing their condolences. "Perhaps, you and Miss Ruthie might want to step out for this part. It's often hard on the loved ones of the departed." Babe had hauled more corpses than he cared to remember, but, in this case, maybe the people from the funeral parlor might be right.

Babe and Ruthie went downstairs. She waited by the stairs while Babe moved into the kitchen, grabbed two small glasses, and poured a dram of whiskey into each glass. He brought it over to Ruthie, who put her hand up. "I don't imbibe," she said with a taut twist of her lips. Babe cocked his head to the side and handed her the glass. "Well, maybe this one time. He'd like a toast." As the men rolled the body bag out to their hearse, Babe and Ruthie raised their glasses in farewell and knocked back the whiskey. "Oh, my!" Ruthie exclaimed as she fanned her face with her free hand.

With instructions in hand, Babe sat on the sofa and called Bjorn. It had been a long time since he'd spoken Norwegian, but he remembered a few words. "god kveld, dette er—" he said awkwardly.

In a husky baritone voice, his uncle responded. "Babe, I've been expecting this call. Good evening to you as well, or I guess it's morning. Rune called a few days ago to say farewell and told me you'd be calling."

With a sigh of relief, Babe spoke, "Glad you speak English; I remember very few words—

"Hah," he bellowed. "Everyone, most of the world, speaks English. You need to visit; see the world while you are young. Ah, but I imagine you have seen much of the world as a Marine. Rune told me he left all his earthly belongings to you; when asked, I told him I needed nothing and to ship anything would be a fortune. I've been to his house once; you were young. It was for the Mardi Gras; we drank and drank, filled to the gills. Hah! The furniture is all antique, you know. Rune amassed great wealth, but I'm sure you noodled that one." The old guy chuckled.

"Yes, sir. He didn't suffer from a lack of money. I have a question. Are there any other members of the family that might want his things?"

Silence. "Like my brother, I've lost my wife and child and have no grandchildren. You and your—" he stopped short.

"My what?" Silence once again.

Babe heard a deep sigh from the other end of the conversation. "Shite. You've caught me with a few drinks and a loose tongue. Leave it to me, the big bag of wind, to break the silence."

"My what? Did my mother have any other children? Do I have siblings?"

"Argh!" he blasted. "Yes, yes, you have a brother somewhere. I believe Mays was removed from your parent's home when he was five. I suspect he's ten or fifteen years older than you, making him—"

"Forty-six or fifty-one. Where is he? Did he know about me?"

"No. You're putting me in a delicate place." He could hear the hemming and hawing.

"Bjorn, now that Farfar is gone, there's no one left who gives a rat's ass, just me. Was he taken because of my piece of shit father?" Babe balled his right fist, the veins in his arm popping out.

"Yes. It broke your mother and my brother to pieces. I don't know about the other side, but from all accounts, I'm sure your father was as he was because of his parents. Let's not talk about this anymore. Open one of those bottles I sent Rune, and we can have a drink together."

Babe could feel the flush of anger rising up his collar. It wasn't his great-uncle's fault, but why didn't his grandfather tell him? They talked about everything else. Perhaps it was a scar he didn't want to bleed again. He grabbed a bottle out of the refrigerator and opened it. "Here's to you, Bjorn, and thank you for sharing the information. It took balls to break the family secret, and I'm glad you did. Mays, you said?"

"Yes. Rune was all about baseball, the great American pastime. He was over the top. Cheers to you, and may you and your wife have a house filled with children and keep the bloodline going. You know we are of Viking blood? Born warriors. Speaking of warriors, I must get off the phone before Ilsa beats me with her shoe. Hah!" he bellowed again. "She's much younger than I, and what a vixen. I hope I die in her arms; then, it will be a most happy death. Hah!" It had become apparent he wasn't kidding when he said he'd had many drinks, and yes, his tongue was getting too loose. What he planned to do with the information of a brother was still up for debate. After a quick farewell, they agreed to keep in touch.

Babe sat in a chair, his head in his hands. Did he want to find Mays, the long-lost brother, or let it go as none the wiser? Decisions for another day; he and Ruthie locked the house and left.

ANOTHER DAY

*H*is routine was off-kilter, but he needed to get to work. As Babe and Gunner, his furry friend, were walking onto the job site, he noticed two of the crew having words that grew into fists and rolling on the ground in a brawl. He grabbed one guy, and the site super grabbed the other pulling them apart. The guy Babe was holding back was a wiry little guy about five-six, but he managed to wiggle away enough to turn quickly and pop the big guy in the face. "Vicarelli, stay the fuck out of my business and keep your ape hands off me. I ain't scared of you; you better watch your back and stay away from me."

With an empty stare, Babe turned and went into the trailer with the dog. The crowd that had formed around the fight dispersed, and everyone headed to their place on the job site. The site superintendent, Glenn Cooper, walked into the trailer. Babe was looking over the blueprints. "Thanks for the help, Vicarelli. I can't believe that piece of shit threatened you; by the way, he's getting pink-slipped today, anyway. I have two write-ups on him already for fighting. He threw a hammer at one of the men, but the guy blew it off, which pissed him off even more. He must have some kind of death wish or something. I brought him on-site as a favor for someone, but that little man has a mean streak. You can see it in his eyes. I tell ya, he's gonna mess with the wrong person one day."

"Happy to help, sir." They reviewed the schedule and the job's progress, determining they were close to the proposed timeline, maybe a few days off. The forecast predicted no rain for the next week, so they could make up the time they missed because of a few rainy days if the report was correct, which was a fifty-fifty chance.

The rest of the day was uneventful, and the wretched little man had stayed to himself. He was a useless piece of crap. As Babe assisted one of the men in lacing cable through a series of holes, the voice in his head brought him back in time. Under his breath, he said "useless" as the thought of the troublemaker traipsed through his mind. *Useless*. What a word, one that stirred memories. The reel played through his mind.

This is my rifle. There are many like it, but this one is mine.

My rifle is my best friend. I must master it as I master my life.

Without me, my rifle is useless. Without my rifle, I am useless, I must fight my rifle true.

"Vicarelli, yo, Vic, the job has you in a trance. It's quitting time, friend."

He looked at the man he was assisting with the pipe. "Thanks."

"Wanna grab a beer or something?" the co-worker asked.

The sack of shit from the morning walked by, scoffed, and said sarcastically. "Him? The yes, sir, man?" He looked at Babe, "ass-kisser. Ya better watch ya back, tough guy."

The co-worker turned to the little man, "Stan, fuck off."

Babe looked up with a cold smile, "Harry, don't waste your time on Stan." He tilted his head and winked, "Not worth your breath. Sure, beer sounds good, but scotch sounds better. I'm heading to Louie's after a shower; you know the place?"

It was about that time that the super walked out and asked Stan to come with him.

"Vicarelli, if I see ya, I see ya; if not, have a good night."

Trinity was up on a ladder when he walked into Louie's. "Hey, Babe!" She looked down at him.

"Little lady, you need to get down from there. What're you doing up there, anyway?"

"Done." She came down the ladder. "Adjusting and wiping down the last camera. Shh. Most people don't know we have them. Usual? Wings, burger, or—"

"Plate dinner tonight, meatloaf and mash, right?"

She laughed, "Yep, you know it. Onions added to that, Babe?"

"Thank you." He nodded and took his seat.

It didn't take but a minute, and she was behind the bar pouring his two-finger scotch. While he preferred the skirt so he could admire her legs, the jeans grabbed her ass the way he wished he could, scooping her up hard and tight. The fantasy needed to shut down and quickly.

"You looking at my ass, Babe?" She flirted, calling him out.

Lie or truth? "Yes, ma'am." He raised an eyebrow and smiled from ear to ear. "Caught me." Babe's ears turned pink.

She put his drink down and leaned closer to him across the bar. " I don't work on Sundays or Mondays; maybe we could grab dinner and go on a real date instead of these half-ass conversations. You interested? Do you want to get to know me better? Cuz honey, I sure want to know you better. Like I said before, you intrigue me."

All he could do was smile and swallow hard. "Yes, ma'am. Sunday, then? Where do you want to meet?"

"Meet, not pick me up? How about Cane & Table or a fancy restaurant?"

"Don't know Cane & Table, so I guess somewhere else; think of where you'd like to go. I don't usually drive, being the Quarter with all its one-way streets; does that make a difference? Unless you want to go to Metairie or somewhere else?" He looked directly into her eyes. The sparks in her eyes created a burning fire inside of him. He thought, *is this getting too close to the edge? Maybe it'd be best to decline the date. No.* He hammered the idea in his head.

"So, why were you on the ladder?" He distracted himself.

"Because of the recent murders, like in the past week, my uncle wants to make sure our cameras are working in case we have an incident in here."

He took a sip of the drink. "Got it. So your uncle owns this place?"

"Yeah, Shep, but it's been in the family forever, just like the—" a clank on the bar interrupted her. "See, a date will be much better." The nightly crowd filtered in.

The day was coming to a close for Trey and Max, and neither was closer to finding the killer. The only additional information was that the perpetrator had suffocated Jessica, according to forensics. They had already figured that out for themselves, but confirmation from Charlotte, better known as Charly, was what they needed for the file. "I'm going to Louie's, Max, you wanna come with, or you got somewhere special to be?" Trey straightened his files and squared everything on his desk, whereas Max left the cluttered mess as it was on his. Trey looked at the disarray and shook his head.

"Yeah, I'll hang. With this new info, you think the perp just meant to force himself on Jessica and accidentally smothered her? Ya know, like put his hand over her mouth to keep her quiet?" While Max didn't come across as a thinker, he was sharp. They made a good team.

They walked to their cars. "Let's say I buy that." Trey went on. "Then, if it had been a stranger, they might have knocked her out, but since there was no forcible entry or injury from a blunt object, I think she knew the person, and if she were left alive, she could give him up. Without any evidence, it's all hypothetical anyway."

Max reached his car first, "Trey, maybe your bromance will be at the bar," and he laughed.

"What, you're jealous now? Bromance, gimme a break. He's an unusual kind of guy. I mean, who goes to Louie's every night?" A few more steps and he'd be at his car.

After parking, they walked into Louie's. Babe was sitting, as usual, at the end of the bar. He did the chin lift guy nod at them as they walked his way. Trey sat on the stool next to him. "I see ya girl's here."

"Not my girl yet." He took a bite of the mashed potatoes.

Max eyed Babe's dinner. "Trey, did you know they do plates? This is good information; way better than fucking frozen dinners or pizza all the time. He leaned forward in front of Trey. "Is the food any good here, or do you come for the visuals?" He playfully raised his eyebrows with a double lift and smiled.

"The food's good, surprisingly, but I can't complain about the sights," half of his mouth upturned, and the tips of his ears flushed. "How's your murder case coming?"

Trinity called out, "After hours, guys or—"

Max smiled and responded, "Two drafts, darlin'. Trey, I got the first round; you get the second."

"What if I'm only having one?" and he laughed.

"Fuck you. Cheap ass." Max responded in his usual crass manner.

Trey looked at Babe, "This case is complex," and sighed. "I think I know who the guy is, but he's not about to confess. I think he finds enjoyment in watching us pull our hair out in frustration. He knows he has us over a barrel—cocky little asshole. I'd do just about anything to get his confession. If we could get the evidence, I'd arrest his ass in a heartbeat."

Babe nodded with a slight wave-like sway. "Look, y'all give me the guy, and if he did it, I'll get the confession; that's a promise." He grinned and took another bite.

"Problem here—I'd have to arrest you because I'm pretty sure your tactics don't fall in step with law-enforcement guidelines, but boy, I wish." Trey stared off into space. "Yeah, I wish. I can't even get a psych eval without probable cause, and I think this guy is certifiable." He thought for a minute, sipping his beer. "How's it coming with" and he nodded in Trinity's direction.

"So far, only in my dreams. " Babe chuckled. "Literally, but ask me again on Monday."

"Sounds like you made progress." Max held up his beer as if to toast.

Trinity stopped to check on the beer progress. She quickly glanced at Babe with a knowing smile. "Detectives, another beer?"

Trey passed his hand under his chin, indicating a cut-off no, while Max spoke up, "Not only another beer but one of them plates like he's got."

Trey stood, "I have a wife to get home to, boys. Enjoy." He handed Max a fistful of ones. "Here's for my round." He waved to Trinity and headed out the door.

The night progressed; eventually, Max left, and it was getting time for Babe to go. Out of the corner of his eye, he saw the same man pass back and forth on the street. He watched the guy; sure enough, it was Stan from work. He could see Stan's reflection in the mirror over the back bar. Babe could only think that he came to make good on his threat. Pretty soon, it would be showtime. A thrill went through his body—the idea of a confrontation with this guy was almost like an aphrodisiac. He settled his bill, nodded to Trinity, put a ten on the bar as a tip, and left. Instead of doing the usual by quickly eliminating the threat, he might play with Stan like a cat with a mouse.

He purposefully walked slower, wondering just how far Stan would follow him and when he'd make his move. He slowed more as he came to a darkened service driveway. *Perfect.* The glow from the streetlamp was ineffective in the darkness of the drive. He could feel the sensation of the man closing in on his personal space. He abruptly turned as Stan raised his arm with a knife in hand. Babe grabbed him by the shoulders and pulled him into the darkened driveway. Stan began to yell, so Babe knuckled him in the throat, disabling his voice box temporarily.

"Stan, Stan, Stan." He shook his head. "What am I going to do with you? Usually, I like a quick snap of the neck, but you've been a nasty little prick to so many guys on the job site; I think I'll take my time. Babe grabbed both the guy's hands and snapped the wrists. Stan let out a guttural sound. "Shh, we're just getting started." Swiping a kick across his knees, the little man fell with terror in his eyes. "Why couldn't you leave well enough alone? Did you truly, in your heart, think you could take me down with that knife?" Playtime was over, and Babe was getting bored. He torqued Stan's neck, feeling the exhilaration as the vertebrae splintered beneath his hands. It had even more power than jacking a load. As Stan was flat out on the cement with his legs twisted awkwardly, Babe did a Weekend at Bernie's and tied Stan's shoelace with his left shoestring. He casually picked him up and put his arm around him like he was helping a passed-out drunken friend. With each step Babe took, Stan's leg would move, and the other leg appeared to be stumbling. As cars or people would pass, he'd quietly talk to the corpse in a quiet, friendly manner. Once at the job site, Babe undid the laces and tossed him in the dumpster. The game that he thought might be entertaining turned out to be a pain in the ass. Next time, he'd do what came naturally. Over and done. Bam.

There were too many people who had a beef with Stan that the police would have a hard time making him for the killer; after all, he had been with Trey and Max at Louie's.

The adrenalin ran through his body; it was a thrill second to none, but the charge he felt from the dreams he explored while thinking of Trinity came close. No other woman had made him feel as energized. All the other women had been a means to an end; nothing self-help couldn't ignite. It was good to be home. He threw his clothes in the hamper and got in the shower. He could see her in his mind, she spoke to him like she had at the bar, and he answered her as part of this imaginary duet. *You intrigue me, Babe. His mind rolled—Trinity, you set me on fire.* He slid into bed, wondering what their date Sunday might bring. Would they merely have a nice dinner, a few laughs, and get to know each other a little bit better, or would she invite him to her bed? *Sleep draw down the curtain*, he begged.

After a restful night's sleep and his morning ritual, he and Gunner took their daily run to work. As he rounded the corner, he saw squad cars, the van from the morgue, and an array of spectators. It was most curious for anyone but him; the street was normally dead, and now here it was with an active crime scene; people came from blocks away to gawk—the old trainwreck syndrome.

Babe tried to go under the crime scene tape, but a uniformed officer stopped him. "Hey, buddy, there's tape for a reason. Move along, thank you."

"I work here." Just then, Trey looked over and saw him.

"Peck, he's cool. Let him through." The officer acknowledged the order.

Babe passed under the tape, gestured appreciation to Trey, and headed for the construction trailer. Opening the door, he said, "What the hell is going on?"

Glenn, his site superintendent, responded. "One of the crew spotted Stan's body in the dumpster this morning. Like I said yesterday, he was gonna pick a fight with the wrong person. How you kept your cool with him after he cocked you yesterday is beyond me. I guess being pink-slipped added to his fun personality." Glenn ruffled Gunner's fur. The dog had become the site mascot.

"Did he cock me yesterday? Is that what that was?" He gave a slight chuckle. "Nah, I shouldn't speak ill of the dead; he must've been having a bad day, and it ended even worse. I'm gonna get back where I left off yesterday." He headed for the door.

Glenn was seated at the desk with his feet propped on an open drawer. "We're gonna have to wait until the police give us an okay to start up again. It's a pity cuz it just puts us behind schedule even more. Did you punch in yet? If not, you need to, boss' orders." After clocking in, Babe went outside and leaned on a sawhorse, checking his phone for messages and email.

Occasionally, the officer from the year of Pre-Separation Counseling would text or email a friendly touch base, which Babe found odd. He didn't know anyone else who had said they'd received communication after receiving an Honorable Discharge, not that he discussed it with anyone.

His counselor recommended verbally, nothing official, that he talk to someone even though he was stable and, from all appearances, healthy. *What a bunch of horseshit,* was his usual thought. Babe took the advice as a precaution and not to cause any ripples. Being a quiet but extremely observant man, keeping his private thoughts to himself sometimes unsettled others, but that was their problem, not his. The doctor he'd seen twice was a stand-up guy, not at all what one would imagine as a shrink. For some unknown reason, Babe's quiet demeanor triggered the medical community to feel there was some manifestation of a disorder, yet The Marines gave him an Honorable Discharge. There was no proof in the pudding, so to speak.

The question in everyone's minds was how he could have come through all he did without significant trauma. He often thought, *have you met my sperm donor?* He couldn't refer to him as a father; his grandfather was more a dad than Gino Vicarelli. Babe was a Marine; he followed orders and would take his duty to his grave. He hadn't been discharged from the human race, after all. The rules still applied; in his mind, if they didn't, then they damn well should.

An hour had passed; Babe could only look at his phone for so long. An idea twigged, and he went on ancestry.com; maybe he'd find Mays Vicarelli. Would he have kept the same name? Perhaps the DNA test could give him some insight. Then, what kind of man would he be? Did the darkness live in him, too? After ordering the test kit, he began looking up facts about genetics, psychopaths, sociopaths, and then PTSD. The more he read about the disorder, the more he conceptualized that if he had it, it probably started way back as a kid and didn't have anything to do with combat. He looked up and watched as the detective headed his way— *phone off.*

"What a way to start the day, eh?" Trey asked as he walked up to Babe.

"You got that right. We're already behind schedule. It sucks." While leaning on the sawhorse, it put Babe an inch taller than Trey, but when he stood, the five extra inches made all the difference.

"You know the dead guy?" Trey asked.

One side of Babe's mouth turned up in an almost smirk. "Everyone on site knew him. He was always picking a fight. My guess is he had little man syndrome," and he folded his arms. Trey couldn't help but notice the bulging muscles adorned with Marine tats.

"I heard you and the super broke up a fight, and then he punched you in the face and threatened you?" Babe took notice; Trey had his trusty pad out. "Sorry, but you're right; he musta had some issues. I'm much bigger than him and wouldn't punch you in the mug. Face it; you're one big guy. Stupid little man." Trey shook his head as though thinking about the victim's poor judgment.

Babe evenly responded. "It was no big deal."

"Well, it was to someone. Whoever the guy was, he smashed his head pretty good; enough to kill him. They'll have to see when they do the autopsy if they even do an autopsy. He screwed with the wrong person. Some guys and girls don't get that you can't go around smacking and threatening people. One day they'll pick the wrong fight and end up like this guy, dead in a dumpster." Trey turned his palm up with a shoulder shrug, punctuating his last statement.

"True," the big man nodded.

"So, how'd it go with your girl after I left?" Trey asked with a smile.

Babe leaned against the sawhorse again. "I'm not what one would call a ladies man. I don't have the gift of the gab, but she asked me if we could go to dinner Sunday night." His jaw jutted forward, bringing his teeth together as he sucked in a long breath. "Either we'll gel, or we won't, right?" He tucked his phone in his pocket.

Trey studied Babe's face. "You been married before?"

Babe laughed, "You could say that; to the Corps."

"You were in; how long?" Babe held up both hands. "Ah, about the same time I got with NOPD. I'm surprised you didn't go career." Trey had an unspoken intensity and watched as the Marine spoke.

"Eleven plus years with several tours and many special assignments, you just know when it's gotten your best, and once my best was used up, I didn't need to be there. Once a Marine, always a Marine, but I knew it was time to step down; I guess kinda like once a cop, always a cop." He laughed. The site super headed his way.

"We finally got the go-ahead, Vicarelli." Babe patted Trey's shoulder and turned to go inside the building, resuming where he had left off the evening before.

On the way back to the station, Trey called Scott. "We need to finish up, Scott." The Spring Breaker seemed cooperative enough.

"I'll be there around noon if that's okay."

"Sure thing; that works." That would give him time to work on the report about the dumpster diver.

He started thinking about Jessica and the weird vibes. The thought of Adam and the interview with him wrenched his gut. Proving it was the deal, and he was at a loss. If something didn't shake loose soon, it'd end up on the shelves of unsolved cases. There had to be an explanation. They'd looked at the video from the eye in the sky; as predicted, it was grainy, and the timestamp was dated the wrong month and year—another dead end.

OPENING DOORS

*B*ack at his desk, Trey attended to the case of the dead guy in the dumpster. From all accounts, Stan, a glorified gofer, was a jerk. He'd get the super to come in and make a formal statement. Once finished filling in the necessary information, he focused on the breakers and poured over the interviews.

Adam's interview spoke volumes about his deep-seated disdain for authority. There were unquestionable markers of a scary personality disorder.

Nonetheless, Scott's interview started to clear up the muddy waters. He decided to sketch it out; who was with who and when? Where did all their little pieces fall into the big puzzle? So, how did Adam end up on the trip?

Fact: Scott considered Adam a close friend. Fact: Scott saw Adam screwing Sloane—was it consensual, and she got caught, so denied it, or was it rape, and she really didn't remember? Fact: Adam was fucking nuts. Fact: an innocent girl was dead. Fact: He didn't have a shred of evidence.

Max called. "Padna, I'm at Mother's; want a debris poboy?" While Trey tried to eat healthy food and work out, there was no way he could pass up debris from Mother's Po-Boy Restaurant.

"Shit! Why ya gotta go to Mother's? Yes, of course, I want a debris, dammit. Thanks." *I'm weak, so weak, poor excuse*, he thought.

Trey called Forensics. "Hey, Charly, it's Trey. You got anything yet with Jessica Lambert?"

"Friend, I told you I would call you the second I had anything. Either the doer didn't fire, or he pulled out in time, but it's strange there was no residue from a condom. Also, I saw no definitive signs of penetration, which is odd, but the bruising on her inner thighs tells me he used a lot of force to pry her legs apart. Like he needed both hands, which begs the question, who suffocated her? Somebody definitely held a hand over her nose and mouth; the bruising around her nose is almost negligible, once again strange. The big tell is the bloodshot eyes and high carbon dioxide levels in the blood. I'm still waiting for the results from the fingernail scrapings, but don't get your hopes up. Trey, this whole thing is weird full of unanswered questions."

He threw his pen down on the desk. "What you're telling me, loud and clear, is that two people attacked her? One held her mouth, and then the other—I didn't see that coming. So, I'm looking for two suspects. Crap. Thanks, Charly."

Holding his head in his hands, hoping to ward off a nauseating headache, Trey looked at the diagram. He closed his eyes and tried to imagine how it all could've gone down. Finn leaves; somebody knocks; she knows them and lets them, two people, into the room. They put her on the bed; one pries her legs apart to do the deed while the other holds her mouth. So, the other person just watched; Charly was right; the whole thing was disturbing and strange.

He called Forensics again. "Sorry to be a pain in the ass, but is there any chance the person covering her mouth accidentally blocked her nose, too, and didn't mean to kill her?"

"Trey, yeah, it's possible, but a stretch, but if she had—wait, I'll call you back."

Max came in with a big smile and Trey's lunch. "Boy, you look bad. Seriously. You're letting this get way too close. Back away and let me take over the heavy lifting." He busily dug in the bag.

Trey spoke with a voice that held a boatload of sadness, "There were two people in Jessica's room; the rapist and the person who held her mouth, maybe also blocked her nose. Charly says she suffocated but is calling right back." His head slumped in disgust.

Max put the sandwich in front of Trey. "Eat. Eat now, or it'll disintegrate in your hands. We'll figure this out, Trey. We always do, right? Well, mostly do," and tipped his head down, eyeing the bag as if to encourage his partner to pick it up.

"Here, give it to someone else" he slid the sandwich to the side. "I can't eat; I'm sick over this. Two people betrayed that girl. I thought for sure, Adam, but did you get any vibes from Desondra or Becca? Maybe they didn't stay at the club. We need to find out what club they went to and show I.D. Where are the breakers at, you know?" Trey had a faraway gaze, almost trance-like.

Max shrugged. "How would I know? Probably still sleeping off last night's party." He went around the desk and plopped in his chair with a grunt.

Trey flipped through his notes. "You got Desondra's number and a copy of her license, right? Call her. I'm not calling Adam yet. Let's hear from the girl first."

"Trey, take at least a few bites of the debris." He gave in, unwrapped the paper, and took a few bites of the sandwich.

"Give the other half to someone or toss it." Max handed the other half to one of the detectives across the aisle. "Enjoy it, Skip," Trey said with a half-hearted smile.

He knew his face looked miserable; even his lips felt heavy like they wouldn't smile no matter how hard he tried. It wasn't just one sick S.O.B. but a betrayal of two friends. While Adam and his utter contempt screamed doer, what if, just what if, it had been one of the guys she'd known and hung with, and then who would've been the one to try and silence her? The scenario was twisted, plain, and simple. Then again, were they barking up the completely wrong tree, even perhaps one in a different forest? They had abandoned the idea of a stranger; why? If it had been only Trey with the feeling that the doer was a friend, that'd be one thing, but Max, who rarely colored inside the lines, always looking in a different direction, shared the friend theory.

The two detectives, both with grave expressions, looked over the diagram. Where had Scott and Sloane gone when they left the bar? They had not interviewed Sloane because of the hysteria and sedation the night of the murder. Her absence from the group on Sunday had somehow not raised any red flags, and she still had not been given a thorough interview. In truth, looking at the list of unanswered questions, the entire investigation should have been littered with red flags. All they knew was that Sloane and Scott were somewhere together, but where, how long, and was there anyone or anything to corroborate their story?

Trey pegged Adam for the rape and murder before completing the interview with Scott; maybe he was jumping the gun. He knew something was unbalanced with the boy, just from Adam's attitude during the interrogation. "Max, we totally dropped the ball here. Is it because they were spring break college kids who seemed squeaky clean other than having a few too many beverages?" They hadn't run background or anything. "Adam's bullshit threw me for a loop; it contradicted his demeanor outside Room One. Our investigation has more holes in it than Swiss cheese." For the next hour, they scoured their notes.

Max would follow up with the bar where Desondra and Becca supposedly danced most of the night. Where did Stevie and Jasmine hook up? What did Gage and Natalie do? Did they really go to the casino; they needed to talk to the call girl that provided the entertainment for Trevor and establish that timeline. Scott was due any minute, and Trey had a list of questions for the boy. He had let himself get taken down the Adam rabbit hole because of the boy's contempt for authority. Plus, Scott was such a likable guy compared to Adam.

"How'd we make such a mess of this? So many unanswered questions." It hit Trey hard in the gut. "Max, we gotta go back to square one, especially now that we know there were two people in on the murder."

Trey's phone rang, "Okay, Charly, what you got for me?"

"Sorry, Trey, I'm glad you asked me if it could have been accidental. The answer is yes, and it looks like that's precisely the case here. Whoever held her mouth didn't know she couldn't breathe through her nose, at least not enough to sustain her life while being traumatized. Sometime in the past, Jessica seriously broke her nose, and either she had a shoddy doc, which I doubt, or didn't realize it was broken; therefore, she didn't have it set. Just the slightest pressure would've caused an occlusion, thus smothering her."

"Thanks, Charlotte."

As promised, Scott returned to the P.D. Trey stood but watched him, this time more as a possible suspect than the boyfriend of the dead girl's best friend. He should have looked at him like that initially, but heartstrings got in the way. In the back of his mind, like a never-ending loop, was the thought *there were two.*

"Right this way, Scott, but I'm sure you remember." He handed the boy a Barq's, still maintaining a friendly attitude.

The boy nodded.

Once settled in Interrogation, Trey began, " We covered some excellent background information in our last visit. Since then, we've made some interesting discoveries of our own. By the way, how is Sloane managing?" Trey squinted his eyes while gently nodding his head in an attempt at sincerity. Trey thought, *Nope, Scotty-boy, not gonna get me again.*

The boy looked down at the soft drink can, gradually rotating it from side to side. "Not well, to say the least. This is the first death she's experienced, and being that she and Jess were best friends adds exponentially to the grief. My grandad died less than a year ago, and I still feel the hole in my heart, and it's not like we hung together all the time; besides, he was old."

Trey bit the side of his mouth, still perplexed at how easily he and Max had derailed. "Sure, she's bound to be sad. We left off talking about Adam and your relationship, but we'll get back to that. Where did you and Sloane go when you left the bar Saturday night, ya know when everybody kinda vamoosed?" He intensely tapped his pen.

"Uh, we went to my room; I knew Adam had gone off with Desondra and Becca. Sloane and I had some talking and making up to do." Scott tilted his head with a slight nod, but his hands twitched. *The boy's nervous or thinking of something he is purposely leaving out.* "After seeing Sloane and Adam, um—" Scott stammered.

"I get it; you wanted to put your mark back on her. Sex, right?" Trey winked with a wicked grin.

"Well, uh-uh, you make me sound so Neanderthal." Scott shifted a few times, seemingly uncomfortable in the chair or perhaps the subject.

Trey interrupted, "Sex is a primal instinct, Scott. Adam had his way with your woman, and you were merely taking her back." The detective shrugged. He was now far more cold, callous, and calculating.

"It wasn't exactly like that—we talked about what I thought I saw. Sloane still denied it, and she followed it up by questioning about Adam's virginity. I was like, 'Uh, no, not at all. He wasn't like the other dudes and didn't brag about it, but he had a girlfriend, and they hooked up all the time.' She kinda looked unhappy, maybe confused about the whole thing. It's a big deal having sex with a virgin, ya know?" He animatedly splayed his hands, emphasizing the importance of his statement.

"Whatever floats your boat, kid. So how long did you stay in the room? Where is your room, by the way?" He pointed the pen at Scott.

The boy started to fidget even more in his chair. "Um, my room is next to Sloane's." His hands began noticeably shaking, and his words almost crackled from a dry mouth, also a symptom of intense nervousness. "We stayed, I guess, about an hour, maybe. Then, we took a walk," his face brightened, "and then, that's when we saw you. Remember? Sloane acted like a—"

"I remember well. So, with y'all being next door, y'all didn't hear anything coming from Sloane and Jessica's room? Like a scream or a fight?" Scott shook his head; his eyes opened wide. "Only an hour for make-up sex as well as talking. Scott, you really need to get better game. Man, you can hear everything usually being next door, yet you heard nothing." Trey scratched his head, pulled out his notepad, scribbled something, and then put it back in his pocket. He noticed Scott wince. No doubt, the boy was holding something back. He knew more than he was telling.

"Back to Adam. How was it that he went to spring break with y'all? No one knows him, and it's not like he had his girlfriend. Why?" Like a dog hearing a squeaky sound, Scott tilted his head from shoulder to shoulder almost in a manic manner.

"He said he wanted to come to New Orleans, and I said as long as he could pay his way. Not to be a dick, but I know how he can be—like I told you."

"Hm. Yep, you told me all about Adam," Trey raised his eyebrows, "not someone I'd want to hang with for sure. I need to talk to Sloane. I'll call a unit to get her. She can corroborate your story, right?" He tapped on the window.

"I don't know where she is," he panicked. "The girls may have gone shopping or to lunch. I don't know," avoiding eye contact.

"Call her. I'm sure she has her cell. Trey called Max. "Step in here for a moment. I need a unit to pick up Sloane Liberto. Scott," he stretched his arm, pointing to the boy, "is getting her exact location." By this time, the young man was coming unglued. His knees bounced enough to shake the table and make his body tremble.

"She's not answering." The boy panicked.

"Text her. Which friend was she going shopping with or having lunch with? We have all the numbers, anyway." He got up, and he and Max left the room, but as they were leaving, he said loud enough so Scott could hear. "Yeah, all of them. All of them need to come in." Trey sat back down. "Never mind, Scott; I'm having everyone brought down here again. By having their numbers, the tech team can figure out their location." Scott's color drained from his face. "Can I see your phone?" Scott handed it over to him. "I'll give it back in a bit." He got up and left the room. The boy's eyes darted like a cornered animal while the nightmare unfolded. This time Trey was on his game.

Twenty minutes later, Max entered the precinct, followed by the overtly disgruntled spring breakers. They sat in the same row of chairs they'd waited in for the first interviews—Trey thought, *more like impressions, we did a shitty job at interviews.*

Max pulled Trey to the side with his back toward the kids. "Desondra and Becca were definitely at Oz until the wee hours. A couple of bartenders remembered them by name. So they can get checked off the list of possibilities."

Another day began. The morning run to the job site proved uneventful, and the breeze, while a little stiff, beat stifling heat and stale air, hands down. The bruhaha from the dead body in the dumpster had died at work. Speculation about the investigation had everyone on the site hypothesizing. The guy had been doused with the little-man syndrome in a major way, making him a thorn in everyone's side, and nobody seemed surprised by his murder.

As he passed residences and businesses, he saw where the dregs from Hurricane Katrina were dwindling; of course, it damn well should have, being that it had been too many years since the devastating Cat 5 crushed the city. He trotted onto the construction site with Gunner at his side.

"Vicarelli, you don't have a vehicle?" Glenn called out as he stepped from the trailer.

Babe smiled as he passed him and clocked into work. "I have an F-250, but I like the run; besides, finding parking is brutal. It's a mile, maybe; it gets the heart pumping, and hell, I barely break a sweat." Gunner raced to the office and the treats he knew Glenn always had waiting. He wanted to say the brief run was nothing compared to training under the harshest conditions with forty-five pounds, sometimes more, of gear strapped to his back, but a civilian would never comprehend. All they pictured was something they saw in a movie, and, for the most part, that was pretty much Hollywood's impression.

As he walked the site, his mind rolled to the adrenalin rush of the Marine Raider competition against teams of six as powerful and conditioned as his. It was hell, but it fit his Type-A need-for-ultimate-control-personality and brought a feeling of belonging back for that moment. His time with the Marines came to a close a month after the new year announced its glory. It hurt to his very core thinking about brothers-in-arms left behind enemy lines. What in the hell was Washington thinking, and what about the military advisors? Somebody needed a good ass-kicking. They'd forgotten what it was like to be boots on the ground; perhaps a two-month deployment might refresh their minds. No, they liked their haughty positions with comfortable leather chairs to sit their lard-like asses.

Memories of missions had plagued his mind for weeks; those executed with timepiece precision but also those where only a few made it back in one piece or even alive. How many brothers-in-arms had he carried away from the threat? Why did he survive and others didn't? Guilt rode him like a runaway stallion. It was during those missions that he excelled; it was instinctual kill or be killed; failure was not an option. One could easily argue that while he came back physically whole, a part of him remained in the execution of the mission. Babe had given all to the Corps—body, mind, and soul. The rage that burned in him from an insane and abusive childhood brought the same intensity making for a laser-focused destroyer and the warrior the Corps expected.

He prowled the work site like a stalking predator, an eye on every detail, and the company expected it, just like the Corps. If someone needed an extra hand, he was there at the ready, but just as he was there for those that worked with the same mindset, his tolerance for slackers was non-existent. Perhaps that was the intense draw to Trinity. She hustled and was a tight little ball of non-stop energy; maybe it could work. He'd have a better feel for it come the night of their dinner away from the demands of Louie's.

A quick confer between Max and Trey yielded nothing more than unsubstantiated theories. With all the breakers lined against the wall, Trey took Trevor next. All they needed was the number of his Barbie for the night. The Trevor issue was almost closed, just a phone call to Barbie's escort service.

Trey spoke first. "Trevor, you seen Barbie again? Do you have a record of the transaction from Saturday night, like proof of purchase?" The detective couldn't keep a straight face. "I know, probably absurd, but I had to ask."

Trevor leaned back in the chair. "Is this some kind of fucking joke?"

Max interjected, "Hold your mouth, Sonny. Respect."

"Give me a second," he pulled out his cell phone. "I'll pull up the info you want. Dad says not to use cash, so I don't." In minutes, Trevor located the information to prove his alibi. Trey snapped a shot of the transaction.

"Well, I'll be damned." Max shook his head. "I've seen it all. Your pops pays for you to get your rocks off? Mine woulda asked me what was wrong with my right hand. Go on, get outta here. Be careful and have fun." They opened the door and escorted Trevor out, then called Gage.

Gage looked just like his name sounded. He could have been the hunky boyfriend in some teen summer love movie. His dark wavy hair set off his bright blue eyes for that real movie star look. The boy appeared confused, "Why am I here again? I told you I went to the casino with Natalie."

"Anyone ever tell you that you look like a young Ray Liotta? God rest his soul." Max asked with a tick of his head.

"Yes, sir, all the time," he said with a polite but unnatural grin. "He was in that Mafia gangster movie, right? My dad likes that movie a lot."

Max nodded, "Goodfellas. Me too."

Trey brought out his notepad. "I have here that you and Natalie went to the casino. What I didn't ask was why; I mean, you just don't come across like a gambling kind of guy. Hell, y'all can barely get in; why there?"

"Because I had to be out of my room. Stevie and Jasmine were, um, hooking up, okay? I figured I'd give him a couple of hours to get whatever he planned finished."

Trey wrote in his pocket pad, then leaned back in his chair with his hands threaded behind his head. "So you and Natalie didn't hook up? I have here that she and Jasmine share a room. It would likely seem that y'all would use her room. No?"

Gage coughed in an almost choking manner. "Are you kidding me? Like, uh, no. Natalie is cute, I guess, but I'm not attracted to her that way. We're in a study group; that's how I know her. That's all I would need to do. My girlfriend is at the beach and wanted me there, but I had committed to the group. We hadn't become a couple when I said yes to New Orleans. She's pissed, and man, I wish I had gone to the beach." The boy looked fed up.

"Any receipts from the casino?" Max asked as he doodled and wrote the occasional note as though the information was of significance.

"Yeah, that's about all I have in my wallet now. I'm so ready to be out of this city. No offense, but it's not my scene. Natalie has a bunch of pictures on her phone." He pulled out a stack of receipts, thumbed through them, and then handed a time-stamped receipt from the casino providing his alibi. Another possible suspect they could strike off the list. They escorted him out.

Trey called Natalie into the room, and they all sat. "I understand, Natalie, that you were with Gage the night of Jessica's murder."

Tears started running down her cheeks, and her breath hitched just short of a staggered sob. It was clear she was attempting to get control of herself. "I'm sorry. I still can't believe she's dead. We were friends." Max handed her a tissue. "Yes, I went with Gage to the casino. I know you know everything already, like about Stevie and Jasmine. Jas is my friend, and she's not a slut, but, um, she does it a lot." She sheepishly smiled with a quick flutter of her eyelashes. "Ya know, has sex. Not that I'm not interested in, well, Gage isn't my boyfriend, and I don't think he wanted

to do anything with me anyway because he has a beautiful new girlfriend."
Trey couldn't help but think, *How much more of this teenage temptation
island thing? Glad Max had the first round with these girls. Ugh.*

Trey ran his hands through his hair. The investigation was going
nowhere and fast. "Gage said you took some pictures of y'all. Could you
show us a couple of them?"

She perked up. "Sure. He's so cute. I wanted pictures to prove he
went with me to the casino. Not that I like him or anything, but going
somewhere with Gage is amazing. I don't know a girl who doesn't totally
think he's the hottest." She rolled her eyes. "I know I sound pathetic, but
we did have a good time." Pictures she had, and he'd had his fill. After the
interviews were over, they still had nada.

NOT A FIRST DATE

*T*rey headed to the bar; by this time, it was nearing nine. He hoped Babe would still be at Louie's. For some weird reason, he felt an affinity with the guy—maybe because he respected his military service or perhaps because Trey felt some underlying current in the man like he was more complex than appearances suggested.

He called Stephanie. "You feel like going out tonight? Like to hang out at Louie's for a drink?"

She sounded excited. "Hell, yeah, I'd like to go out, but Louie's? You don't have your other wife, Max?"

"Very funny. Max is following up on our dumpster diver guy to answer your question. See you in fifteen minutes. I love you." She'd been aloof since the murder, and she resented the many hours he was gone working the case. They hadn't had much time together, but such was his work and the life of a detective's wife.

His mind floated back to the interviews. The interrogation with Sloane went nowhere. Just the mention of the murder and the girl went to pieces, but it was almost a little overboard. There was more to the chick than met the eye, and further chats with her were a certainty. What Trey couldn't get was, according to Sloane, she and Jessica had been best friends since before Ole Miss. He felt a genuine admiration from the girl regarding her dead friend, but there was a slight hint of jealousy. Maybe Jessica had been the inexperienced virginal girl Sloane secretly wished was her past. No doubt, Sloane had been the recipient of several home run bats. Was he detecting remorse? Maybe it was sadness that she had given in so quickly to peer pressure and the need to fit in and be popular. Sloane was a beautiful girl with black hair, dark, mysterious eyes, full pouty lips, and a figure any girl would envy. She came from money but so had Jessica.

The next time he interviewed Sloane, he would ask to see pictures of her and Jessica together. Maybe he could bring it closer to the heart, delve into their past friendship and not have the mere mention of her friend's name conjure a waterfall of tears and hysteria—a little too rehearsed or exaggerated to feel authentic, but he could be wrong. There was much to ponder, and things were far more complex than initially thought. Nothing was simple.

Then there was Adam, and while he was a dick and dislikable, Trey's original findings seemed more and more an unlikely conclusion. Adam was the kind of sneaky prick he would have preferred as his lead suspect, but such was not the case. Something very hinky occurred in Jessica's room while she waited for Finn to return with the pizza and beer. Trey thought, *Finn, now there was a good kid.*

He pulled up to their bungalow, ready to jump out, when Steph came out the door. Since he was in a police unit, while unmarked, it was still off-limits for joyriding or dates. Besides, the squawk of the radio was a constant noise only those on the job tolerated well. They climbed into Steph's Jeep and took off for Louie's.

"You look gorgeous, too hot for Louie's. How'd your day go? Anything interesting?" he asked.

"Just ya basic day. Nothing too glamorous." She held his hand, stroking her thumb delicately over his.

Trey brought the back of her hand to his lips. "I'm sure you're wondering why Louie's; it's not like we go there, but—" She gave him a sideways glance; she knew. "I know I'm off the clock, but I'm hoping some spring breakers will be hanging around. I want to observe when they don't know I'm looking at them. Oh, and the guy I told you about, Babe, will more than likely be there. When you meet him, you'll see what I'm talking about; he could be the poster child for the Marines. His biceps have to be this big around," holding up his hands to indicate the massiveness of Babe's arms.

She laughed. "Trey, I love your muscles just the way they are; I really don't get into the muscle-man look."

He glanced in her direction. "Usually, I wouldn't think anything, but it goes with this guy. It's part of him." Steph watched him for a second and smiled. She'd swear her husband had some weird fascination with the man, but such was his nature. He was a people watcher and tightly tuned to what made them tick, making for a skilled detective.

They circled a few blocks looking for a parking spot. "Trey, pull into a garage. We could be circling all night and never find a parking space." She pleaded.

"One more pass around. It galls the hell out of me to pay thirty bucks to park. Fuck that." Just then, a car pulled out of a tight spot a block from Louie's. "Ah-ha, the gods are smiling on me." He maneuvered the vehicle and slipped right in. "I got mad skills, ma girl!"

Steph raised her eyebrows and held a quirky, sarcastic smile. "Mad skills, indeed, but I guess parking as well." His eyes shifted to her, just catching the double entendre.

Hand in hand, they walked the block and turned down the street toward Louie's. "I'm gonna have the hottest date in the place. Girl, you look so good; you're smokin'. We could turn around right now and go home." He had a bright blush about his face and a devilish ear-to-ear grin. "Have I got plans for you!"

"C'mon, stud, let's go observe your breakers." She squeezed his hand.

Louie's never changed, maybe the clientele had different faces, but it drew a particular kind of crowd. The younger set came to experience the anything-goes city, and then there were the every night regulars, a dichotomy for sure. The steely-eyed old-timers bellied up to the bar for simple conversation about the heat, the crime, and the corruption, while the younger crowd engaged in table talk, darts, and suggestive flirting. The dynamic provided a most interesting combination and gave the feeling of home away from home. It didn't have the feel of a tourist trap but rather a neighborhood bar and grille like the TV show Cheers, the bar where everyone knows your name.

The kids started to split their time between trolling on Bourbon, visiting strip clubs, going to Pat O's for Hurricanes, and not spending so much time at Louie's. Since Jessica's death, the cops have popped in too much. Because of the close proximity to their hotel, it was easy to meet each other at Louie's, making sure all were okay before heading out to other places.

Sure enough, as Trey walked into Louie's, he spotted his newfound friend in the usual spot. Babe silently watched the crowd, but his heightened sense never left Trinity. He nodded to Trey as he and Steph made their way over. "How ya doin', Babe? This is my wife, Stephanie. Darlin', this is Babe."

She smiled politely at the hulk of a man. "Trey's told me about you. Thank you for your service and sacrifice."

Babe smiled back, "You're welcome; it was mine to do."

She hiked her hip on the stool next to Babe. "Yeah, I always called Trey babe, but when he told me about you, he said it somehow didn't fit anymore. I see now. Great art, by the way." She touched one of his tattoos. "Kinda scary, but pretty nonetheless. So, you were a Marine." He nodded.

"Yes, ma'am. I hear people call themselves former Marines, but I feel once a Marine, always a Marine, kinda like the cop thing. They never truly retire; it's in their blood, part of who they are, right?" He gave a half-cocked smile and put his drink to his lips.

Trey put his arms around her waist. "Steph, what do you want? Wine? Beer?"

"No, just some ginger ale with a lime, if they have it." She smiled back at him.

Trinity came down to their end of the bar. "What you having tonight, Detective?"

"Bourbon with a splash of coke, and my wife wants a ginger ale with lime. Y'all got that?" Trinity nodded. "Also, we'll have some loaded skins if the kitchen's still open."

"You got it." She smiled at Steph, "Hey, I'm Trinity. We love having your husband here, and it's about time he brought you. Besides the skins, Detective, you want anything else? We actually have a menu. Other than the daily plates, most of the menu is bar grub, but good, and I'm sure I can get them to do something special."

"I'm good. Thanks." Steph watched as Trinity hustled their drinks and placed the order. *So,* she thought, *the big guy has the hots for tiny Trinity. They certainly would be an odd couple.* The bartender was attractive, with black hair that touched the small of her back platted to the side with three-inch gold hoops. The gold was stunning against her caramel-colored neck. Her eyes had an enchanting sparkle, and her body was perfect without an ounce of fat, just tiny. The rope-like muscles of her arms were enviable. What a pair they would make; Babe, handsome in a rugged military way, and Trinity, organically sensual.

"Anything much going on around here?" Trey asked Babe. "I see the college kids on spring break aren't here tonight."

"No, sir. They've been romping the quarter, stopping in on the way back to the hotel. How's the investigation going?" He put his tumbler to his lips.

"Could be better," Trey said in an almost whine. "The thing is getting the proof," he snapped his fingers when he said 'proof.' "Shit, we're up to our necks in a lot of nothing, but we know there's something," he said, clearing his throat.

Trey watched the big guy's eyes quickly dart, "They're back, boss." The detective slowly turned his head and cast his eyes across the crowd. Surprisingly it was Scott with Jasmine. *Interesting,* he thought. Not the couple he figured it would be. Why would Scott be with Jasmine? Moments later, Adam entered, adjusting his shirt. They ordered their drinks and sat at a table.

"Steph, I want to move closer to the three that just came in. Close enough to hear but be inconspicuous." He took a long draw of his drink. "See the guy in the blue shirt? He's supposedly in a committed relationship with the dead girl's best friend, but here he shows up with another chick and Adam, the other guy. I know he comes across geekafied, but he's definitely a head case—bad news in a big kind of way."

While Stephanie and Trey talked, Babe got up and went to the men's room. A few minutes after he disappeared, the two boys got up to go to the can, chuckling amidst comments to each other. Their expressions screamed arrogance, and it was obvious something mischievous had gone down between the boys.

Trey put his hand on Steph's elbow and led her to a table in the corner. Hopefully close enough to hear the breakers. While sitting with his back to a door was uncomfortable and most unusual for someone in law enforcement, he made the exception to stay unnoticed. He heard as the boys returned to their table, then a heavy hand landed on his shoulder. "Trey, got ya answer; y'all come back to the bar unless you want alone time but at Louie's? Detective, take your wife somewhere nice and put down the shield for a night. See you at the bar."

Flashes of tortuous behavior jetted through his mind. What had Babe done? Trey looked at his wife and asked, "Back to the barstool or stay at the table? Your choice."

"Really?" She grinned as she tilted her head in question. "I say, let's go back and sit where we were, eat the skins, visit for a few moments with your new friend, and then pick up Chinese and go home. Like you'd hate my job; I would totally suck at yours, but I would take a day off now and then. You don't always have to be on the job. C'mon, let's hear what your big friend has to say and then bolt. We don't even need the Chinese; I already know what your fortune will be." Her laugh was sexy and alluring. Stephanie's voice had a slight rasp, creating an electric wave through his body. Suddenly, he could think of nothing but getting her home and into bed. "Trey Kimble, I can tell where your mind went; it's plastered all over your face. Let's hurry up, get the skinny, and go."

They moved toward their original seats. "And, you completely nailed it—he's the ideal image of a poster boy for the Marines. He's freakin' huge but seems like a really nice guy."

"He's something," he put his tongue in his cheek, raising an eyebrow. " I admire him, but I'm not so sure about nice guy; I can feel he has another side, a very dark one. From what I gather, Babe's the guy they call when they want to take out a hostile enemy by means of clandestine missions. Even the military likes to hide him in the closet. He's badass; no ands or buts about it."

Babe watched as they made their way toward him. Looking over the top of his tumbler, he sipped his drink. His eyes had an excited twinkle like shimmering mirrors. As they got closer, he said, "Boys will be boys and reminisce about their conquests. Don't know about the girl's side, as far as her thrill, but they had themselves a threesome. Detailed enough, I wanted to smack their heads together like a clapboard."

"They talked like that in front of you?" Trey looked shocked

Babe smirked, "They didn't see me; I was in a stall. I knew they'd come in; I just had a feeling."

Trey looked at Stephanie, "Threesome. You hear that? At that age, what 21, I counted myself extremely lucky to have a twosome but usually only a onesome," and he laughed. His mind flashed back to Sloane. He wondered what she might think of the whole threesome thing. While Scott came across as polished, genuine, and a good kid, things like cheating and threesomes smacked of something far more ugly. There was way more than met the eye concerning Scott. What was the deal with Adam? Scott all but said having him along was a mistake.

Throwing the last of his drink down the back of his throat, Babe stood, stretched, and said he was heading out. He signaled to Trinity that he was leaving. She quickly made her way to the end of the bar. "Aw, dang, I was hoping to be at this end a bit more. If I can get Samantha to switch shifts with me, you want to get together tomorrow after you get off work? I mean, we'll still have our proper date for dinner like planned; this would be hang time. You live close? I could meet you after work at your place." If one stood close enough, they probably could hear the gears grinding as Babe weighed the idea.

He was hesitant but relented. "Pen?" She handed him one clipped to the front of her top. The neckline on her tee shirt pulled ever so slightly, revealing a peek of more skin. Trey laughed to himself, finding mirth in his observant giant friend. Babe's eyes twitched just barely; the big guy hadn't missed anything. He scratched something down on a napkin and handed it to her. "No judgment."

"No, indeed. None here. See you about six?" Her smile turned up like a bow.

Trey and Stephanie said goodbye with intentions ever-present in their minds.

Once in the car, Stephanie began to prod. "Okay, sport, you've had a shit-eatin' grin since that barmaid came onto your friend. I have such a hard time calling him Babe; I know it's his name, but c'mon, it's hard. What kind of parent names their baby Babe, like a real name; I get nick-name. Find out his middle name; maybe I can call him that or make up a name." She reached over to his seat and rubbed his crotch. "Ha! I thought so. No Chinese, I take it?"

Trey gave her a sideways glance, but the smile across his face spoke volumes. He pulled into the driveway, barely stopped, threw the car in park, and made tracks to get in the house. As soon as the front door closed, they started stripping off their clothes. "Crap, no shades." With long strides, he picked her up and raced back to the bedroom. He lathered her with deep, hard kisses moving down her neck to her breasts, navel, and beyond. She rested her legs over his shoulders and welcomed his passion. Pleasing as it was, she wanted all of him, rolled him onto his back, and straddled his hips, grinding his penetration deep inside her body. It was a symphony of sensuality as their bodies moved in an almost choreographed performance.

Trinity glanced at the napkin, noting his place was on the far side of the Quarter and that he'd included a phone number. She grinned and stuck it in her pocket. Throughout her time behind the bar at Louie's, countless men and even a few women had asked for her number, invited her to dinner, and made unwelcome advances. Babe had been coming to Louie's for over four months, and for the first two months, all he did was say thank you, yes, ma'am, and order his drink. After discovering they had daily plates for the offering, he added his dinner selection to his conversation repertoire. Despite the non-verbal interaction, his eyes spoke volumes. Even though the man watched her, he didn't gawk or make her feel uncomfortable—a mystery. Without saying a word, he had created the vibe that warded off likely flirters or working girls and guys.

She had fantasized about her handsome military man. What was his deal? Was he merely wanting a drink and some dinner? He'd never had a friend with him, and it wasn't until the murder of the college girl and the investigation that he engaged in any conversation. Everyone warned her that it was the silent ones a girl had to worry about, not the players that tried to chat up the girls at the bar.

"Finn, grab the bar for me for a minute, please." She had asked him to help on the rare occasion when she needed to use the ladies' room or deal with a demanding guest, so he paid no attention to the request. Leaning against a wall in the restroom, she punched in the number.

One ring was all it took. His husky voice answered, "Vicarelli."

"Hey, it's me, Trinity. I thought since you gave me your number, it was only fair that I reciprocate, that's all. So, now you have it." Silence.

"Okay." He responded. "Call me anytime you want; I gotta warn you, I'm not much of a talker." She swore he chuckled after the comment.

"No shit, Sherlock; it's okay; I talk enough for both of us."

"Hm. See you tomorrow, but if you want to cancel or need me for anything, you have my number. Goodnight, Trinity."

"Goodnight, Vicarelli." He felt an electric pulse, or maybe it was what people called butterflies. Anticipation was reasonable, but the sensation he felt was complicated.

The exchange with Trinity was the most he'd ever had with a woman, other than a female comrade on a mission. He didn't date in school and didn't date anyone in the military. There were always working girls who didn't expect to talk, which was okay with him; consequently, he'd only kissed a couple of girls in his life once because someone had dared the girl. He knew how to fuck and had become proficient, but intimacy was a whole different creature and one that scared the hell out of him. If Trinity had wanted to engage, he was pretty sure she'd expect some kissing, caressing, and closeness. Maybe this whole thing was a bad idea. His mind churned over, and his gut gurgled with the what-ifs. *Where is this even going? Maybe she'll cancel.*

Laying there thinking of Trinity gazing into the nothingness of a dark room, his mind began to wander. Memories of his first time at Louie's popped into mind. Babe had been a civilian for three weeks, sorely missing the Marine life and the desire to make a difference, eliminating the threats. While working out and running fulfilled one need, his body demanded physical contact, more like returning to battle. He'd heard a woman scream, but when he turned the corner, it had been a laughing scream and not a cry for help; he turned back around after realizing the situation.

The adrenalin rush raised his pulse, increased his oxygen intake, and left him wanting like a gnawing pain in the soul. Across the street was a bank of open doors that wrapped around the corner. He read the name of the establishment, Louie's Tap. A pour of scotch might quell his desire to sift out the enemy and destroy. The inward debate he'd had so often began again. *Is it the killing or protection of the weak that motivates me? The Marines made me a beast; I'm nothing more than a killing machine—like a fucking shark. If I were a lion on the prowl to feed, that'd be one thing. No, some people don't deserve to live; all they want to do is prey on the weak because they are worthless. Survival.*

From the moment he saw her, his heart did a double tap. Her brown skin glistened with sweat. She looked at him when he entered, and it was obvious she had taken note of him. Her smile— spunky, friendly, and sensual, aroused him, completely removing him from the internal berating. "What strikes your fancy tonight, big guy?" She called out. He walked straight to an open spot at the end of the bar. She met him, "What ya want, darlin'?" His first thought was 'you,' but he refrained and replied appropriately. "Two-finger Gle—"

She teasingly retorted, "Your two fingers or mine," and flashed her eyes in an almost taunting way. Oh, she had teased him alright, creating the need to adjust himself. She tantalized and ignited him; she was sheer perfection in one tiny package.

He needed to shake the memory, stripped, and cranked the shower. No need to conjure a scenario or imaginary sexy banter; he exploded with just the slightest grasp. "What the hell am I doing? I can't even imagine her without ol' soldier-boy standing at full attention, and the salute comes all too fast. What the fuck?" He sat on the floor in the shower and lifted his head toward the pulsing spray, accepting the surges of water directly into his face. "This whole thing is a mistake, a huge mistake." Why the need to beat himself up? He had delivered excellence to the Marines and protected the country—hadn't he done enough to warrant the attention of a beautiful woman? He stood, toweled off, slid into the bed, and drifted to sleep with thoughts of her.

The phone buzzed at three in the morning. He answered, "Vicarelli."

"Sorry to wake you, Vicarelli. I just got home from Louie's; all I can think of is you. I don't know what it is about you, Babe Vicarelli, but you got my engine revving. Want company tonight? I don't bite, well not very hard anyway."

Think. Think. "Yes." He inhaled deeply.

"On my way." He could hear her smile. *The boys have already made a strike, so the siege may last for a while. Excellent, I think.*

There was no need to straighten anything; his place was always ready for inspection. It was a tribute to his comrades and his country, with a flag on one wall, multiple Marine posters, and an assortment of framed photos of him with different teams in an array of countries. His place was small, with only one bedroom, a living room with a sofa, a weight bench, neatly organized free weights, a suspended heavy bag, a table with a lamp and his computer, and a TV. The kitchen was the size of a postage stamp, but the owners had done a great job with the bathroom. He threw on a pair of jeans, still shirtless, when the knock came. She had on a slip of a dress and booties. A strap barely hung onto her shoulder, which he could scarcely see amidst her head full of black wavy hair.

"Hey, Vicarelli. I hope I don't scare you."

One corner of his mouth turned up. Trinity reached up, pulled his head down to her, and kissed him. He gently kissed her back, then pulled her closer; he wanted to kiss her; he wanted the intimacy, and all those years of lacking were coming out. He picked her up and brought her to the bed. "Do you—" he began to ask.

"Oh, yeah, I do, you bet." She pulled her dress over her head, exposing her total nakedness, and began undoing his jeans; he inhaled with studdered breaths. He stripped them quickly. "Your body is amazing; I knew it would be, Babe."

He delicately touched her, studying her breasts, and slowly his eyes absorbed the sight of perfection before him. "I'm no good at this, Trinity. I don't want to hurt you—you're so tiny."

"Military man, I don't break; in fact, I like—"

That was all the confirmation he needed. He sat on his knees on the bed, gave her the condom to roll on him, then pressed into her, beginning with slow waves of penetration. He wanted the moment to last forever. Being inside of her was all he had imagined—tight with a strong clamp squeezing hard around him. He pushed deeper and harder, her body welcoming each thrust. Her body matched each piston in kind. His intensity accelerated; no matter how hard he fought to restrain himself, his primal need took over. He lifted her petite body onto him, and together they performed in perfect harmony, her legs tightly wrapped around him. She looked up and kissed him deeply as their passion soared. As it was, he realized he didn't need anyone to teach him intimacy; it came naturally as breathing. Her full lips were soft while her tongue probed, then, just as the moment was but a second away, she sucked on his tongue with purpose. Whatever the technique was, his body complied with propulsions filling the wrapper.

"Girl, you got some skills."

"Yeah? Well, Vicarelli, you ain't so bad yourself. I've known since the first time I laid eyes on you that I wanted to be in your bed. I'm gonna say something bold, which might, but I hope not, freak you out. I felt like I'd be your girl from day one. Then, after a few times at the bar, I figured you were single since you never brought anyone. Am I right?"

"Yes, single, unless you're my girl." He turned his head and smiled. "I've never had a girlfriend; not so sure I know how to have one."

When Trinity mentioned she could talk for the two of them, it was a fact. She was surprised that he hadn't had a steady relationship at some point in his life. He was the king of yes and no answers. Eventually, they fell asleep. Lucky for him, thunderstorms began around six in the morning, so no work; he returned to the bed where she was sound asleep and climbed in next to her. She automatically moved closer to him, and they slept for the next few hours.

GETTING NOWHERE FAST

The rain came down in sheets making the streets of the Quarter seem even muckier than usual complete with loud rumbling thunder like the heavens were bellowing. A lightning show of bright bolts and vivid spidering veins of silver danced across the sky—a perfect setting for snuggling under the covers instead of picking apart the discrepancies in the breaker's stories. Only a few of the puzzle pieces remained beyond reach.

"What're we missing here? I have a gut feeling that there is a significant element that we're overlooking. God, I feel like we need to get justice for this girl and her family." Trey fiddled with the pen, using it as a back scratcher. In a jerky-fast motion, he brought the pen into view. "Max, I got ink all over my shirt?"

His partner gasped, choking on a sip of coffee. "Moron. Stephanie's gonna love this one. You and your damn pens. Click-click, click-click. You are the most aggravating son-of-a-bitch; here, use my pen; it has a fucking top instead of the click-click spring thing!" Trey stood and turned for Max to look. "You got lucky this time; no ink lines." With a sigh of relief, Trey sat back down. Max rested his chin in the palm of his hand, his jaw set and an alertness in his thought. "What do we know about the vic?"

Trey rocked back in his chair. "Not much. We need Sloane to come in with some pictures of her and the deceased. Fill in some of the blanks. Ya know, our favorite boy, Adam, said something about Jessica controlling, or I gotta look back through the notes. I do know; he said lesbian lovers. No, it was Jessica's possessiveness of Sloane. I'm picturing Jessica as the proverbial good girl, ya know, waiting for marriage, yada, yada. Trevor said those exact words and even emphasized that she was the girl he hoped his little sister would become. Adam has a warped moral compass." He picked up the phone and called Sloane. "Good morning, Sloane; this is Detective Kimble. I know it's crappy weather out, but remember when we talked about you and Jessica and how y'all had been close friends for a long time? I want to talk more about Jessica since you knew her best." He winked at Max.

"You want me to come down during this thunderstorm?" She sounded groggy like he had woken her.

"Hey, we can pick you up, me and Detective Sledge." Max mouthed 'thanks' and held his middle finger in Trey's direction.

Sloane cleared her throat and asked, "Can Scott come with me?" Her voice trembled.

"Sure." He purposefully didn't mention that Scott would not be a part of the interview. *Okay,* Trey thought, *maybe I didn't paint the whole picture, perhaps even misled the girl.* He was willing to do whatever it took to find the answers.

"You don't need to pick us up; we'll catch a cab or Uber. I'm still in bed, so it might take me a couple of hours to get to you." Trey rolled his eyes at the comment causing Max to chuckle silently.

"It's better if we pick you up; see you in a couple of hours." Trey hung up the phone.

Max rocked back in his chair. "Go pick her up? From what I heard, she seemed hesitant, maybe rattled by the phone call or idea of coming down here. There's something she's hiding, which may be the key to unlocking the shit-show. Padna, you got a strange look on your face. What's going through that twenty-pound growth on your shoulders?"

Trey looked Max square in the eyes with determination. "I think our impression of Jessica is way off the mark. What if she and Sloane shared more than friendship? God, I wish I could get ahold of her phone and check out her camera roll. Wow, I pegged this all wrong, I think." He closed his eyes and hung his head for a moment as he sized up and organized his thoughts. "If it was just Jessica and Finn, the busser from Louie's, why would she order an extra-large pizza? She expected company?" He ran a hand through his hair.

Max leaned forward toward Trey's desk and suggested in a low voice. "Set up the Spoof app with Scott's number. Since he won't be in interrogation, she'll see he's calling when her phone rings and answer, but there'll be no one on the line. Dollars to donuts, she'll want to come out and talk to him." He slowly nodded with sly, squinted eyes. "Yeah, spoof it. Hopefully, she leaves the phone on the table, unlocked. Padna, you need to be lightning-fast, scrolling through her camera roll. Maybe I can delay her, but you better be quick. Then, ya see, you can take questions down a different vein. Who would know if they were, let's say, experimenting with the other side of the bread? Would Sloane tell Scott? Or—"

Trey interrupted like a light switch turned on. "What if it was a threesome? Ol' Scotty-boy likes the group sex thing. I saw him, Adam, and Jasmine come back from the game of who's doing what and to whom?" He got on his computer and started typing away. "I'm YouTubing what the younger crowd considers sex. Me, I like one-on-one, you?"

Max cocked his head with a broad smile growing across his face. "I haven't before, but if it were two hot babes and me, I wouldn't turn it down, but me and another guy with one woman, nah, I ain't got time for dat. Hm. Two women." He rocked in his chair.

The video started, and Trey hurriedly tried to turn the volume down, but it took him a minute, and by that time, he had a crowd around the desk. One of the officers started a commentary that resulted in a host of crude comments. "Kimble, I never pegged you as a swinger, and with that pretty wife of yours—"

With a tight frown, he looked at the officer. "Maronne, as if. I'm working a case. Any words about my wife better never come out your pie-hole again." Trey hadn't taken his eyes off the screen. "Ain't no way a person can bend that much. She's like a fucking pretzel." With tightly closed eyes, he commented, "I've seen enough of this shit." The crowd around his desk started to boo when he stopped the video. "You watch this crap on your own time." He waited for the group to disperse, then began hypothesizing with Max. "So," he said in a quiet, smooth tone, "Jessica is waiting for marriage to have her cherry popped, but maybe she doesn't think of oral play as sex. Technically, as long as there wasn't penetration, she's still a virgin. Just looking for a minute, everyone's going oral on each other and not calling it sex or cheating—only the horizontal mambo qualifies. Boy, do I feel out of touch." He reviewed his information again, making notes and highlighting noteworthy things.

Max watched as Trey manically reviewed the notes, clicking his pen the entire time. "You're wound way too tight; it's not gonna help, maybe give you an ulcer."

In a whisper, with his hand cupped on the side of his mouth, Trey asked Max, "You ever wanna suck someone's johnson? Maybe I'm old school, but that's the last thing I'd ever want in my mouth."

Max walked around the desk to Trey's side, and in an almost inaudible voice, he said, "No, but I'd probably get off on watching girls doing each other. There's something about girl-on-girl action that's hot. You?"

"Nope." He wanted to ask Sloane if she had a thing with Jessica; perhaps the suffocation was an accident. Sex gone wrong.

"Vicarelli, you awake?" Trinity asked in a soft-still-sleeping voice. Eyes closed, she snuggled into him, draped her arm around his waist, and cuddled even closer. She was still naked, but since he'd already been awake and started to dress for work, he was in his boxers when he slid back into bed.

"Yes, ma'am." He didn't want to roll back onto her, afraid he'd hurt her, but he wanted to look at her. Somewhere in his psyche was a scared kid—vulnerable; she had broken through his defenses with minimal effort. He wasn't sure what to do with those feelings; it was odd even to have feelings about something, let alone someone, in a good way, in that way. It amazed him that someone so tiny could have such a strong hold on him. Swinging his feet to the floor, he asked, "Are you hungry? I have eggs and orange juice if you'd like." He turned in her direction. Indeed, she was beautiful, gutsy, and in his bed.

"No, sir, I'm looking at what I want for breakfast. She threw the covers off of her while he watched. "Do you see anything you desire?"

He knelt by the side of the bed and pulled her to him. "Do you have any objection?" He'd never performed oral sex; he knew the basics of the proposition, but the working girls always serviced him, and that was the end of the story. "Let me know what you like and don't."

Trinity propped herself up on her elbows. "I'm sure whatever takes your fancy will be fine with me. Big guy, I may be small, but I don't break." She spread her legs and exposed the finer workings of her body with her hands. He required no more encouragement and stroked her with his tongue. The primal instincts reared again, and he was ravenous to explore her body. For the first time out of the gate on this new adventure, he could only think about pleasuring her. He craved what she had to offer, making her body his for over half an hour. She grabbed his hair with both fists, drawing him closer. Her body responded to his endeavor. Her moans became louder. "Mercy, yes!" The muscles in her legs became rigidly taut for a few moments and then released. "Come on, my man, get up here on your back. It's my turn to bring you to the breaking point."

"You sure? I want everything to be for you." He climbed into the bed and let her work her magic. She was equally as skilled as the pros, but the emotional part of the experience brought him to the highest pinnacle ever. He held back as long as he could, then nature took over, and he allowed himself to surrender to completion. Babe padded his way into the bathroom with his legs weakened from the morning's activities, turned on the water, returned to her, grabbed her hand, and led the way to the shower. How many times had he imagined a scenario with her under the spray? Softly he spoke the words of his imagination. "I want this to be all about you." He slid her body up the tiled wall; she weighed maybe a hundred pounds, if that. In response, she wrapped her legs around him, settling him into her. The hammering began, just as always in his imagination, only he didn't have to imagine this time. She was there for the taking, and he had her with determination. They toweled off, and she grabbed one of his tee shirts.

"If you're still offering," she said. "I will have some eggs and juice, or we can grab breakfast somewhere."

He fastened his jeans and looked at her. "It's up to you. The weather is pretty bad, and I have eggs here."

Trinity moved closer and put her arms around him. " I'm sure everyone tells you this, but, Vicarelli, you have an impressive body. I think your biceps are as big as my waist, but then, you're huge everywhere. Just how tall are you?" She put her size four-and-a-half foot next to his. "My foot looks like a child's next to yours. What size shoe do you wear?"

"Eggs—then answers." The sides of his mouth faintly turned up, but his eyes glittered in amusement.

"Scrambled, dry. If I embarrassed you, I'm sorry. I guess you hear it all the time." She sat cross-legged on his sofa, picked up the remote from the table, and turned on the TV. The first comment they heard was a report regarding the Americans trapped behind enemy lines. "I bet you got all kinds of opinions on the matter."

He stood at the stove. "Yes, ma'am, I do." She heard the crack of the eggs and the sizzle as they cooked. Then she heard more cracks but no added sizzle sounds. She turned to look as he drank a cup of raw eggs.

"You got to be kidding me. I could vomit right here on the spot; you're drinking uncooked eggs. That's disgusting. Probably poisonous." Her nose scrunched, and she had a look that indicated stomach uneasiness. He found it amusing. After pouring her juice and plating her eggs, he washed the pan, walked to the pull-up bar, and commenced his morning routine.

"Now I know how you keep those muscles bulging. You do this every day?"

"Yes." After the pull-ups, free weights, and sit-ups, he started to do the push-ups. "Sit on my back, please." She obliged but laughed the whole time.

After his routine concluded, she walked around the room, looking at the photos on his walls. "You're some badass military man. You went on secret missions? You miss the excitement?" She turned with her hand on her hip and gazed at him.

"Sometimes, but mostly not." He halfway lied.

Getting conversation out of him took some skill. Finally, after several dozen questions, he talked a little about one of his last missions, not the details, only that out of eleven men, only two returned whole and alive. He became even quieter as though slipping into another space and time; she watched in awe as he somehow placed himself back into the mayhem. She could see every muscle tense, and he took on a faraway gaze in his eyes. Trinity didn't intend to send him back to the nightmare, but innocent or not, she had. He crouched down, tensely alert, eyes scanning whatever he saw in his mind, then Babe jumped quickly and brought her under him as he lay hovering his body over hers. "Shut it. I got you, Blocker. Shhh." He waited with such a stillness to his body that his breathing hardly caused movement of his shoulders or back. Trinity wasn't sure if it was best to snap him back to reality or remain still and silent. She chose the silence and observed. She'd heard of vets returning to the war in their minds, with many unable to handle it and taking their lives. Making a mental note, she decided missions or time spent in the military would be off-limits in the future. The last thing she wanted to do was torture him with the past. The spell passed, and he rolled on his back, staring straight at the ceiling.

"I'm sorry, Babe, I—"

"No. It is what it is. When I returned and de-briefed from the last mission before coming home, the shrinks told me to talk about it; easier said than done. I'll have to work through it because I'm not going to some doctor that has no idea of the situation we left. We carried the team one by one, their mutilated bodies, with and without life, to the stealth copter. With the new technology of the rotor blades, the sound gets muffled and distorted, so we got in close. A few of the guys I'd worked on several special assignments with, while for others, it was their first high-level mission and their last." He went into a different zone when discussing his missions, leaving him with a clenched jaw and an intense stare.

Trinity climbed on top of him, putting a hand on each side of his face. "You listen to me, Vicarelli; I'll listen whenever you want. I'm not a kiss and tell and believe me, I hear some shit behind the bar. I'm not afraid of you, and I know you won't hurt me."

"You don't know that." He glanced into her eyes, "I don't know that." She leaned down and kissed him, forcing herself on him. At first, he was cold, but it didn't take long for him to accept her affection. "No news, okay?"

"You got it. How about a stupid sitcom or game show?"

It was well past twenty minutes when Scott and Sloane showed up. Max saw them first, exited the vehicle, and walked toward the couple. "Good afternoon; glad you could make it." The sarcasm was thick, but neither of the breakers noticed. As he drove back to the station, Trey was ensconced in his mental hypothesizing. Max directed, "Sloane, follow Detective Kimble; Scott, you can sit there," pointing to one of the chairs against the wall.

Sloane looked around, almost panicked, "But you said Scott could come down here with me."

"Absolutely, and he can wait right there." Trey looked at Max, "Show Scott to the machine; he's a Barq's fan." Trey opened the door and directed Sloane into an interrogation room. "Do you want something to drink?"

"No. Let's get this done, please. Talking about Jess is hard for me; I can barely control myself when I think of her." She dropped her head, her chin almost touching her chest. Trey couldn't help but think *a bit too dramatically.*

The detective sat across from Sloane. "I get it." He pulled out his pocket pad, opened it to a blank page, looked at her, and began the interview. "How long had you known Jessica?" He sat back with his head tilted to the right, looking her directly, eye to eye.

"Since before high school, sometime in the eighth grade. Jess' dad transferred from Alabama. "She moved in down my street, so we rode the bus together, went to school together, and hung out in the afternoon. We played on all the same teams and even did dance together. She's my roommate." She was a tad abrupt.

"So, you know, uh, knew her well. Wouldn't you say?" He nodded as he spoke as though confirming the answer. His eyes squinted with intensity.

"Better than anyone." Her voice wavered slightly. "What was she like? Did she have a particular boyfriend, like you have with Scott? He leaned forward, shifting to the left, resting his head on his clenched fist like he was utterly invested in the conversation.

Sloane batted her eyes as though pretending to hold back non-existent tears. "We knew everything about each other. She dated Trev for a little while, but he's a player in a big way. I knew her secrets, and she knew mine—best friend kind of things."

"M-hm. When did Jessica break her nose?" Point blank.

"She didn't," her brows furrowed.

Very calmly, Trey responded, "Oh no, she did. The M.E. discovered the fact during her forensic examination. See, we thought the rapist suffocated her, but our forensic specialist said there wasn't proof of rape and that when the attacker put their hand over Jess' mouth, she couldn't breathe. At some point in her life, she broke her nose, making her nearly unable to breathe through her nose." The girl's eyes got wide as saucers.

"W-wait. I thought the guy hit her in the head, like with a lamp or something, and then raped her. Ya know that guy from the bar? She was a virgin."

Trey pursed his lips, shaking his head no. He drew a deep breath making a rattling, sucking noise. "Nope. Suffocated most definitely, and as far as our examiner could tell, there had not been any penetration. So technically, she died a virgin." Sloane could barely swallow, and her hands trembled. Trey held his phone under the table and hit the programmed spoof call. Sloane's phone vibrated on the table. Trey nodded, giving the okay to answer.

"Scott, hey. I can't hear you. Hello?" She became extremely nervous. "Can I go see him? It might be important."

Trey waved her out of the room, grabbed her phone as quickly as possible, and tapped into her camera roll, scrolling as fast as he could. Bingo, Sloane had some compromising pictures of her and Jess kissing, touching tongue to tongue with big smiles, then the crème de la crème; there was a picture of Sloane kissing Jess' breast. *Yep*, he thought, *a picture's worth a thousand words*. He quickly snapped the incriminating photos. The trick, now, was to get a confession and find out who else was in the room—someone needed to sketch out how the whole thing had gone down. It wouldn't be first-degree or second-degree murder; no, it was manslaughter, maybe even reduced from there. They were playing, more than likely. He just needed to hear the words.

Sloane returned to the room, her phone exactly where she left it, and no one any the wiser to the spoof trick. Trey continued. "Everything okay?" She nodded. "So, back to the question about the broken nose."

The girl sighed loudly, "The only thing I can think is that in a volleyball game, Jess caught a hard spike in the face, her nose bled a lot, and her eyes both bruised badly, but the bleeding stopped. I guess it could've been a broken nose, but it's not like it was all crooked. She didn't even go to a doctor." She became quiet momentarily, then cleared her throat and spoke again. "I heard the guy forced her legs apart, and she had bruise marks all over her thighs. How do you explain that? That's what the other detective told Natalie."

Trey wickedly grinned, changing the subject. "Why do you think Jessica ordered an extra-large pizza if it was only her and the guy from Louie's? That's a hell of a lot of pizza for two people. You may or may not know this, but there are other ways people can have sex without penetrating the vagina. It's quite common, especially when girls want to keep intact, so to speak." He looked to the side, feigning discomfort with the subject.

"Yes, of course, I know that, but Jess wasn't like that." She became perturbed.

"Y'all never practiced kissing or anything with each other?" He warmly smiled at her.

"Why would you even think that? She wasn't into girls; she liked boys a lot, just didn't fool around. She kissed a bunch of dudes; maybe some of them might have touched her, but not down there. She wanted to wait for the right guy."

"I see." He stayed quiet for a minute as he watched the girl become fidgety, unable to sit still, every muscle and sinew taut as a guitar string. "Talking about oral sex with my partner gets him all hot and bothered. You?"

Sloane came unglued. "That is completely inappropriate, and I want to tell your captain that you have been sexually harassing me and accusing me of things that aren't true."

Trey raised his hands, "Whoa, I'm sorry if I made you uncomfortable. I certainly didn't mean to imply anything disrespectful. I only wondered if you and Jessica might have experimented, that's all. Because if y'all had, maybe she had with someone else, and maybe that someone went to her room, but with that humongous pizza, it looked like there might have been a party in the works. Look, I know a lot of people your age have sex parties. Some kids were behind the movie theater a few years back doing some rainbow thing. The girls would put on heavy lipstick in bright colors and, well, perform," he shook his head in a nodding fill-in-the-blank way, "with their guy friends. No harm, no foul. It was just a game, ya know, playing around. Certainly nothing serious."

The girl rolled her eyes. "Yeah, I've heard of skanks that did that. Jess wasn't a skank." She tightened her lips in a scowl and crossed her arms.

Trey picked up his phone as though a call had come in and asked, "Do you mind if I take this, it's important?"

With a look that screamed hate, she answered, "I don't care." No doubt in his mind he had struck a nerve. The picture was becoming clearer, and his theory was panning out. He stepped out of the room.

He called down to Charlotte. "It's your favorite pain in the ass. Can you tell if dried saliva was on her private parts for DNA purposes? What about fingerprints?"

With a heavy sigh, Charly responded, "Yes and yes, and I've already swabbed, but Trey, it'll be at least 72 hours, hell, maybe longer. We can maybe determine who created the bruises on the girl's legs and if there is dried saliva on her labia. Do you think it's a thing?"

"I do, but more than that, I'm going to use the threat of DNA potential findings. Maybe it'll loosen some tongues, no pun intended."

Trey walked back into the Interrogation room. "Sorry, it was Charly from forensics telling me she was waiting for the DNA results. Like everything else, 24 hours turns to 72; who knows? I'm sure you'll be relieved to know we'll have the results soon and can put this all to rest." Sloane looked like she was about to jump out of her skin. Her breathing had picked up, her hands started trembling again, and her posture had taken on a look of defeat.

"Don't look so gloomy. Hey, why don't you show me some pictures of you and Jessica together so that we can end this on a positive note? You sure you don't want something to drink?" So far, between Trey and Max, they had collected seven cans and two water bottles. Charly had them swabbed, fingerprinted, cataloged, and in the capable hands of the lab. It wouldn't be long before they had the answers. He preferred a confession, especially concerning this particular case. His heart said it had been a playful accident and, sorrowfully, one they'd have to live with for the rest of their lives.

"I just want to leave if it's okay. Are we done?" He'd snuffed her over-confident attitude like a blown-out candle.

THE THRILL OF
THE CONQUEST

*T*rey had some pep in his step. The interview with Sloane proved en-
lightening, and he felt sure would oil the squeaky wheel. He wondered whose saliva and fingerprints would be listed in the report. His gut
said Sloane, but who was the other person? Scott and Adam were the only
two left without an air-tight alibi.

Given that Adam and Scott had enjoyed Jasmine's company and
talents, that's where he laid his bet. The part he didn't get had to do with
Jessica's involvement. Had she been a willing participant, or was it coercion
or assault?

Like a doting parent, Max advised, "Trey, you look beat. Go home.
That was a long-ass interview, but from what you said and what I heard
eavesdropping, you hit the lottery."

"Yeah, stick a fork in me. See you in the morning, and pray for no call-
outs tonight." He straightened the folders on his desk, grabbed his water
bottle, and headed out the door.

A stop at Louie's had become almost routine given this case, but he'd even
welcome a break in the routine. He turned the block and cruised for a
moment, his mind rambling. Walking down the street, he spied Hulk-

man walking beside tiny Trinity. Their difference in size was somewhat comical but nonetheless sweet. He watched as she playfully pushed him; she bounced like a ball off a wall. He knew the Quarter would look cleaner in the morning after the deluge washed away all the funk-nasty. He pulled alongside the couple lowering the passenger window and shouted over the blaring music from the open bar doors lining the street, "Hey, y'all."

Babe turned, his body blocking Trinity, but upon spying Trey, the giant took her hand and pulled her in front of him. The couple walked up to his car. "You off or on?" Babe asked.

"Off, thankfully. Y'all headed to Louie's?" Not that Trey planned to go there, it was for small talk.

Babe leaned into the car. "She's off, so no way. We're going to the new pizza place, Fat Boys, next to Pat O's. See you there, or you headed home?"

"Headed home, but maybe I'll stop and pick up a slice for Steph." He pulled out and turned off Bourbon Street at the corner. Undoubtedly, they would arrive before him. It made him smile to think of them together. *Who knows*, he thought, *something might develop*. He parked at the first available spot, put the NOPD parking permit on his dashboard, and walked to Fat Boys. He called Max, "Hey, stopping by Fat Boys to pick up a slice for Steph; I ran into our military giant with none other than our favorite Creole bartender, Miss Trinity Noelle. I thought you might find that interesting."

"No shit. The big guy's dream is coming true; gotta love it. Now, Padna, I need to find a good woman," he laughed.

"You've had your share of women, and it didn't fair well—"

"Yeah," Max interrupted, "but I said a good woman and none of those bitches were good. If I can find decent parking, I'll see ya there; if not, see you in the morning. We got a lot done today. It was a win. Take it and go see Steph."

By the time Trey made it to the pizza joint, Babe and Trinity were already sitting at a table. He placed an order, grabbed a beer, and sat with them. Trinity talked a mile a minute as the giant held on to her every word.

She wrapped up her explanation, "And so, that's how I came to work at Louie's." She smiled at the detective. "Vicarelli, I been talking non-stop; it's your turn."

A little upturn of his lips fueled twinkling in his eyes as he looked at her and then spoke to Trey. "How's it going?" He nodded with an uplifting of his chin and eyebrows; it was a guy thing.

"I hope I'm not intruding on a date. Max may or may not be coming; I just stopped to pick up a slice to bring home to the wife and say hi." They didn't have their food, so it might be a longer wait than Trey had anticipated. "It was a good day, but I'd love to be a fly on the wall to listen to them after today."

Babe took a long draw from his beer. "You know some rooms have ears. What made it such a good day?"

"Police crap and stuff," he couldn't say too much as this was an active case. He'd probably already let go more than he should, but he was exhausted and all out of give-a-fucks.

Trinity tilted her head and asked, "What do you mean? Rooms have ears? Uh, not at our hotel, dude." Trey wondered how that conversation went when she told him she was a Noelle, as in the Noelle family. All Babe could respond with was a hm, and what that meant was anyone's guess. Trey wondered what it was like inside the military man's head. He knew the guy had seen way more than he had and had done things he couldn't even imagine. *Yeah*, Trey thought, *the guy the military used when the missions were on a need-to-know basis with little to no one needing to know. I'd bet my last dollar that he's a fucking scary kind of guy.*

It didn't take long before they had their food. Trey waited for Steph's to-go while shooting the breeze with them. Trinity chimed in, "I guess y'all are waiting on DNA and all that tech stuff you see on TV."

"It's a lot different in real life, but yes, we're waiting for hard facts. Personally, I think it's better for everyone when there's a confession. No oopses or questions about the chain of evidence." With a far more relaxed demeanor, Trey asked Trinity, "Where do you live? In the Quarter, warehouse district, Metairie, uptown, mid-city, or the Lakefront?"

She giggled, breaking off a small piece from the gigantic slice. "It's fair to say, some n'some. I have a house in Lakeview that I rarely see and an apartment connected kinda to the hotel. I'm fixin' to sell Lakeview; I'm never there. My ex and I lived there for the few years we were married." She scarfed another bite of the enormous piece.

Trey's mind started rolling, "Why don't you work at the hotel instead of Louie's? I'm sure it would be better hours." He took a slug of his beer.

His comment nearly made her choke, "The clientele. I like my regulars." Her eyes shifted quickly to Babe with a smile, "Besides, working with family, like sister, brothers, and Dad, definitely isn't for me. They are a pain in my ass. My uncle, Shep, is laid-back, roll with the flow, and doesn't hassle me about anything. I love working at Louie's; I meet some interesting people, that's for sure."

Babe watched her, not missing a word, bat of the eyes, or flirty glance towards him, but, all the while, was thinking how he could get a recorder into the friend's room. He'd create that fly on the wall. The murder investigation and romping with Trinity had controlled his urge to right the wrongs in his natural way, at least for the time being. He'd thwarted a would-be robbery with his presence a few days before. He had observed a group of three young boys setting up to rob a tourist, but when he made his presence known, they dropped their plans like a red-hot iron.

Ten minutes later, Trey got his to-go order, bid farewell, and headed home. Even talking with Babe and Trinity started to feel stale; he needed a break. The murder or accidental death of Jessica Lambert and all the truth twisting, lies, deception, and betrayal from the Ole Miss spring breakers had soured him. While the breakers were adults, it felt more like dealing with a bunch of spoiled high school brats.

On the walk back to Babe's place, he and Trinity began a discussion about where to spend the night. He knew he had work the next day, so his place was the best option, but he wanted to get a recording of the girl's best friend. He had a feeling that something would come out once they were out of earshot of anyone else.

During her disclosure about her last name and the hotel, Trinity mentioned that she had a master key and could access the entire hotel. Babe's next step needed to include getting Trinity's key. Which room was it? He'd heard on the second floor, but that was over twenty rooms, he suspected. The timing had to be perfect.

Walking hand in hand, with more than half her piece left over in the box, he said, "I wonder if the girl stayed in the same room where the murder took place. Not that it would bother me, but I can see where a young girl may not be okay with the thought. Oh, being a crime scene, I guess not." He looked down at her.

Excitedly Trinity responded, "I went to my sisters on Sunday after Mass. Bethany told me all about the murder. I told her there was no way my Finn raped the girl and certainly didn't kill her. From what she said, the girl didn't want to release her room or move, but because it was a crime scene, they had to move her to two-ten. She stayed with a couple of other girls for a night. I don't know what it is about two-o-six, but it's got some bad juju. A few people have died in that room, and now one more. One man had a heart attack, another died of alcohol poisoning, and an older lady fell in the bathroom and hit her head. You ask me, ain't no way I'd stay in that room. They need to leave it locked forever."

He chuckled, "Bad juju? You believe that?"

She turned around to look at him and continued walking, only backward, "Hell, yes, I believe it, and you should too, my big friend. The spirit world is nothing to fuck with, I know." He took her hand and spun her in the right direction.

"Okay, whatever you say, lady. I'm on your side." He made a mental note of Room Two-ten. Just like that, he formulated a plan. "You've seen mine; now I want to see yours, apartment, that is." He briefly huffed a laugh.

Grinning from ear to ear, she said, "I was about to say, we both got a good look at each other's, ah, but you want to see my place. Warning, it's nowhere as neat and tidy as yours. I clean it once a week, and I missed my last cleaning day."

Babe's mind started processing. He'd have to find an electronic store, perhaps Best Buy or maybe one of the touristy stores on Canal Street. Surely they would have something to fit the bill. He'd have to line that up while finding an excuse to get Trinity's hotel key card. There had to be a way he could plant a recorder in an inconspicuous place and retrieve it later. Leave it long enough that maybe he'd catch one of them saying something. His curiosity was piqued. Depending on the success of his mission would determine if he'd ever disclose the findings to the detective. If it were to go to court, which he didn't think would happen, the recording would be inadmissible. For once, his law degree came in handy. Maybe it might shake someone up, though, or give the detectives another route for questioning, and they could use it.

Her apartment was only a few blocks away, and they made it in what seemed to be minutes, but probably more like fifteen with their banter. Babe opened up to her more than anyone else in his entire life. He told her about his grandfather and the conversation with Bjorn about a brother somewhere. She was easy to talk to and didn't register judgment. The fact that he had an episode in her presence and was never spoken of again said a lot about her character.

While one of his last missions had succeeded without team casualty, the one prior haunted his night and daydreams. All too often, in the recesses of his mind, he heard his commander's voice.

Vicarelli, you are a fighting machine, a one-man mission success story. You've given your life and loyalty to the Corps, which is the only way, but you have done it flawlessly.

He wondered, *did they consider the fateful mission a success? Yes, we eliminated the target, but at the expense of Marine lives. I didn't deserve the accolades or a pat on the back; I let my team down. I led them to certain death, and they followed. Why did I survive? It was my duty to lead and protect them.*

"Hello, in there. Where you at, big guy?" Silence. "Oh, no you don't. You come off that battlefield, my friend; your future is but one step followed by another. Honor the fallen by being the man they knew and respected."

His eyes were laser-focused ahead, and his senses were on high alert to everything around them. He looked down at Trinity and confessed, "I kill people."

She jumped in front of him and stopped him. "You," and she used air quotes, "eliminated the enemy and did your job, but it's over; let it go." They entered the hotel and went down a hallway through an employee-only door leading to an outside brick corridor, still part of the hotel but separate. Two flickering flames brightened her doorway; she unlocked the door with a pass of the plastic key card, and they entered. Her place looked like a display from a magazine, clean and perfect. He hated to put the leftover box of pizza on the counter. She grabbed it and put it in her near-empty refrigerator.

"This is a nice place and not what I'd call a disaster." She took his hand and pulled him toward the closed door to her bedroom, which was, as she said, a mess. Trinity had clothes strewn all over the floor, a rumpled unmade bed, and the opened closet resembled a war-torn country. He laughed from the deepest part of his belly—something he couldn't ever remember happening. "You're not kidding, girl. You're a fucking slob; this looks dangerous."

"I told you, so like you said, no judgment. See, my bed is ready to plop in, mister. I have a fee for staying the night here, though." She walked up close to him, their bodies touching as she gazed upwards toward his face. Keeping eye contact, she undid his belt and pulled on it, sliding it through the belt loops with ease. She folded it in half and, in a sexy manner, slapped the palm of her hand. "Snap to it, Marine. I wanna see your body; it's unbelievable." She pushed against his abs, tracing the muscle definition with her finger. "Do a muscle man pose, you know, like—" She made a stance flexing her biceps.

"What?" He laughed again. "Do you really want me to flex?"

"Yeah, baby, strike a pose, but first, get naked." He pulled his shirt over his head, unbuttoned his jeans, and started to unzip when she stopped him. "Stop, pose like that; you look so hot." He stopped with a huge grin. She made him feel alive more than ever before; reluctantly, Babe raised his arms, curled them at the elbow, and flexed with a cheesy smile." Her eyes became round with a popping-out look. Then, he bent in half with a laugh.

Babe pointed at her. "Ya know, you've got some serious muscle in your arms, Trinity. That's one of the first things I noticed, oh, and that tight round ass; I did a lot of fantasizing about that. Now, it's your turn to do as I ask. I gotta say, I'm glad you dropped my belt because I'm not into the whole pain-for-pleasure action. No, ma'am, just pure pleasure; I've endured more pain in my life than I care to admit, starting as a kid. It's why I bulked up, hit the weights, and started intense training. I was always a big kid; I just got strong." Enough talk; you ready for some action?"

"And you haven't even seen my bathroom!" She stood with a hand on her hip and a face of attitude. He peered in the bathroom doorway, and it was just as much, if not more, of a disaster. "Now, I am more than ready for some action."

Morning came, and his day began much earlier than hers, so he quietly left the bedroom after kissing her on the cheek.

Babe jogged home, leashed Gunner, and continued to the construction site. Glenn was in the office looking through the plans. No one else had made it to the site yet. " Good morning, Vicarelli and Gunn. You're early, but I could use the hand. After that crappy day yesterday, we have some major water to sweep out before the other men arrive. That way, they can get right to it and hopefully make up some of the lost time from yesterday. That was some kinda storm we had."

"Yes, sir." The two walked out of the trailer, and sure enough, there were some puddly patches. He picked up a push broom and began at once to move the standing water. After thirty minutes, they had swept most of the water, some men had arrived, and the site was again vibrant with the sound of construction. The morning zoomed by; it was nearly time to implement his plan. At the beginning of lunch break, Babe told his site super that he had to hit an appointment and would be gone an hour. Gunner stayed in the trailer with Glenn. As predicted, it wasn't an issue, and he took off breezing through a couple of stores on Canal. Jackpot, he found a camcorder of sorts with a six-hour battery life. "Ready-charged" was advertised on the box. He quickly paid, headed to Louie's for the key, and lastly to two-ten.

Babe hoped the guest in two-ten had left so he could plant the recorder and be on his way. The scheme went without a hitch, and before long, he was back at Louie's returning Trinity's key. "Glad to have my belt back on. Working construction with no belt is a bitch; I've been pulling up my jeans all morning." He winked at her as he turned to leave.

She came around the bar, "Uh, I don't think so. No kiss?" He looked around. "I don't care who's lookin', big guy. They got a problem; they can talk to management or deal with you." She giggled. He swooped in for a quick peck and turned to leave. "I'll see you tonight after you get off work?" He nodded.

The DNA still had not come in, and as each hour passed, Trey became antsier and antsier. The breakers had only a day and a half left in New Orleans. Of course, he could always extradite them, but if what he believed happened was the case, then it would have been an accidental death, and no one was to blame. It was unfortunate circumstances that left a hole in the Lambert's heart, and life would never be the same. Perhaps after all was said and done, they might find comfort in knowing it hadn't been a brutal rape and horrendous murder.

Max looked at Trey, who was pacing like an expectant father. "Boy, you gotta relax some. This isn't the be-all, end-all case. Yes, it's sad, but we've seen far worse. You've let yourself get too emotionally invested."

"I know." He said while still wearing out the floor with continual pacing. He finally sat and called Sloane. "Good afternoon, Sloane. This is—" she stopped him. "I'm calling to check my notes. When is it y'all are leaving New Orleans?" She confirmed his thoughts, which gave him the day and the next to solve the puzzle, but then they were heading out the following morning.

The Captain stepped from his office and called, "Kimble, Sledge, in my office." Both detectives hopped to the request. "There have been three kidnappings in Mid-City in the past twenty-four hours. It's not our precinct, but keep an ear out. It's gonna be the focus of the six o'clock news tonight. One kid from City Park was abducted, and two from the adjacent neighborhood. Not that we have a lot of children residing in the Quarter anymore; we do get families with kids. I'm assigning more officers to the French Market, Jackson Square, the Aquarium, and Royal Street, as those are the more kid-friendly areas meaning I'm pulling a few officers from Bourbon. Moving officers around translates into a need for more police presence. We have an allocation for overtime, first come, first served. What the hell is going on with the spring breaker case? Have we put the debacle to rest yet?" He looked from one detective to the other, obviously irritated. "You two are slipping; put it to bed; we got cases out the ass."

"We're close, sir," Trey answered. "Like breathing down the neck close, but I don't think it's what we thought it was initially. I'm thinking there was no foul play, only accidental death."

District Captain Bull Turner, a long-time veteran of the NOPD, cradled his head in his hands. "Another fentanyl overdose?" He sadly shook his head.

"No, sir, no drugs. I think it was, but I'm not sure yet—"

"Spit it out, Kimble. You're wasting my time. Thoughts?" He stared holes through his detective as if saying go on, get to it.

"Sex games, sir. The deceased couldn't breathe through her nose, and no one knew. She suffocated." Trey had his hands laced in his lap.

"This is a cluster. Get back to me pronto; if you want any OT, better grab it. Dismissed." He looked back down at his paperwork.

Walking out to their desks, Max asked Trey, "Why in the hell would you tell Cap? We got nothing to stand on yet, Trey. Stupid. You gotta learn to keep your head down, and your mouth closed. You better check with Stephanie before you go taking OT, or you'll be one miserable son-of-a-bitch. Trust me, don't piss her off. You know what they say, happy wife, happy life."

No matter how tempted and impatient he was, he was determined not to call Charly. He looked at Max. "We need answers; we need them now."

"I'm going for a spin around the Quarter. How about we take a drive, see if any degenerates are lurking around? Get your mind on something else, boy; you're a mess. This one really got to ya. Every now and then, a case grabs your heart. Don't know why; we've seen some horrific things, ma man. Remember the case where that crazy loon doctor went on a rampage, killing a lot of the street kids, all because his daughter dyed her hair pink and polished her nails black? Remember that? He made a mess of their bodies. Sliced them open, gutted like pigs. Remember? You didn't get shook at all; you kept your head down and plowed through the case until you caught the sicko; that was all you who caught the doc. C'mon, let's take a ride. Clear your head up a bit." He grabbed Trey's coffee cup and walked to the door knowing his partner would be close behind.

The workday ended, and Babe went straight to Louie's. Trinity smiled big when she saw him. "I got an idea; lemme see your key. I promise to bring it back before closing time."

Rolling her eyes, Trinity asked, "What're you up to? Don't go cleaning my room; I like it just like it is." She turned toward a guest. "Another gin and tonic? Slow down, Tiger; they'll kick you in the ass if you're not careful." She giggled. Babe could see that the older man was eating up the attention, and he thought, *good for him*. After handing her customer his drink, she returned to continue the discussion of her room.

"There's no way I would even consider cleaning your room; that's all you. No, it's something different." He nodded with an exaggerated wink.

"Ya know, I don't give my key to just anyone." She playfully teased.

"I should hope not." He threw it right back at her. Her silent military man was beginning to have a voice and reveal his personality. What she didn't realize was that it was a revelation to himself. He'd never seen this new side and wondered where it had been hiding for his thirty-six years. Babe couldn't recall even playing as a child but was sure at some point he must have been a normal kid; then again, given the parent situation, maybe not. Uncle Sam didn't call for playfulness. Sure, he'd spoken to some of the people he'd been on missions with and maybe chuckled at a crude joke, but he was never one to instigate conversation unless it was commands or directions.

After relinquishing her key, Babe headed out. First, he bought a bouquet of fresh flowers and a vase, then placed them on her entry table so it was the first thing she'd see when she got home. He'd seen the breakers at Louie's, so he knew the coast was clear to retrieve the recorder. He then went home to listen; the picture was an up-too-close of the fake ivy plant he'd hidden it in.

The first ten minutes involved the girl getting ready to go out and singing along with a song from her phone. Then came a knock. "Scott, thank God you're here." He heard the door shut. "That detective called again, asking when we were leaving. We need to talk; I keep reliving the night in my head and my dreams; I can't let it go."

There were muffled sounds like he was moving something and then a creak of a chair as the boy sat. "I'm not talking about it anymore. Quit, or I'm leaving."

They talked about going home for the next hour and how different things would be. Everything went quiet for a while, with some moaning and grunting. Babe fast-forwarded the recording. The sex was over; he heard the zip of a duffle bag and then a whirring of a blow dryer.

"I told you I don't want to talk about it. Dammit, Sloane."

She was getting angry; he could hear the venom in her tone. "Look, if I hadn't babbled in front of Adam about how Jess asked me to touch her."

"I'm going." He could hear rustling and grumbling but nothing distinctive.

Sloane raised her voice. "Scott, listen, none of the going down on her thing would have happened." Babe's jaw dropped in surprise. The girl started to cry.

"No, it's not your fault. Stop crying, please. Adam's the jerk by pushing the issue, almost prodding you. Jess was pretty buzzed." He tried to console her. There was mumbling from what sounded like Sloane.

"What did you say?" He was pissed. "No more talking about it. She's fucking dead; let it go."

"No. Why don't you go back to your room? You don't give a fuck about my feelings like you didn't care about Jess' feelings."

"Oh. No, you don't. No blame game, Sloane. She was pissed that you told me and then Adam. Get over yourself." The girl began to sob. There were hushed murmurs. "Sorry, I guess that was mean. If you think about it, it's kinda Jess' fault too. Remember, she said, 'What the hell, like anyone would believe us, anyway.' Think about it. Every time you put your face down there to show us, she squeezed her legs together, laughing so loud she could have gotten us in trouble for being so rowdy. I had no choice but to put my hand over her mouth. Christ, she bit me, just playing, I think. So I held her mouth tighter. It was Adam that forced her really by prying her legs apart, and you did your thing. Look, Sloane; she liked it, I could tell; she was moaning and squirming. Adam got so turned on by the girl-on-girl stuff that he had a hard time. That's why he wanted to get in on the action. I thought she'd had a major 'O' when her body went limp. I had no idea she was dead."

He heard a loud squeak and thud like she'd thrown her body on the bed and began to wail again.

Her voice hitched, and through sobs, she said she was going to tell the cops. "That one detective is pretty young, and he might understand. None of us thought she'd die, or we would never have done it."

The sound of a canned drink popped in the background. "You won't get mad at me if I tell him? The only thing is Jess' parents can't ever know. Oh my God, they'd come unglued, for sure." She started to sob again. "I miss her so much."

"Sloane, was that the first time you did that to her?" There was an uncomfortable silence, squeaks caused by someone shifting in the chair, and a rustling of sheets. "Well?"

"No. It all started with kissing, and well, one thing led to another. We made sure her virginity was intact. I don't want to answer any more questions, Scott."

"Just bi?" He said sarcastically. "Did she get you off as much as I do?" *Whoa. What an insecure little bastard* was all Babe could think besides being completely blown away by what and how things happened. *Trey is gonna love this one.*

Riding along, Trey and Max passed a huddled bunch of grunge kids; they pulled over. Max spoke, "Break it up, break it up. What's going on here?" A few of them scattered, hurling police slurs, leaving three. In the center of the circle of kids was a young boy. He'd been beaten and was unconscious but somehow looked vaguely familiar. "Y'all do this?" He didn't think they did, but they'd seen something. The three teens immediately denied any involvement. "Trey, you know this kid?"

"Nah." Trey leaned in to feel for a pulse. "Call a bus; I got a thready pulse. What happened here?" All at once, the remaining three started talking. "One at a time, pick a spokesperson." A blonde-haired girl with a head full of dreads and dirty clothes answered.

"We were like chillin' here, minding our own business, and some ride pulls up and rolls this kid out of it." Her arms animated with flicking her wrists like she was hyped up on something or just teenage-girl-dramatic. "He looked pretty bad; we were about to call for help, but like you dudes pulled up." They started backing away like they were about to bolt.

Trey had his trusty pad and clicky pen out. "Stay put. Answer my questions. What kind of car? Do you remember what the driver looked like? Man or woman? Maybe a license plate? Do you know this boy?"

The girl raised one side of her upper lip with a look of disgust. "Too many questions, dude. All I saw was a woman driving a blue van; someone in the back slid the side door open and rolled the kid out. She almost pulled onto the sidewalk, and I was like, 'bitch, watch where you're goin'. She was so close I could smell weed; she musta been like wasted the way she was drivin'. I don't know about no license plate, but she had gobs of stickers all over the back of the shitty old van."

One of the remnant three, a tall, lanky black kid, said, "It was a Mississippi plate, and I saw a couple from Biloxi, some mermaid saying something like Keep Off My Tail. Oh, and I don't know the numbers on the plate, but the first three letters were B-L-U. Funny cuz the van was blue." He pointed at the kid on the ground. "Bro, he's a lot younger than us, like maybe ten or twelve, I think. He sure don't hang with us."

The paramedics pulled up and took over with the boy. Running through Trey's mind was that if they wanted to dispose of the kid, why drop him next to a group of people, even if they were grunge kids? Trey looked through his phone at the pictures of the abducted kids; sure enough, he was one of the kids. "Max, this is one of the three kidnap victims. I'm calling it in. Cap's gonna be happy we got at least one of the kids. Maybe he'll get off our ass." The blonde girl said the van took a left at the end of the block. He asked her, "Did you see the woman's face? Like, could you describe her to a sketch artist?" The girl shook her head no. Was it truly a no, or was she trying to avoid getting involved? Once the kidnapped boy was on his way to the hospital and Trey spoke to the Captain, he and Max continued patrolling. "See, I told you, Sledgehammer, driving around would be a good thing."

"Wha—" Max began to say.

"Yanking your chain, Max, you're way too easy. I know damn well you were trying to pull me out of my obsession." Trey turned up the force of the air conditioner. "I'm hot, you?" He could see the sweat running down Max's face.

They made the left and traveled down a few blocks. A few cars parked along the street had been side-swiped. They stopped and called it in, but from the appearance, the color of the paint left on the hit-n-run cars was blue. Trey scratched his head. Max piped in, "Man, what's the deal? These people trying to get busted? It's like fucking Hansel and Gretel with the breadcrumbs. I got a feelin' we gonna catch these weirdos. Unfortunately, their breadcrumbs are kids and sideswipes. "

After forty-five minutes, the uniforms arrived; none too happy that they had to mop up behind the detectives, Max and Trey took off again. Before they knew it, they were on Esplanade. They rode toward the French Market. A call came in that they needed to report back to the house. Trey became animated with hopes of a response from forensics. They made it back quickly; Trey nearly raced in with Max hollering for him to slow down. He called Charlotte, "Yeah, you got something?"

"No, Trey, I told you I would call, but I'm hoping sometime today." He became almost disheartened until he saw an envelope on his desk. He carefully opened it and found a thumb drive. He plugged it in, unsure what would be on the USB. The techs had already installed audio from a previous case, so when he inserted the drive, he heard a few crackles and then the conversation between Sloane and Scott. He listened for a few minutes, fast-forwarding through the silence, meaningless banter, and sex. "What the fuck can I do with this?" He asked who had dropped off the envelope, but no one seemed to know, probably a rookie from the reception desk. Trey brought it into the Captain's office. "Ya gotta hear this, but I don't know what I can do with it or where it came from." The Captain glanced a few times at Trey as they listened; both men were without words during the playback, glancing back and forth at each other.

"Bottom line, Kimble, we can't do anything with it unless we can track down the source. And you say we have no idea where it came from? I hate to say it, but you gotta tell the girl forensics confirmed your suspicions, and maybe she'll spill, but without an actual forensics report confirming, if she pushes back, you'll be shit out of luck. How lucky do you feel today?" He rocked back in his chair.

Trey pursed his lips, raised his brows, and nodded, "Pretty damn lucky; we found a kidnap victim and followed a trail of side-swiped cars damaged by the kidnappers." He turned his hands up with a shrug of his shoulders.

"Go for it and cross your fingers that Charlotte comes up with the evidence to substantiate the recording. It's got me curious about who recorded and delivered it." The Captain rubbed his temples with his eyes closed. "Some days, I think I picked the wrong job. It was either the Fire department or the police. I bet they don't have half the bullshit."

When he returned to his desk, Max, who had heard the recording with Trey, asked, "You gonna call the girl?" He nodded and pointed to the phone.

"Sloane, it's Detective Kimble. I need you, Scott, and Adam to come in; this'll probably be the last time."

To his surprise, she answered, "I wanted to come talk to you anyway." She sniffled.

Glenn called the day at noon, something about inspectors. Babe stretched to begin his run back to his place for a quick shower and then to head to Louie's for dinner. All went as planned; he had a sweaty run after being on the construction site most of the day, and a shower was most welcome. He peeled off his drenched clothes that stuck to his skin. There was almost a slick plastic sound as the pants came off. "Fucking heat, and it's not even summer."

He padded around naked, trying to lower his body temperature. He thought *only one sure way to do it.* He turned on the cold water in the shower and stepped in, "Mother fucker." He grabbed his genitals to keep the cold spray from hitting them. Gradually he added a little hot water and lathered up, hoping to remove the workday stench.

The coldness of the water plunged him back to the freezing temperatures and heavy snowfall of Afghanistan. He could clearly remember the mission. They crawled on their bellies, despite the icy conditions. The adrenalin was pumping through their bodies, and they could see the security on the walls surrounding Aarif Sayed's compound. Orders: Bring back Sayed, dead or alive. The powers-that-be were back on base monitoring the attack, so why the need for a body? It wasn't his to question but to implement. The team braced for the fight, and in twenty-two minutes, they had attacked, retrieved the threat, injured but alive, and were headed back to base with their prisoner. The team was still intact, with no injuries or fatalities. Perhaps, that was the coldest he'd ever been, but because of the adrenalin, he didn't notice until back on the Blackhawk.

He dressed with haste looking forward to seeing Trinity. Where this newfound personality had been hiding was any man's guess; he had no idea. "Gunn, stay." The dog had learned some commands. With food and water, his furry pal would be good for at least six hours.

As he crossed the first street, a blue van ripped toward him, screeched to a stop, dumped something, and started to take off. Something was wrong with the picture. Babe jumped to the side and managed to grab the face of the driver through the open window, causing the van to smash into a fire hydrant, throwing the driver into the steering wheel with great force, disabling her while he checked the something thrown from the vehicle.

It was a young girl, maybe eight; if he had to guess, she was in and out of consciousness. He called nine-one-one and hopped back in the van. In the back, trying to hide, was a man cowering in the corner and another younger, apparently unconscious child. He shook his head at the man, who raised and pointed a gun at him. Babe threw him down, straddled his body, and snapped the man's neck with a quick torque, then carried the other child and laid him by the first victim. Quickly returning to the vehicle, he smashed the driver's already bloody skull into the steering wheel, crushing the side of her head, creating a hideous deformity. He felt for a pulse; she, too, was dead. His rage was icing on the cake.

Two uniforms arrived; Babe apprised them of the situation and said that the driver and the adult passenger were dead from all he could tell. He had placed the kids on the sidewalk next to each other, waiting for help to arrive. Babe explained that the van drove erratically down the street, dumped something, which turned out to be a child, and went out of control and plowed over the old hydrant. The situation was aggravating, and he could've kicked himself for hanging around and getting involved, but someone needed to stand guard over the children, and the two pieces of shit in the vehicle were a moot point. They got what they deserved. No guilt whatsoever; if anything, it made his heart rest to know that there were now two fewer monsters on the street.

While appreciative that he had called in the emergency, one of the officers said he would have to go to the station and make a formal statement. Going to the police station was not on his list of things to do that evening, but he agreed, telling them he was on foot, so it may take time. The officer called another unit to take him to the precinct. The other uniform was busily reporting the accident, stating the vehicle matched the description of the kidnappers.

The last thing he wanted was to go to the police station; he knew Trinity would be looking for him. *What is it with the girl? When did I get so soft?* He rode to the station; they led him upstairs, and his eyes met Trey's when he walked in.

"What're you doing here, friend?" The detective asked as he stood.

Babe shook his hand. "I witnessed an accident and pulled a kid from the vehicle. There was a man and a woman, but they didn't survive the crash, at least I don't think. Anyway, your fellow officers asked if I would come down and make a legit statement. Here I am. Where do I go from here?" Trey pointed to his chair and handed him a pad and pen.

"Was it a blue van?"

"Yes, sir and it stunk of weed." He smelled his shirt to ensure he wasn't carting the smell of marijuana in his clothes—no residue scent. "They rolled one kid out of the vehicle but had the other in the back when they ran into the hydrant. They were swerving all over the street; it's no surprise they lost control—good thing they did, or who knows what would have happened to the other child."

Babe noticed the USB on the desk and grinned inside. He wondered if they had been as shocked as he had been. The world was getting hinkier by the day—threesomes, group sex, wasn't his thing. Getting laid had never been an issue, but consistent sex with the same person was a new concept for him. Speaking of—thinking and not doing was wasting time. He jotted down his statement and handed it to Trey, whereby the detective asked some fill-in questions, then he was out of there with a thank you and a handshake to see his girl. *My girl?*

On the way out, he spotted a police car pulling up to the station with three spring break kids and watched as they got out with the officers escorting them into the station. His hand at espionage seemed to create a dialogue. The mission now was Trinity and food as his stomach growled. No one offered to give him a ride, but it didn't matter; he could easily walk from one side of the quarter to the other with little effort and fast.

He strolled into Louie's. Trinity had her back turned and was swaying with the music, her hips and shoulders moving in an alluring manner.

Silently he observed her, a distinct thumping in his chest and immense heat developing below the belt. Yeah, she was his girl. No doubt. No other woman had ever moved him like the tiny Miss Trinity—a ball of sexy energy.

Her face lit up when she saw him. "Boy, you are a sight for sore eyes. I'll get you set; think of dinner while I get your drink." It was obvious to everyone sitting at the bar that her world had stopped when she saw him.

After he sat, she brought his drink and asked, "Daily plate or something different?"

"I don't think what I want goes on a plate," he winked at her. "Can I get a piece of meat, potatoes, and a salad? Also, some water with lime, ma'am. Their eyes met, and just at that moment, a heat wave moved through his body, creating a tickle and a flinch. "Cold water, please." He smiled.

"Your wish is my command," she said with a bat of the eyes and a hearty laugh.

When she could break away, she did, but it was fleeting; nonetheless, it was a thrill for him—this new life. After a couple of interrupted hours, it was time for him to leave. He needed to get back to his routine; spontaneity wasn't his norm unless it was relieving the world of another ne'er-do-well, and that just came naturally without thought or emotion. He signaled her with a point of his finger, "Gotta go." She nodded, grabbed his shirt, and pulled him toward her for a goodbye kiss. Some of the older men at the bar whistled and said things like, 'Yeah, you right,' and 'hot-damn.' He smiled and walked out.

A WORD OF TRUTH

Rather than wait for Sloane, Scott, and Adam, Trey and Max had a patrol officer pick them up. It was interesting because Sloane had said she wanted to talk. Babe had left; they had his statement regarding the kidnapping, so that case was closed, and the Captain would be happy. Trey rocked back in his chair with a yawn, "S'cuse." He knuckled his eyes, and when the blurriness cleared, he saw Sloan, Scott, and Adam walk through the door. Sloan appeared upset, and all Trey could think was, *here we go again!*

Trey's face was somber when he walked toward them. He brought them into the conference room at the precinct instead of interrogation. Captain Turner and Max joined them. The Captain sat at the head of the table with a stack of paperwork.

Everyone sat, and Trey began, "I called you Sloane because we have some forensics that indicates you were more than friends with Jessica Lambert. It also reflects that Adam was part of the sexual activity and that Scott cupped her mouth, accidentally obstructing her breathing, resulting in her death. I know it was all accidental or could be considered homicide by misadventure which is unintentional. I'm not quite sure who will describe the encounter to Mr. and Mrs. Lambert. It's touchy. We are not going into the details; they have sustained enough sadness." Sloane raised her hand. "Yes?"

"None of us would have ever hurt Jess." The tears started rolling down her cheeks. "Her mom and dad can't know. It would crush them."

The Captain spoke gruffly, "Missy, they're pretty damn crushed already. They need closure." Sloane started to sniffle again.

Trey cocked his head, "Do y'all have sex parties a lot? I mean, is this common?" Trey was perturbed, and it came out in his clipped speech.

Adam weighed in with a monotone drone, "More common than you probably think. Look, I didn't know the girl, but we were all laughing, including Jessica; no one knew anything went wrong until Scott yelled that Jessica wasn't breathing, so we covered her and left. It wasn't like we could bring her back to life. We were all freaked out."

Scott and Sloane were twitchy, unable to sit still, whereas Adam sat perfectly calm with no look of emotion. The Captain matter-of-factly addressed the group, "There will be repercussions from this tragedy, and a Grand Jury will look at the evidence and decide what happens next." He looked at the older detective. "Max, can you hand me three pads and pens?" Then with a stern look, not a trace of a smile or warmth, he spoke to the breakers. "I suggest you describe the incident and intention as thoroughly as possible. If it were me, I'd make sure to note that it was a party of sorts among close friends, and it was all light-hearted. You are all adults and will be treated as adults; it is your decision to disclose this information to your parents or hire a lawyer or whatever you see fit, given your personal situation. I can't promise what the outcome will be. Still, the way I understand the situation, I don't see where there will be incarceration, perhaps monetary compensation. We will let Jessica's parents know the cause of death was by misadventure." The Captain remained controlled and to the point. "Sledge, Kimble, put them each in a room to write their statement.

Sloane looked weary, her face void of any glow or sparkle in her eyes. "She was my best friend. Will we be able to go home or back to school? We're supposed to be home the day after tomorrow. Is Jess' body still in New Orleans? I'd like to see her." Trey knew the dam was about to break, and the rush of sobbing tears was eminent. No sooner did the thought cross his mind than the dam burst. Scott had kept silent during the discussion.

With his head lowered in shame, Scott began, "If anyone needs to be in trouble, it's me. I held her mouth closed, but it was because she was laughing loudly, and I didn't want other guests complaining. I didn't know. I'm sorry. I'm so so sorry." He ran his hand under his nose, wiping the snot. Max slid a box of Kleenex his way, to which he eagerly pulled a tissue and wiped his eyes and nose.

Trey asked, "Curious. No one tried to resuscitate her? What about calling 911?"

Sniffling again, Sloane said, "We freaked. We were all drunk; I mean, nothing woulda ever happened, but everyone was drunk. I told Jess at the bar that I'd told everyone to come to our room. She wasn't thrilled at the idea but said she'd order a pizza. I told her Scott and I were gonna head back to the hotel for some alone time, and then we'd meet her in two-o-six. We had no idea who would come, but then Adam knocked and entered; after all, it was his room, too. Scott and I had already dressed. Scott told him about going to Jess and my room. Adam made some comment about Jess being frigid and well—"

Adam defensively piped in, "Yeah" he looked at Sloane. "According to what you said y'all did each other, I wanted to watch." He looked back at Trey. "I'd never seen that like live in front of me. While I watched, Jessica kept staring at me, so I figured she invited me to join. She didn't even try to close her legs, so I knew she wanted me, but when Scott screamed that she wasn't breathing and was dead, we covered her and got out of there. It wasn't something we wanted anyone to know about, ya know. It's not something you want to tell people, or at least I don't. That's why everyone thought I was a virgin—like Jessica. I figure you either do it or talk about it."

"So, you didn't want to tell anyone that Jessica was dead or about the sex stuff?"

"I guess both." Adam stared at Trey without a wince or any emotion.

The scene was pathetic and sad. No one asked to see the forensic report, and just as well. Charly still had not sent it to him.

After the incessant rambling, the detectives took them individually into separate rooms; there'd be no comparing notes. The detectives looked through the glass into each room, noticing that Sloane and Scott had broken down a few times, but Adam was just matter-of-fact. Adam knocked on the window. "I'm done. Can I go now?" Trey opened the door as Adam continued, "The chick died; it's a shame; she never got to experience my abilities; it would have rocked her world." His cocky attitude was repulsive to Trey.

Standing by the door, pissed off, Trey looked down at Adam. "You are a piece of work. What's your next move? You gonna seek legal counsel? I think you should, just in case."

"I don't have the money for that. Besides, I did nothing wrong." Adam bristled.

"Butthead, if the captain wanted, y'all could be charged with omission or knowledge after the fact. Since y'all didn't attempt CPR or call 911, there is culpability. Think about it and grow a conscience while you're at it." Trey was fuming, and Adam's arrogance had set off his last nerve. He was the kind of guy he wanted to take out back and pulverize. *What a piece of crap.*

"Whatever." The boy had the gall to roll his eyes. "Yeah, for sure, I'll think about it," shaking his head with an audible chuffed sound. *Prick,* Trey squared off his eyes, picturing in his mind perhaps five minutes teaching the kid about the world. "If you were my age, you'd have jumped all over the chance to join the threesome. Group sex is the best; you ought to try it; maybe it'd pry that stick out your ass." If Trey wouldn't open himself up to a lawsuit, he would have popped the kid in the mouth. Other than extreme psychiatric care, a boot up the butt or pop in his smart-ass mouth might have helped as well.

Scott finished his statement about a half-hour after Adam left. When Trey read over it, the words came across as a confession, not a detail of the relationship. "Scott, let's sit. What you gave me is an admission of guilt, and it sounds like you purposefully smothered Jessica. You need to describe more." Trey had crossed the line by imposing his opinion.

The boy could hardly look Trey in the eyes, but in a muffled manner, he said, "I wanted to keep her quiet. She was drunk, too, and laughing, almost screaming about being tickled. Even though the act was sexual, it was more playful, kinda like a more grown-up version of playing doctor." Scott blew his nose into the tissue and cleared his throat.

"See, that's exactly what you need to write down. Not 'I held her mouth closed to keep her quiet.' Can you hear the difference? She was your girlfriend's best friend, and you liked her. Write this again." Scott sat and stared at the blank page for a few minutes. "What are you not telling me?"

"I know I saw Adam with Sloane, it wasn't a nightmare, and I finally got Sloane to admit it. I hoped it would even the score if I encouraged the sex stuff. I planned on," he put his head down and started to cry.

"Planned what?"

He looked up with an intense look of anger, almost like a completely different person—a personality disorder and a scary one at that. Maybe this was his punk persona, like when he was with Adam. His demeanor and posture were all wrong. "To do her, get a virgin notch on my belt."

Trey pushed his chair back from the table. "Wow." He ran his hands through his hair, set his jaw, closed his eyes, and in a guttural, angry tone, said, " Maybe your first statement might be closer to the truth. Kid, you need some counseling or something. What the hell is wrong with you? Maybe you didn't mean to kill her, but you planned on forcing yourself on her, all for a notch on your belt? Sick."

Scott banged his fists on the table. "Sloane was in on it too. It was a payback for what she did with Adam. We were all going to have a turn, you know, like a fuck fest. It would be full-fledged orgy time; maybe even get the guy from the bar in on the action. At least that was the plan until she died, but Adam and I still managed a threesome on this trip." He grinned.

Max slipped into the next room after listening to Scott and Trey's conversation. "Sloane, Scott says you were equally involved in the plan for an orgy? Do you have anything to add or rebut Scott's perverse story? Tell me; you were going to allow Scott to force himself on your best friend?" He coughed. "Some best friend. Glad you're not mine." She looked away. "It's all peer pressure; you need to be bigger than that."

An hour later, after the breakers had left, the analysis came. If they needed proof, they had it all. The evidence proved the happenings of that sex-party-gone-horribly wrong. They could have hit them with the omission of fact or culpability after the fact, but one life was gone, and no one would see the justice in three more lives ruined. As it was, they would have to live with the knowledge every day for the rest of their lives. Maybe not for Adam, Trey thought, as he suspected the boy was a sociopath, but that would come to light at some point in his life. He didn't come across as a person who would receive happily-ever-after love; frankly, it didn't seem like he'd care one way or the other. After the Scott revelation, Trey wondered how twisted the kids were and if it had become a culture thing, but now it was in the hands of the judge and the attornies. If they needed him to testify to something, it would be at a much later date. His ass was onto the next investigation while prioritizing the stack of cases he and Max had. This one had been a humdinger, and he was glad the nightmare was over, at least for him.

PRESENT, PAST, AND FUTURE

*T*rey remembered the first time he and Steph had sex. It wasn't her first time; he was only her second partner, so to speak, and while he had been around the block, he wasn't what one would call skilled or accomplished. Because they were both scared out of their minds of being caught and living up to each other's expectations, they had taken things slowly with a ton of foreplay, making sure their decision was mutually agreeable. In his mind, he compared the group he'd just investigated to his and his wife's first encounter. He'd choose what he and Steph had every day and twice on Sunday as opposed to the breaker's way of life. Max had surprised him with his obvious thrill of thinking about girl-on-girl action. Was he the square peg in the round hole, or were they? He loved his life and his wife, and if they weren't part of the in-crowd, he really didn't give a flip. What they had was real, and "until death do you part," there was no doubt about it.

It had been a long day, emotional, and filled with so much ambiguity and overall weirdness. He called it quits for the afternoon and headed for Louie's. *What was this new Louie's thing,* he asked himself. When he strolled in, he sat at the end of the bar where Babe usually sat, but a chair over.

Trinity came over with a big smile. "Your dog died today?"

"Huh?" Trey cocked his head with furrowed brows and confusion.

"You look like your dog died or someone pissed in your Cheerios. What's up? You seem down. Is it about that murder case? Whatcha drinking, friend?" Her smile lit up her eyes. The sudden flood of questions, although simple, momentarily stopped him.

After a slightly elongated pause, "Bourbon straight up." He watched as she turned to grab his drink. Only a few other people were hanging out at the bar, so when she brought his bourbon, she leaned against the countertop, waiting to hear. As she saw it, that was part of the perks of tending bar.

He slugged down the drink and handed her the empty glass. "Again."

Trinity looked him in the eyes, "You sure? How 'bout I get you some French bread and olive oil to go with your drink?"

Trey shrugged his shoulder, "Sure, why not."

In a flash, she had his drink, bread, and olive oil-garlic concoction for dipping. "So, you wanna talk about it? Y'all got the murderer?" She wiped the bar top with a towel as she looked at him.

"It ended up being something totally different—no rape, no murder, death by misadventure. Basically, a bunch of kids were having a party, and the girl died. It's a different world than when I grew up, and I'm only in my thirties, so I feel like I should be more in touch with the trends. Kids today have weird parties. I'm not expecting pin the tail on the donkey or things like that, but they get into some kinky shit."

She smiled and nodded. "I'm younger than you, and what I see here when college kids come to the bar shocks me. Groups come in, and one day they're paired up in one way and the next different. I've seen it all, or a lot." She snickered lightly. "Yeah, as the old-school song says, 'baby, baby, it's a wild world.' Just getting wilder and wilder. I have a brother in his forties, and he's having a hard time with his teenage kids. He says it's way different than when he grew up, and my parents are real old-school. The way these kids speak to their elders would've warranted a smack with the belt." Trey laughed and agreed.

He had never been a bad kid, sometimes mischievous like rolling people's houses, but nothing terrible. No dope, no drunk and disorderly, and definitely no fuck fests. Couples were couples. Straight or gay didn't matter; people paired up and were actual couples with some degree of fidelity until they broke up. Yeah, people cheated, but it wasn't accepted or the thing to do. He thought, *Yes, Miss Trinity, it's a very wild world.* They talked about the early heat wave going through. The low-nineties for April were hot. Like so many pondered, the question was, did that indicate a busier than usual hurricane season? His eyes were drawn to an open door. Her smile was bright, and her eyes were loving. Max must have called Steph. She walked to him with a big hug and whispered on his neck that she loved him. His belly flip-flopped. Trey wasn't an overly emotional person, or so he thought, but the fact that his wife came out to find him overwhelmed his heart. Their love was pure.

"Wanted to check on you, my love. You okay? Max mentioned the case had gotten pretty wacky and that you seemed particularly disturbed. Just know these are other people's kids, not our little one on the way; you'll have more control there."

He was about to say something, but he froze. Trey looked from her belly to her eyes and back again. She smiled big. "Yep. I've been waiting to tell you once I knew it was going well. We're about twelve weeks, poppa." The tears filled his eyes, and there were no words to say. His chest filled with emotion, staggering his breath, all he could muster was a hug and an I love you, and even then, his voice cracked. "I thought today might be the perfect day to tell you. Make your day?"

Trey cleared his throat a few times, "Day? No, it's made my life. I'm guessing you're sure."

"Positive. It's why I had ginger ale the other night and haven't been drinking wine. The case has had you wound so tightly; I bet you didn't even notice." She pulled a small chunk of the bread and dipped it in the oil and garlic. "This way, we both have garlicky breath," she said with a laugh.

Trinity walked over, "Good afternoon, detective's wife. Ginger ale with lime? I'm not good with names, but I usually remember what people drink. Your husband is one patron that throws me for a loop. It's been water with lime, bourbon and coke, beer, and now, straight bourbon. He needs to get some consistency." She winked at him.

Just then, Max strolled in. Loudly he said, "Now that I'm here, it's a party, y'all. Trinity, I'll have a draft, and what's the plate special? Meatloaf and mash?" She responded by saying stewed chicken and rice. "Dang, that meatloaf was incredible."

"You have a choice then; if you have to have meat, do an open-face roast beef sandwich or debris poboy, it's not Mother's, but I'll put it up against most poboy places. Our chicken and rice is something special, one of my faves. While you decide, I'll get ya beer."

It was ten minutes until knock-off time. Babe watched as the crane lifted an iron beam to the third floor; the massive metal girder slipped slightly, almost unnoticeably, in the chain. Without a thought, as his site super walked in front of the crane, Babe ran full speed and tackled him, throwing them far away from the machine just as the steel slipped completely out and hit the ground. Glenn looked around in a dazed stupor. "You're okay, sir. I might have left a bruise on your shoulder, but you're okay." All the crew stood with their mouths agape.

The site-super, regaining his composure, exclaimed, "Jesus, Vicarelli, I feel like I got hit by a train, but thank you. You saved my life." Karl, the crane operator, had jumped down from the machine and ran to check on the situation.

"Sir, I don't know what happened; I thought we had it securely hitched. I don't know what to say other than thank God for your boy here." He patted Babe on the shoulder. "Man, you got eyes like a hawk." His voice was still trembling with the thought of the tragedy that could've been.

More than ten minutes passed while everyone on the site contemplated the what-ifs. "I did what anyone else would've done. I think it's knock-off time." Babe suggested.

The super chimed in, "If it's not, I'm making it so. Shit, y'all wrap up and go home. See you tomorrow. Vicarelli, got a moment?" The two men stepped into the trailer. "You saved my life. I can never repay you for your actions."

"It was mine to do," Babe replied. "For all I know, the beam would have swayed, and that would've been the story. You probably would've thought I was out of my mind, maybe even fired me for tackling you. Things are instinctual with me, and I act. One day, it'll be to my detriment."

Glenn patted him on the back and said, "You'll always have a job with me, Vicarelli. Always." He opened a metal filing locker and grabbed a bottle pouring two plastic cups with a swig or two of the whiskey. He handed one to Babe, "To friends." The big man smiled and nodded.

He hurriedly swallowed the drink, gave Gunner a treat, and parted, double-timing to his apartment, the shower, and Louie's.

By the time Babe made it to Louie's, Trey had already knocked back four tumblers of bourbon and was three sheets to the wind. Seeing the condition of the detective, he glanced at Trinity with curiosity. She shrugged and raised her eyebrows at Babe, letting him know she, too, was puzzled by the detective's flurry of drinks and lack of sobriety. Max whispered to Trinity, "Water them down, please. He may have had a rough day, but he won't fix it by getting drunker."

Babe put his hand on Trey's shoulder, "You okay, boss?"

Trey took a deep breath in and shook his head. "Today has been one of the best days in my life; Steph's expecting, and it's been a shit show the rest." His words slurred. "The girl didn't need to die. They had a fuckin sex party, and she was the main attraction. But get this," he nodded, leaning against Babe's shoulder and in an attempt to whisper, "She's a virgin 'cause she hasn't done the big deed, but she's been letting people perform oral sex on her, oh, and she on them. That's not exactly what I call a virgin, ya know." He began to mumble.

Trinity came around the bar and pecked Babe on the lips. "Between you and Max, maybe y'all can get him to his wife's car. Everyone has tried to get him to eat to soak up some of the bourbon. So far, nada."

Babe smiled, "I got this." He looked at Trey, "Looks like you have a bunch of fuel in the intake. Shit happens. We had some on our site today. Split a poboy with me? I'll also get some skins. Congrats on the bambino."

Trey closed one eye and held up his glass. "You eat that kinda shit. I figured you to be all about protein. I mostly do keto, but I hardly have your build. Where you work out?" He started to slip off the stool.

Steph had her fill. "Time to go if you're not gonna eat."

He frowned at her, his eyes glossy and half-cast. "Don't be like that. We need to celebrate."

Finn brought out Babe's skins and po-boy. Trey eagerly grabbed one of the skins and, with a mouth full of food, turned to Stephanie, "I'm eating, okay?"

"You're a mess, Trey Kimble. Straighten up." She glared with all seriousness, saying there was no option other than to sober up.

"You don't know. All those kids looking so clean-cut all-American are fuckin twisted. You ever wanna be with a girl?" He swung his head down and focused his eyes on her. "I'll know if you're lyin'." He squinted his eyes.

"Trey Alexander Kimble, you get yourself together, or I'm leaving here. You already know the answer to that question. Stop it."

Looking at her, he grabbed half of Babe's sandwich and laid it on some napkins. "Happy?" He took a bite. Trinity brought a glass of water with lime, and he took a big swig— then smiled at Stephanie.

"Better." She stood with her hand on her hip, watching his every move. After several bites of the poboy followed by slurps of water, he seemed to slowly be coming out of the sloppy drunkenness, still blasted drunk, just not as sloppy. She looked at Babe, "So, what were you saying about a near accident at work?"

"It was nothing, ma'am. I tackled my site super out of the way of a metal girder; it slipped out of the cable. " He gave a half-smile.

"That's not nothing. Wow. Good thing for your boss."

"Yes, ma'am. Turned out that way." Stephanie excused herself and went to the bathroom.

Max stood behind Trey. "Hey, youngster, you're acting like one of them spoiled brats. Straighten the fuck up. Your woman has this great news, and all you can do is get wasted to shit. Paging Captain Trey-hole."

"Fuck you, Max." Trey retorted.

"No, Padna, I ain't married no more because of shit like this. Get your act together, or me and this big guy are gonna throw your ass in Steph's Jeep and call it a night for you."

Trey motioned, pushing both hands down. "I'm getting my shit together. Okay?" He waved at Trinity. "Y'all got coffee, hon?"

"Coming right up, detective." The tiny woman moved with lightning speed, and before he could say anything else, she had a cup of joe right in front of him. He added some sugar but kept it black and took a few sips. "Thanks, and sorry 'bout my drunk ass." She turned and waved him off. It certainly wasn't the first time she'd dealt with an intoxicated police officer, and it wouldn't be the last. She'd never seen Trey so out of control. He must've made it too personal, is all she could figure.

Stephanie came out of the restroom, and from the smile on her face, it was apparent she was happy to see the coffee, mostly eaten poboy and remnants of a few skins. It was the rare occasion that a case so took her husband. He usually managed to keep it all at an arm's distance, but this one sunk straight to his heart. Maybe because he bought into the pure, innocent girl betrayed by friends only to find she wasn't so lily-white. Was he perhaps picturing Jessica to be like Steph had been in college?

While she hadn't been pure, she was most definitely one of those girls that didn't fool around. She'd had one boyfriend, Tommy, but like most first romances, it didn't last more than a year. She'd given him her virginity, but he hadn't dragged her name through the mud; they parted as friends. Not long after that split, Trey became the love of her life. He knew he'd been on her radar as a kid, but for some strange reason, she thought, he was beyond reach. When she told him that, he remembered his beer shot out his nose as he tried to hold back a laugh. She thought he wanted someone a bit more worldly and experienced. It wasn't until their first date, which ended with coffee and two hours of conversation that she found he wasn't a player. From that moment on, they were inseparable. Now, they were going to be parents, and she knew he would be an outstanding dad. Since she'd known him, he had a thing for babies and younger kids, which wasn't normal for most teenage guys, so she knew whoever ended up with him would have the best father for their children, and he was hers—it was all meant to be.

Eventually, Trey, Stephanie, and Max left, giving Babe a moment to speak with Trinity without ears. She leaned into the bar and said in a quiet voice. "I don't know if I ever thanked you for the flowers. At least I know not properly. Stay at my place tonight?" He agreed but said he'd first go home to get his stuff for the next day and would probably be sleeping when she got back from work. With a quick kiss and thoughts for later, he left Louie's and went home to gather a few things.

Walking back to his place, thoughts of the weird day and evening passed through his mind. Some of the voices in his head were starting to die off, which was good, maybe? Undoubtedly, he was changing, but he wasn't sure if it was who he wanted to be. From the day's work incident, he obviously was still finely tuned and acutely aware of everything around him, but the feelings part was a whole new concept, and he wondered if it would interfere with his mindset. He wasn't one to plan a future. Everything was the here and now, other than the twisted memories that struck without warning. Still, Trinity had never brought up the couple of episodes he'd had around her, but she made a point of not letting him talk about the past too much or at least not as in-depth. He knew the day would come when he would speak to her about the worst operation he'd ever had, where there was heinous, indescribable, and needless death to so many innocents—the mission that took the best out of him.

As she left work, she tucked her tips deep into her left pocket and walked with determination, not glancing from side to side but trying to keep aware like she did every night. She only had a few blocks to walk and would be inside the hotel.

Steps approached from behind; she struggled to retrieve her mace from the right front pocket of her jean skirt as the pursuer picked up speed. The footsteps following her sped up as well, and before she knew it, someone had grabbed her from behind, picked her up, and thrown her behind a pile of restaurant garbage bags. He climbed over the refuse and pinned her to the ground with his hand around her throat. She sprayed the mace in his face, which caused him to back away, choking, and he ran. Trembles filled the inside of her body, and all she wanted was to get home; he had shaken her to her core. She imprinted his face in her mind, speaking aloud, "Dark shoulder-length hair, a Saints ball cap, white skin, wiry build, and he had a snake tattoo on his left forearm." Again, she repeated the person's description. Her voice wavered, and her body tensed. Nobody had ever hassled her walking home in all her years at Louie's. The occasional patron flirted uncomfortably, but she could shut that down. She didn't recognize her attacker. He was maybe in his twenties or thirties; the cap hid a lot, and it was dark.

Trinity walked into the hotel; the attending front desk manager, Lexington, ran from behind the counter. "Miss Noelle, are you okay?" She nodded. "Looks like someone messed you up. You got jumped?" She nodded. "I'm calling the police."

"I just want to go home, Lex." He put a sign on the counter that said,

'Please ring bell for assistance.' He walked her to her front door. She'd given Babe her pass card; the manager used his. "Thank you."

Once the door closed, she sat against it on the floor and cried. The night manager had been right; she was a mess. Her legs were scraped and bleeding, and she had fingernail scratches on her arm where he had grabbed her. Other than dirt and nasty foul trash funk, she was otherwise not too bad off. She heard him open the bedroom door.

Upon seeing her, he squatted and picked her up, placing her on the counter. "Trinity, we have to call the police. What happened?"

Her body began to tremble. "I-I got jumped. Lex already called. I just wanted to get home."

Babe decided to call for himself. He called the police station and asked that they contact Trey or Max. The dispatch responded that they'd send an officer; what was the address? "Maybe I didn't speak clearly; call Detective Kimble or Max; he couldn't remember Max's last name." The response was even less impressive, stating the officers would make that call once they arrived. "Dispatch them to the Hotel Noelle and have them get the night manager to lead them to Miss Noelle's home." Silence for a few seconds, and then she responded that Detective Sledge would be on his way. Satisfaction. He made his point, and she received it loud and clear. This attack had a different flavor to it than the average nightly jumping. He lowered his head and said, "I'm sure you want to bathe, but you need to stay as you are for any DNA testing. The scrapes on your legs aren't too bad; leave them open, no bandages. Did you get a look at the person?" She nodded. "Any chance you scratched them?" She shrugged at first.

After a few minutes of thought, she answered, "I maced him with my right hand, and I'm pretty sure I grabbed his arm when he threw me."

"He fucking threw you? Oh yeah, you'll have his DNA all over you. Did he hurt you anywhere else, Trinity?" She shook her head no. His fists clamped tight; she could see the veins popping out all over him; he was beyond pissed. His chest had turned bright pink, and she knew if the guy had been near him, Babe would have pulled him limb from limb, but he maintained his cool. He kissed the top of her head. Thoughts exploded in his mind. *When they get the guy's identity, it's on. He'll be one tortured and dead motherfucker when I get finished with him.*

She closed her eyes as he tried to put his arm around her, "I'm nasty, don't touch me. The guy threw me behind a pile of garbage, and I wreak. The bar grunge smells bad enough, but this is foul. Max better hurry up, or I'm taking a shower. DNA or no DNA; this is revolting."

It hadn't been much longer when there was a rap on the front door. When Max took one look at Babe, he knew something was very wrong. "She was attacked." Babe gritted his teeth together, setting a hardline to his jaw.

He led Max into the kitchen. "Girl, you're a mess. I can take you to the hospital, or we can call for a wagon. Either way, your giant friend can tag along." He smiled at her. Just Max's presence had a calming effect. As Trinity described her attacker, Babe went to the bedroom to put on a shirt. In a quiet voice, Max said, "Your friend's built like a brick shithouse, and those tats, whoa. I knew he was big, but damn, girl!" She grinned; he knew it would lighten things—given the situation, it was such a stupid thing to say.

"But he's tender and gentle, at least with me. I hope y'all catch this guy before Babe does. I have a feeling—" Just then, Babe entered, and the conversation came to an abrupt halt. As crazy as the big guy was about Trinity, if he got the guy, it wasn't gonna be pretty, and he wouldn't blame him. Lord help the son-of-a-bitch, if it was his girl. Bang, one shot right between the eyes and weighted with blocks in the river—end of story.

Tucking his shirt into his jeans, Babe asked what the decision was—riding in the cop mobile or ambulance. Trinity didn't want the mayhem and looky-lou's gossiping about Hotel Noelle again, like the murder only a week before, so they rode with Max to Touro Hospital at her request.

"After the hospital does their thing, they'll send the labs to our forensics department, and we'll hopefully find out who the bastard is that did this. What could have been the motive? I'll want you to meet with our sketch artist, but as your friend said, he probably left a bunch of DNA on you." He winked at her, "We'll get the guy." He turned to Babe, "And if you happen to find him before we do, let us handle it, okay?" Babe only smiled.

LONG TIME NO SEE

*A*s promised, any evidence went straight to Charlotte. It would take a few days to process for a sure-fire identification. Other than the scrapes and bruises, Trinity was okay, a little shaken. They decided somebody would escort her to the hotel for at least the next couple of weeks.

She needed to return to Louie's as soon as possible for things to feel normal again. Babe returned to his routine with his furry pal, Gunner. The dog hung out in the cool a/c of the office trailer with a clean bowl of water and plenty of food—Gunner had it good with lots of attention.

Five o'clock rolled around; Gunner and Babe made their way home to ready for the delights of Louie's. By six, they walked to the bar.

Trinity waved, brought him his drink, and took his order but seemed distant. She wasn't her usual bubbly self. It had been a few days since the attack, and she'd appeared herself the day before; something had happened. He pensively observed, sizing up anyone that entered the bar. In the far corner of the bar sat a guy with slicked-back dark hair tied in a ponytail. He had a couple of empty beer mugs, which Finn was about to clear. Babe noticed an exchange between the two, then the man left.

He watched as Trinity took note of the man leaving. Her shoulders dropped slightly, and her bounce slowly returned. Babe unobtrusively cupped his hand, beckoning her with a twitch of his fingers. His curiosity was acute and his senses alert; something about the guy from the corner didn't sit well with him, even though he had left the premises. She moved his way with a fake smile. "How's my girl today?" he asked her.

"Fine, why?"

"Just asking." Their eyes danced in question, an answer she held back.

"I'm fine, Babe, just another night at Louie's, ya know?" She tilted her head to the side with a hand on her hip. "Are you alright?" The corners of his mouth turned up with a sarcastic smirk. "You sure you're okay, big guy? Wanna stay at my place tonight?"

He nodded in reply, then cleared his throat. "I guess we'll talk then." One of the old-timers waved her over for another drink, and off she went. Finn brought his food out. "Was the guy in the corner harassing you?"

"Nah, just the usual questions I get nightly from newcomers about Trinity, but he had more questions than usual. Without saying the actual words, I basically told him she was off-limits. Babe, I got orders out the wazoo, the kitchen's hopping; all's good in da hood. I watch out for her. If Shep hadn't cut me early, I woulda watched her walk to the hotel the other night. I told the boss I leave when she leaves, not that I can tell him what's what, but I tried. He got it. Gotta git before I don't have a job." The kid coughed up a laugh and headed to the kitchen. A series of dings sounded with impatience.

The night pushed on; the unknown gawker hadn't returned. Babe wanted to stay as long as she did but realized it wasn't practical. 5 A.M. would come fast, and she didn't get home until two or three. "Trinity, I'm leaving Gunner with you; he'll walk you home, but if you feel like something's not right, call me or get someone from here to watch you home. Who was the sleazeball with the ponytail? He was over there in the corner." His eyebrows raised, and his head jutted toward the now-empty corner.

She shrugged, "Not sure. I've seen the guy here before, but only once or twice. He reminds me of someone; I can't put my finger on who, but it'll come to me. No matter how quiet I am, you always wake up when I enter the bedroom." She winked at him and blew him a kiss. Babe was handsome; his dark brown hair had grown some but still screamed military, and his eyes were constantly darting around, sizing up situations or strategies. "I'll try to be quiet."

He leaned over and tousled Gunner's coat, instructing, "You're on duty now, boy. Keep your senses acute and protect our lady." He patted the pooch, leaned in, kissed Trinity goodbye, and started his path to her place. The back-and-forth sleeping arrangement resulted in his and her clothes at each other's place; he just didn't have his weights or lift bar. On his way to the hotel, he passed the dark driveway flashing him back to the fifty-dollar jackass and the guy with the shiv. Now that the breakers had returned home, he thought about the strange behavior and the volumes it spoke about the world and the country's future leaders. He doubted their idea of a party differed from most of their contemporaries, not that he was particularly familiar with parties. The world, in many ways, had become a cesspool. Where had the values gone?

Three men emerged from the darkness of the driveway—two in the five-eight height range and one six-one, thin like a matchstick, but they were punks. Their posture and body language screamed trouble. "You boys need to be on your way; don't pick a fight you can't win."

"What you gonna do, G.I. Joe?" The arrogant spokesperson said.

Babe stood still, observing the trio of no-goods, calculating who'd be the first to attempt a strike. "Go about your business. Do yourselves a favor and leave."

The three laughed, hurling slurs at the military man. Babe had a chuckle on the inside but maintained a straight face. His nerves were tingling on heightened alert, and most ready to fight. Pulling out a knife, the spokesman stepped forward, followed by the other two. The three descended upon him. He grabbed the knife-bearer and, in a blink, had him turned, facing his associates. Babe manipulated the man's right hand, which held the knife, plunging it deliberately into the stomach of one associate, and kicked the other in the chest, sending the man flying backward, landing with a hard thud on the pavement.

The next thing he knew, Gunner was on top of the man on the ground, snarling, defying the man to move. The sweet, happy-to-have-attention canine was like his human companion—a natural-born killer ready for a fight.

The sidekick of the initial assailant looked in horror at the knife stuck in the side of his gut, while the ballsy one who'd pulled the blade was at the mercy of Babe, who had him in a tight headlock. "You," pointing to the man horrified by the knife in him, "leave the blade where it is, or you'll most likely bleed out. And you," he jerked his hand to tighten the hold. "I could snap your neck so easily." The man stayed statue-still. "Now go. Don't bother me again." The three stooges scuffled away in wide-eyed bewilderment. Here, boy," he called to the dog. He turned to go back to Louie's and saw Trinity with her hands cupped over her mouth and a look of horror in her eyes.

She ran to Babe crying, "Gunn bolted, like all of a sudden, and then I saw your silhouette and those men. Are you hurt?" She looked him up and down, scanning for any sign of injury. "Oh, my God, Babe," she held on tightly. "Should we call the cops?"

"No. I was about to walk Gunner back to you. I'm fine, promise. A couple of stupid guys picked a fight with the wrong person. I warned them to leave before some heavy shit came down, but I didn't kill them, which means they'll heed the warning or try again." He kissed the top of her head. "The Quarter can be a dangerous place, but sometimes that's for the bad guys. Now I really need to tuck in for the night." He looked down at the dog. "Good boy, now stay here and protect our lady."

Babe gave her a quick peck and resumed his walk to her place. Gunner watched as he walked out of the door.

The weekend was upon them, and while Trinity had a busy Saturday night, Babe hung out at the bar until she closed for the night. While sorting the till, she watched while he played with his dog. They were the last to leave as the morning crew arrived. "Babe, you don't have to stay here with me every night. I've been doing this for a long time. I'm twenty-eight and been tending bar since I was eighteen, but I hung here bussing tables and being a general pain in the ass to my uncle since I was sixteen. Louie's is more a home for me than my place." They headed toward the hotel.

Her entire hand fit in his palm. "You're so petite and perfect." He stopped and looked her in the eyes, "Do you not want me to come to Louie's? Is it a problem with Shep or your job?"

She cleared her throat. "No, it's not a problem, but I want you to have a life. You work all day and then come hang out with me. You need to do things that make you happy, ya know. Everybody at Louie's loves you; I'm just thinking of you, Babe, that's all."

His mind rolled over; he'd been to the grocery in Metairie, gassed up his truck, brought Gunner to a dog park, did a run in Audubon Park, and worked out. What else was there to do? He didn't have friends, nor did he want them. He had Trinity and Gunner; that's all he wanted. Since leaving the Corps, he'd had only a few conversations with Hurley, a guy from the Corps days. Most of his brothers-in-arms had wives and were glad to be done with their duty. "It's best for me not to sit in either of our places for too long. I get out and do things. Shit, I have a job; many of the guys who return don't find a job right away. I got lucky; Glenn's brothers were military. Uncle Sam paid for one to go to med school, and the other one, I think, is a truck driver. I'll loiter somewhere else if you prefer," and he smiled. "Did you hear that, Gunn; she doesn't want us hanging at Louie's. I guess we're cramping her style."

She nudged him as they walked, "I did not say that; you know better. Just thinking of you." They walked through the hotel and to her place. "I'm getting in the shower; you can join me or do your own thing."

He observed as she removed her clothes; he reached out and pulled her to him. "You're not going anywhere just yet." He ran his hands over her body, stopping at the highlights.

Wriggling away, she laughed, "I am nasty; I gotta shower. Now, you either join me in the shower or—" She walked into the bathroom. Babe could feel his heartbeat in his throat; moments later, he joined her under the spray of the shower. "I was hoping you'd take me up on the invitation."

She put her arms around his waist. "Sometimes you go somewhere in your mind, and bringing you back is hard. I know many of your memories aren't happy ones—do you have any good memories you could reminisce about instead of the bad?" She looked desperately into his eyes.

"Good? Hm." He thought for a minute. "Fulfilling, yes. I don't believe the good started until you." He kissed her, filling his nostrils with her scent. " I guess I had thrilling moments, and unlike those I served with, it hyped me when our drill instructor barked commands. My heart would pound, and my body was itching to go. I know a lot of the guys hated our commanding officers or any of the powers that be. I thrived on their force and commitment, and those times roll through my thoughts too, but the bad ones are nauseating, and they haunt me, as you well know." A lump formed in his throat. "Nope." He spoke aloud as though answering some question he had in his mind. Then leaned over and kissed her, holding onto her like a storm was brewing around them. They drifted to sleep.

Sunday morning came, and it was their day to laze in bed, snuggle, and quietly chat. She stroked the side of his face and lovingly studied his expression. "I'm sorry I pried last night; I just want to understand and help."

"There's no help for me, Trinity. The demons are far too big and loud." He became still for a few minutes, but she could tell he was having an internal debate and wondered what side would win. He cleared his throat and spoke quietly, "Here it comes; fair warning. About a year and a half ago or longer, when I was in Afghanistan, we had orders to capture or kill an important person in a terrorist cell. You're sure you want to hear? It's gruesome and plays in my mind sometimes, enough to make me vomit. You sure?" His eyebrows raised with a look of sincerity. She nodded slowly with intent. "We had intel on the location and managed to get into the compound. It was a miracle we made it that far without detection, so we got to the exact room where he was hiding. Harding, a young man from Illinois, went in first, and I was right behind him. He froze for a fraction of a second when the shots pierced the silence, and he went down, splattered by a rain of ammunition. I, along with the rest of our squad, lit it up—" He squinted his eyes, bit his bottom lip, and inhaled deeply. "The fucking coward used his wives and children as a shield and blazed his weapon, instantly killing them, taking down Harding, hitting me with a through and through to the deltoid, and one of the other guys took rounds in his quads, splintering the femur, but we opened up on the fucker. They, our superiors, deemed the mission a success; we brought the dead body of the terrorist back with us. We lost good Marines that night, and two of us sustained injuries. One of the guys carried the body of our enemy, one carried Harding's body, and I carried Bishop, who later had his leg amputated, not because of the femur or wounds but other complications. The other fallen rode back in the chopper with us. If possible, we never leave one of ours behind." Her jaw had dropped by this time, and tears trickled down her cheeks.

"He killed his kids to kill y'all and protect himself? That's sick; he knew y'all would have a hard time shooting through children." She wiped her hand under her nose. "I'm sorry, that's beyond horrible."

Babe rolled on his back, staring at the ceiling. "Yeah, it's a fucking nightmare, but you do what you gotta do or end up like Harding. I can't fault him; he was the first to lay eyes on the sickening sight. He froze. I don't know if I would have, and we'll never know. The one thing I know for sure is that I don't have trouble or regrets taking down an evil person, but that sight was shocking. In my head, I hear my instructor say, 'We fight for those who cannot fight for themselves.' That's how I got Gunner. I watched this guy kick the shit out of the dog and then smack him in the head. I had him follow me into an open garage door, kicked him in the gut like he had the dog, and when he pulled a knife on me, I snapped his arm and knocked him down. I wanted to kill him but didn't. I have no regrets about doing it—"

Her eyes widened, and she took a deep breath, "you broke the guy's arm?"

"Yes, ma'am, and I'd do it again. Do what you like with that information and think what you will, but I stood up for a defenseless dog. The leach on society intended to kill me, but the difference between average Joe and me is that I'm a trained killing machine, Trinity." Her facial expression registered disapproval and horror, but her eyes emanated love. "As long as you're with me, nobody, and I mean nobody, will ever hurt you." With a slight hesitancy, she cuddled against him, nestling under his arm. "Of all the things I witnessed and all the skirmishes I experienced, that one mission, by far, was the worst, and that's when I decided I'd given my best and started the process for Marine separation. It's a fuckin process, like at least a year. Those kids had no idea their father would shoot through them to kill us. The gunfire was so fast that I hoped they didn't have time to be afraid. Trinity, I'm not afraid to die." He rolled on his side to face her twirling a lock of her hair around his finger.

She sniffled, "I am so sorry that you had to go through that, and the info about Gunner, I guess I get it, but I'm not wired that way. I don't know what I would've done. Probably screamed at the man, and if he drew a knife, I would've yelled for help, and he probably would have killed me before help arrived." She lay quietly petting his chest. She sat up abruptly and looked at his shoulders. Not that she didn't believe him, but she had never noticed the scar hidden amidst all his ink. She traced her finger over it. "You do know, Babe; I'm falling in love with you. I hope that doesn't terrify you. You may be what you said, a killing machine, but you're also a loving machine. You try to right the wrongs of this world."

Monday morning came, and he was off to work, following his usual routine. Trinity's words about falling in love with him rolled through his brain. He didn't know what to do with that information. Did he love her, was he falling in love with her, or had he already fallen in love with her? He had never had the flushed feelings inside his being before; was it love? He hadn't told her he loved her but knew he'd never felt like he did when it came to her. It was beyond description. Just the thought of her spiked his temperature and made him long for her. Was that love? It wasn't just that she stirred him sexually; it was so much more. He reflected on the night she'd gotten jumped, and his heart took on a sinking feeling. Maybe that was love.

"Gunner, you're my best friend." He smiled at his lab mix breed. "Do you think I'm in love with Trinity? I know I've pondered the thought many times before, but now that she has said it aloud, I need to respond to her about the notion. Don't you think?" The dog looked up at him, and whether it was from panting or not, he found it amusing that the pup had a look like he was smiling. "You're as much of a sap as I am, Gunner. I've never had time for these kinds of feelings, and according to some shrinks, I'm incapable. I call bullshit on that hypothesis." They slowed the run as they turned onto the site.

Trinity relished her off days even more now that she had someone in her life. She retrieved her Mercedes SL from the parking attendant and tootled toward Lakeview. Memories flooded her mind from the years she had been with Joey. He was drop-dead gorgeous with a winning smile. After a year in college, he surmised that school life wasn't for him and that he really wanted law enforcement. Joey did great at the academy, completing at the top of his class. He thought that once he was on the job, Trinity would stay home, have babies, and be a dutiful wife. Plain and simple, Suzy Homemaker was not her thing. She loved Louie's and the energy of the French Quarter. Thinking of him jogged her memory, and she realized that the ponytailed guy reminded her of Joey's brother, Philip. She thought, *no way was it him.*

Trinity hadn't spoken to Joey in over seven years. His family loved him marrying her and thought it would up their status. It was a sheer disappointment for him and his family. Trinity had no desire for the echelon her family enjoyed, which pissed them off in no uncertain terms. They accused her of being hard-headed and spoiled, forcing her way. It was bad enough that her family badgered her about her free-kickin' lifestyle, but to have him and his family constantly on her ass was more than she could bear. After the divorce, all communication ended. They had been two kids with no idea about life and two very different opinions about the future.

She pressed the garage door remote and pulled in. She had to admit, it was a beautiful house, and as property in Lakeview was at a premium, she should sell it. The house, while ten years old, still smelled of newness. They'd only lived there for three years, and it remained empty other than the occasional night. She'd make it by every so often to pick up the mail the postman had inserted through the mail flap in the front door. It was all junk anyway; her postal address was her home in the Quarter.

There was a distinct scent when she first walked inside like someone had been there. Instinctually, she knew she needed to get the hell out, but curiosity got the best of her. Quietly she tip-toed into the kitchen. Someone had most definitely been there as dirty dishes filled the sink, and the Keurig was popped open with a used K-cup. A few pairs of shoes littered the living room floor, and her bedroom door was closed. Finally, good sense kicked in, and she thought it best to leave. Trinity turned, heading to the kitchen, and almost reached the garage when an arm grabbed her from behind. "If it ain't the spoiled little bitch." She recognized the voice, and it was most assuredly Philip. He had his hand over her mouth, but she managed to move enough that she bit him, and he pulled his hand away.

"What the hell are you doing in my house?"

He cocked his head with his chin tucked. "Remember, princess; y'all gave me a key? I just got back in town a coupla weeks ago and thought I'd crash here since you're not staying here."

"I want the key back and you out, you hear me?" She had both hands on her hips, flexing her bad-girl attitude.

"No, I ain't leavin', and neither are you." He picked her up easily despite her thrashing and brought her into her bedroom. He threw her on the bed and straddled her body. She bucked her body upward but couldn't get from under him or knock him off her. He punched her in the side of her head, and that was the last thing she knew as everything spiraled rapidly into darkness.

Upon waking, Trinity found herself gagged and restrained to her antique iron bed with a throbbing head. The house was silent, with no sounds of any movement. Had he left? The whole thing seemed like a bad dream. She didn't know Philip all that well, and he was considered the black sheep of Joey's family. He was into drugs and wild living and had knocked up one of the neighborhood girls. Joey had been the one to toe the line, and while their marriage didn't work out, she had no animous feelings about him or his family.

Examining the strategy he had used to secure her, it was apparent he had no idea what he was doing. She slowly pulled on the nylon rope restraining her left hand; it gave a little. She remembered being on her father's sailboat, and the ropes or lines were made of nylon because they were durable to the elements, but they also stretched. She gradually worked the nylon cord pulling it looser bit by bit until there was enough slack to slip her hand through. He had used another type of rope on her right wrist and legs, which had zero give. She was practically useless with her left hand but spat in it and rubbed it along the rope, hoping the dampness might yield its inflexibility. If it had given any, it was very little, and what took only fifteen minutes with the nylon would take hours with the cotton-like rope. Did she have hours to wriggle out of the hold?

Trinity's heart pounded harder when she heard him in the kitchen, opening the refrigerator, turning on the faucet, and then the grinding sound of the ice dispenser. She slipped her left hand back into the loop of the nylon rope, testing how fast she could manage, then dampened the restraint on her right hand again, slipped her left hand in again, and closed her eyes as his footsteps crossed the living room.

"Still not awake?" He shook her a few times; she kept her eyes closed. Philip left the room and went to the kitchen, where she heard the cabinet open and then the tap running. His steps were quiet, but she heard him in the living room again and knew he was planning on dousing her with the water to make her come around, but it would also make her situation more uncomfortable.

Being gagged, she couldn't speak, but she screamed as much as she could, which wasn't much.

Philip came in with a grin, "Tsk, tsk. It's only me. How about we get to know each other better?" He put the cup of water down and started to unfasten his belt. She continued to make noise. "It won't do you no good. No ones gonna hear you, and I doubt anyone is even looking for you." She thrashed as much as she could in the bed. He coughed out a laugh, "Oh, you gonna try to fight me? What you don't understand—" He began pacing back and forth at the foot of the bed, "is I got all the power. I can do as I want, and there ain't nothing you can do about it. I'm holding all the cards this time."

Trinity pleaded with her eyes, letting a tear roll down the side of her face onto the pillow. She tried to talk, and only muffled sounds came from her mouth, causing her to gag.

"You gonna choke yourself if you don't shut up. I bet ya didn't know I've been in jail. Yeah, OPP, and I ain't played nobody's bitch. Know why I done this to you? I bet you don't, you probably don't even care, but you killed my brother, bitch." She knew she had a surprised and sad expression; that was the first time she'd heard that Joey was dead. "Oh, you didn't know he died. You're so caught up in your bubble that you don't pay attention to the rest of the lowly world. Yeah, Joey's dead, and I didn't even get to tell him goodbye. After you broke his heart, he started drinking and one night ran his car into one of them big trees on Marconi. They said he was dead on impact, so at least he didn't suffer then. You broke him, and now I'm gonna break you. Payback is a motha-fucka, ya know, Trinity?" He was getting off on the terror in her eyes. The fact was nobody knew she was missing or where she was. It wouldn't be until much later that anyone would figure she'd gone missing. Someone from the family would eventually think to look in Lakeview, but it'd be too late, and terrifyingly she knew it all too well.

She hadn't even told Babe the address, only that she had a house in Lakeview. "This is a real nice place; ya got here. Too bad you couldn't be a good wife to Joey, ya know, give him some kids and normal life. No, you had to stay working in the Quarter like all the rest of them whores. Whatcha rich Daddy think about you still working at Louie's? I seen ya the other night, chatting up the old men and dancing all sexy. You ain't gonna prick-tease me, no ma'am; I'm gonna take what I want, and then when I'm done, I'm gonna do you like you did my brother."

Trinity again tried to speak, the gag growing damp in her mouth, rubbing the corners of her lips raw. He dropped his pants and stepped out of them, climbing on the bed and her. Philip ripped her shorts open, but the inseam held tight on the right side. He pulled again but to no avail; he released her right foot, trying to pull her shorts down, making her available for his purposes. She had to go for it, so with all her strength, she tried to kick him in the face but missed clipping his jaw, which threw his head back, causing him to lose his balance and fall to the floor.

He jumped up angrier than before and attempted again as she thrashed her right leg and pulled her hand loose, striking him as hard as she could, but his strength overpowered her, and he took her mercilessly, punishing her with every thrust. The tears streamed from her eyes, and no matter how hard she hit him, he continued the abuse, smacking her in the face. She could feel her right eye swelling and taste the blood running from her nose. He finished in what felt like hours but had been mere minutes. Once finished, he secured her foot and tied the nylon rope tighter around her hand. He didn't get that she stretched it—she would loosen it again. The violation made her sick to her stomach. She swallowed the vomit as it rose in her throat, knowing that she could easily choke to death if she didn't get it under control.

Trinity was a strong-willed woman, talking herself through other offensive situations, none quite as appalling as this; nonetheless, she began an internal pep rally. *Get a grip; it's not like it's the first time you've experienced rough.* Replying to herself, *yeah, but this is the first time things were beyond my control. When I slipped my hand from the rope, I showed my cards, mistake number one. I should've just laid there and taken it without trying to fight; that only amped him up more. With the gag, my mouth is not an option, but if he does undo it—when I slip my hand, I will whisper to Alexa to call the police; hopefully, he won't hear, and she can call before he says, 'Alexa, stop.' I'm as good as dead. One thing at a time, control what I can, and focus on good thoughts.* Her mind was flying through scenarios like shuffling a deck of cards.

Philip returned to the room with a washcloth and ice. He wiped her face of the blood, then held ice on her eye. "I'm doing this for Joey; he'd want me to take care of you." *Oh jeez, he's a schizo.* "If you promise not to scream, I'll undo the rag." She nodded. " He untied the gag; she moved her jaw from side to side and opened and closed her mouth. The freedom from the cloth was immense.

It amazed her that such a simple thing could have a massive impact. The intense tightness of her body relaxed a smidge when the gag came off. *Control and calm*, she thought. The emotional rollercoaster was something she hadn't experienced often as her life, while filled with activity, was sure and steady. She could hardly compare herself to Babe, but they gelled because neither one surfed the waves of controversy, and both were self-reliant, not dictated by anyone.

Trinity calculated what she thought to be the time. She woke around eight-thirty, puttered around the house for a couple of hours while watching the news, then called for her car and drove to Lakeview, maybe taking twenty to thirty minutes, making her arrival at the house somewhere around eleven. Her interaction with Philip went on for ten minutes when he clocked her. How long she was out was up for debate, and the assault, while feeling like forever, probably was a half-hour given the ripping of her shorts, the fight, and the rape—best guess twelve-thirty, which meant it would be hours before anyone noticed her missing.

Philip sat on the bed as though nothing had happened and rambled about his mom, dad, sister, and then Joey. When he mentioned her ex's name, she saw the anger build, his posture change, and his entire essence became something beyond scary. In her calmest, sweetest voice, she tried to soothe the situation. "I'm sorry you're having a hard time and were in jail. It must've been awful."

His eyes shifted to the corners of his eyelids. It was downright frightening, almost demonic. "You have no idea, Miss Trinity Noelle," he growled with a graveled voice. Her heart sank; it wouldn't be long until he began another assault. The look on his face was the same as it had been during the first violation. "You think you're better than me and my family; you're nothing but a whore." Still naked from the waist down, she could tell the monster side of him was ready for another go at her. "Tell me how you like this, you slut." He climbed back on her tiny body and pounded into her with aggression. "Is this how all the other men treat you? My brother was too good for you, and now he's dead because of you." He slammed into her over and over. Yes, he was hurting her, but more than that, he scared her. She planned that if he stuck his penis in her mouth, she would bite it off; she figured he would kill her anyway; at least she would be satisfied with bringing misery to him. Philip slapped her across the face. "You like this? You want me to hurt you, I can, and I will." He swung hard with a closed fist, and the darkness overcame her.

AND THAT'S HOW IT'S DONE

*B*abe was surprised that he hadn't heard from her all day. She usually called at least one time, but nothing. It rolled around to five; he and Gunner headed to her place. She had mentioned something the night before about tidying her room. That was going to be an undertaking, which was more than likely why he hadn't heard from her. They walked in the door and peeked into the bedroom. She had not touched the mess. If she'd gone to the store, he needed more eggs and juice. He called her. It went straight to voice mail before a single ring. He tried again, with the same result, so he texted her.

Are you at the store? If so, please pick up two dozen eggs and some orange juice. Thank you. See you soon.

Moments later, his phone dinged. The message was chilling, triggering a madness he couldn't quench without someone paying the ultimate price.

No, you won't. Soon? How about never?

The lump in his throat couldn't be swallowed down or coughed up. His heart raced as the fire rose inside. He walked out and crossed into the lobby.

"Lexington, you heard from Trinity?"

"No, sir, but I just came on. Jeff hasn't left yet; you can ask him."

Lex stuck his head in the office and asked Jeff, the day manager, to come to the front desk. Babe once again asked, trying to keep his anger undetectable. "Miss Noelle called for her car about ten or ten-thirty this morning, and she hasn't been back since."

"Are any of the family here?"

The manager from the morning skewed his face and looked up as though thinking. "One of the boys might still be here; I'll call." He picked up the phone and punched in a number. "Good evening, Rose Marie. Is Neville or Charles in?" Silence. "Louis or Chance?" Pause. "Good. Mr. Vicarelli would like to speak with him. I'll tell him. Thank you." He pleasantly smiled at Babe. "He'll be with you momentarily, sir."

Chance looked like a male version of Trinity, only bigger and much taller.

Babe had met most of the family members once or twice in passing. "Chance, have you seen your sister? Or know where she might be?"

The man had a puzzled look on his face. "Did you try her at home?"

"Yes, I was just there. I called Trinity with no answer, texted her, and got a disturbing response. Any idea where she might be?"

Chance shrugged, turning up his hands. "Maybe she went shopping or to her favorite coffee shop on Harrison Avenue, then to her house in Lakeview, but that's a long shot. I know sometimes, on her day off, she runs over and picks up the mail. What was the message, if you don't mind me asking?" *Yes, I do mind*, he thought.

"Something a bit awkward, and it didn't sound like her, but I don't want to alarm anyone; she could be playing with me just to get a rise." He forced a smile. His gut told him she was in trouble. "I don't know her address in Lakeview." Chance took out one of his business cards and wrote the address on the back.

"You know Lakeview?" He asked; Babe answered no.

"It's two blocks from Canal Boulevard; take a left off the interstate, or if you're going Orleans—" Babe raised his hand to stop the incessant directions; he'd use his GPS. "My number's on the front if you can't find it."

Babe thanked him and ran to his truck, avoiding other pedestrians.

Traffic in the Quarter and probably everywhere else in the city was slow-moving. He feared every minute was vital. He felt a rolling boil in his blood as it traveled through his body. In the back of his mind, he pictured the guy with the ponytail. If he were the man holding her captive, he'd kick himself for not addressing the threat when he had the chance.

Weaving in and out of the traffic flow with a myriad of blowing horns, he made it to Canal Boulevard and followed the map app. It said he had four minutes left. He punched the accelerator; he had eight blocks to go before turning.

The sun coming through the curtains had a different cast which meant it was getting close to evening. She prayed by this time that Babe would have figured out there was a problem. Her right cheekbone throbbed, and her eye swoll closed. It was hard for her to keep a clear thought; everything seemed jumbled. He'd tied the gag back on her. Philip was ranting to someone, hopefully not in the house, if it was one of his psycho friends or fellow convicts. His footsteps gained volume the closer he came to the bedroom.

"Look, you know the people, I don't. I say we sell her to them, and then they can do what they want. Bro, she'll be a gone pecan, and no one will ever find her." Silence. It sounded like Philip was pacing, still on the phone, as she heard a few uh-huh. "Yeah, I was gonna, but then I got to thinking, maybe I could make a buck or two and sell her." Silence again. "You gonna contact your people and see if they want her? She's hot with a tight little body. She should fetch a pretty penny. Come get her around eleven tonight so neighbors don't see."

Babe drove by her house. There were lights on, but he didn't see her car; maybe it was in the garage at the back of her property. Most homes he noticed didn't even have a garage, mainly driveways and carports, which would have made it easier to tell if she was even there. He made the block, pulled up a few houses down from hers, and then walked down to a gate. His gut was beginning to have doubt. Did he make it in time? Was she even there? Thoughts of how he'd punish whoever had her created a slide show in his brain that most people would have found disturbing; he relished the pictures of it—that is, if anyone had laid a hand on her. The acid purging up the back of his throat confirmed his feelings. He silently opened the gate, forced a window open, and then slinked in silently. His adrenalin surged, and his training instinctively kicked in. Hearing a man's voice echoing through the house, he followed the sound.

Philip entered the bedroom after finishing the phone call. "Awake again, I see. You're looking pretty bad, Trinity. I hope you behave yourself so I don't gotta beat you again" He was smiling so happy and smug, thinking he was in control. "I'm gonna have my fun, but then it's the end of the line for you, so you might as well enjoy it; I know I will." He snickered. "I crack myself up. You ready for another round?" He straddled her again, and just as he was about to plunge inside, she saw Babe quietly come up behind him. He made not one sound; complete silence from him as Philip started his crude, disgusting comments. Babe lifted the man up by the neck in the flash of a moment.

When he saw her beaten face and obviously ravaged body, he decided he couldn't elongate the death with torture; Trinity needed to get to the hospital. He dropped Philip on the floor and stomped on his neck. The crushing sound was audible, then he squatted, and with every ounce of strength, he jerked the man's neck so that his face was nearly on the wrong side of his instantly limp body.

She began to cry. Babe removed the gag and untied her, wrapping his arms around her. He had to get through to her, "I love you, Trinity." He grabbed the top sheet off the bed, covered her, and carried her to his vehicle. "I'll deal with the body later, and no one will ever know." He placed her inside, rounded the truck, and drove away quickly, but not alarmingly like the trip there. He had to consider Trinity's shattered nerves.

Babe drove straight to Touro. She faded in and out from exhaustion or perhaps brain trauma. He wouldn't let her fall asleep in case she had a concussion, so he nudged her anytime her eyes closed. She muttered, "I'm okay." She saw Chance's card in the console and asked, "Chance?" Her petite frame was trembling; he held her hand.

"Yes. I'm gonna let him know I have you." She shook her head and grabbed his phone from a cup holder.

She punched in the numbers, and on the second ring, he picked up. "Chance," the sobs began again, and she handed the phone to Babe.

"On our way to Touro. She said something about Dr. Landry." Chance said he had it from there and would let the family know. "Her ex's brother."

She took the phone back. "He—" her speech studdered in concert with her crying. "R-raped and beat me; I think he broke my nose." He asked her a few more questions. "Please call Dr. Landry and have him meet us at Touro."

Babe took the phone when Chance began speaking again. "No, I don't know Bethany, but if you describe me to her, I'm sure she'll find me. I'm not leaving Trinity's side until one of y'all get to the hospital." His senses were keen as he glanced straight ahead and to the sides, zipping in and out of traffic.

Once Babe's conversation with her brother was over, she touched his hand. "There's something you need to know. Philip has someone coming at eleven. They were gonna sell me. That's why he didn't kill me." She cried with mournful sobs. "He blamed me for Joey's death, but that's BS. He did it to himself."

When they arrived at the hospital, a host of medical personnel met them. Someone tugged on his sleeve, "Are you Babe Vicarelli?" When he turned to look, there was no doubt the person was her sister; she wasn't as tiny, but she was smaller than average and had light eyes instead of Trinity's ebony color. "She looks bad? I saw her at a glance. Thank you for finding her and getting her here." She wiped her nose and eyes. "Oh, my God, I can't believe this has happened. Dr. Landry will be here momentarily."

She started to lose it, "Who would do this? We have to call someone so he won't do it again."

He pointedly said with a severe deadpan face, "He won't, and that's a promise. I have to leave to take care of a few things, ma'am. Please don't leave her alone. She's got a feisty spirit, but right now, she's shattered. If the hospital insists on calling the cops, tell them we already have detectives on it."

Through the glass, he saw Trinity burst into tears. She asked the nurse to get Bethany. Dr. Landry arrived about the same time as the rest of the family members, all thanking Babe for saving her.

"It was mine to do. I'll be back later tonight; y'all are staying with her? Bethany, please keep me apprised. I should be back by midnight." He left.

Driving back to Trinity's house, he started talking aloud, "I hope that motherfucker comes to the house. Anyone that would agree to sell her has to be vile." Perhaps he should call Trey and let him witness how to be the judge, jury, and executioner. Those were roles he was most adept at bringing to fruition, but no, he didn't want to end up on the wrong side of the equation.

Babe parked halfway down the block and went into the house. He purposefully left the door unlocked, giving the bastard a sense of confidence that the plan was coming together. His entire body tingled as the nerves ignited synapses. Once again, the question popped into his mind. *Is it the kill or a means of justice?* One way or another, the asshole was going down. Maybe he wasn't the one to brutally accost her, but he was willing to sell her. Once he'd seen her and known his friend raped her, he'd also have jumped on the wagon. He knew those kinds of men; he'd punished a few. Those thoughts made him seethe even more. *How dare anyone lay a hand on her?*

Babe sat in a chair in her bedroom, waiting. He allowed the energy to pass through his body, not that he needed any boosting in the exterminating business, and viewed this as just another mission. If he let the guy off the hook, there was no doubt he'd assault someone weaker than himself somewhere down the road. Decision made.

Looking down at the dead body, he wished he had the opportunity to torture him as the ponytail guy had tortured her, but given Trinity's condition, he needed quick elimination. It made his heart ache. He knew the brutal capabilities of humans. There was no emotion in relieving this world of the likes of such an animal.

He heard the door open, and footsteps track through the kitchen. "Phil, where you at?"

Babe coughed to disguise his voice. "Here."

The guy followed the voice and walked into the bedroom. He saw blood on the fitted sheet, then noticed his friend's dead body and a looming individual leering at him from a chair. "What the fuck? You killed Phil?" Babe smiled, his gaze drilling through the man. He knew he was a frightening sight and hoped the guy was scared shitless. He knew Trinity must've been confused, scared, and feeling vulnerable. "I don't want no trouble from you. Where's the girl? I got everything lined up. Give me the girl."

Babe stood, and the guy started begging, "Look, I'll leave, forget about the girl. Don't worry, I seen nothing. Phil mighta been dead when you got here. I'll just ease right on out the door." He started backing up.

"Not that easy; don't take another fucking step; you got me? Your friend, Phil, picked the wrong lady to fuck with; ya feeling what I'm saying?" He squinted the corners of his eyes, emphasizing his words. "Your friend raped and beat her mercilessly." Babe slowly shook his head, narrowing his eyes again. "There's always a consequence for every action, and you motherfucker crossed the line. Want me to shoot you? That'd be fast; there are so many ways to kill you. I know countless ways, but go for it; what'll it be? You have a preference? My favorite is a quick snap of the neck. I love that feeling of shattered bones beneath my hands; nothing quite like it. Shooting you or slitting your throat is too messy; nah, a quick torque, and it's over. Plain and simple." He stared at the man. "Ten, nine, eight, seven—"

The man started crying and begging. "Please, mister, you don't gotta do this. I won't tell no one. I didn't do nothin', man, nothin'—" He crumbled in a heap.

"Six, five, four—I'm waiting for you to decide." The man remained collapsed at his feet, but in a quick move, he lunged toward Babe and stabbed the massive man in the forearm, who looked at the wound in his arm, shook his head, and smiled. "Stupid motherfucker." He kicked the knife away, crushed the man's hand under his foot, leaned over still with his weight on the man's crushed hand, and grabbed his head with a quick snap. The ordeal was over. He stepped over the two bodies and retrieved his truck.

Reversing into Trinity's garage, he went back inside, wrapped both bodies in bedding, threw them in the bed of his truck, weighted them down, and took off toward New Orleans East. Jetting off the interstate onto the service road, he drove to a deserted place in the East. It was known as an area for torched vehicles providing the perfect place to blaze a couple of bodies—nobody would notice. It was commonplace.

The return to Touro took twenty minutes; moments later, he made it to the E.R. waiting room, where her family sat pensively.

Her father was the first to approach him. "There are no words to express our gratitude. Is everything handled?"

"Yes, sir." Babe wrinkled his forehead in concern and asked, "Where is she, sir?"

The man had jet-black hair with slivers of silver at his temples. "Dr. Landry just finished with her; her mother and Bethany are with her right now. She's been looking forward to your return; go see my girl. I know she'll be happy to see you. Hey soldier, while you're there, have them check that arm of yours."

"It's just a scratch, sir. No big deal." He'd let the soldier thing go, never soldier, only Marine. The brothers all nodded at him as he passed by them. Undoubtedly, there would be much discussion about the big man.

Through the sliding glass door, he saw her mother doting over her with Bethany at her other side. Bethany signaled for Babe to enter. "Mama, this is Mr. Vicarelli, Trinity's boyfriend."

Babe held out his hand, which she promptly shook, but then wrapped her arms around his waist, eyes filled with tears. "Thank you for finding my baby girl, Mr. Vicarelli. We were scared out of our wits, but you did it. I didn't think I'd ever see her again. To think it was Joey's brother, I know his parents must be destroyed. Even though she divorced their son, they still loved her, but who wouldn't, right?"

"Yes, ma'am."

Trinity pointed, beckoning him. She had tape over her nose and stitches on her eyebrow. Her eye was almost closed from swelling. She was obviously medicated and babbling with slurred, unfiltered words. "I know I look like crap, but Dr. Landry said I wouldn't scar and my nose would be perfect. My vajay's okay, too, if you're curious. He wasn't that—" Her mother cleared her throat.

"Mr. Vicarelli, Trinity has had Demerol; please excuse—"

He politely nodded but stayed silent.

"Babe, thank you for saving me. What happened when you went back?"

He kissed her forehead. "Shh. We'll talk at another time. Right now, just get better."

ALL'S WELL THAT ENDS WELL

*T*hree weeks had passed since the major debacle. While Trinity was an easy girlfriend, she wasn't pushy, demanding, or whiney; he started reconsidering the complications of having someone in his life. There was no doubt that he loved her, but as intense as the love was, so was fear of something happening to her, like the incident with Joey's brother. Nonetheless, he sat at the bar, sipping his glass in hand with a plate of stewed chicken in front of him.

He saw the two detectives enter through the open door, edging their way to him. Trey sat next to him; Trinity automatically brought Max a Diet Coke. "What you having, Detective Kimble?"

"Water with lime, thanks." He looked at Babe. "Haven't seen you in a while, but you came up in a discussion at the precinct. Okay, here's the thing, not that it really matters. Did you, by chance, drop a thumb drive at the station during the spring break ordeal?" Babe started to answer, but Trey put his hand up and stopped him. "Dude, remember, you're very easy to identify."

Babe looked him directly in the eyes, "What if I did? Your point?"

"Why? How?" Babe put his hand up to stop him.

"Some things are best left a mystery, Detective. Who knows, that could have been a music recording or beach snapshots. The thing is, as you so put it, does it really matter? The answer there is no." Babe sipped his Glenlivet and winked at Trey over the top of his tumbler. "I have a question for you. Knowing what you know about the crime on the streets, how do you stay sane knowing your wife is out there? Don't you worry?" Babe cleared his throat. "You can't protect her twenty-four-seven, right?"

Trey pursed his lips, bowed his head, then looked back at the giant. "Blind faith. You got religion? Ya know, trust in God? If you don't, maybe you should try to get some; it'll do you good. There are bad people everywhere, and I'm sure to some you're no picnic in the park—probably more like a fuckin' nightmare." He paused, "Babe, would you consider yourself a good guy or a bad guy?"

The story continues, and for a Sneak Peek of The Identity Lie, Book 2 of Fit The Crime series, turn the page! Remember, if you liked The Innocence Lie, please write a brief review on the site of purchase. Make sure to visit my website, corinnearrowood.com, like, and register for the newsletter to get the latest scoop on new releases and freebies.

FIT THE CRIME

The Identity Lie

QUESTIONS AND CONSIDERATIONS

*T*he feeling of uncertainty bubbled from his stomach to his soul. Trey's question held gravity in his heart. Was he a good guy who needed to fix the wrongs of the world or a bad guy who reveled in the thrill and adrenalin rush of cold-blooded stalking and killing? And what of this God thing?

Where was God when he hid in the corner of his closet, listening to his father beat the living shit out of his mother? As a boy, he prayed for invisibility with hands clamped around his ears. Where was God once his father turned his menacing violence on him, only ten years old, with nightly ruthless beatings? He'd cried out to this supposed Creator called God. Concerning the horror and atrocities of combat, he knew that was part of what he signed up for, so he gave the God entity a pass on the brutalities of war. There certainly was no sign of goodness there, but that was okay; one wouldn't expect it. His biggest question was, where was God when Trinity was beaten and raped? There were too many twisted fucks out there to claim there was an all-knowing, all-powerful, all-loving God. His grandparents were the only people who truly cared about him as a child. His grandmother would tell him, "Babe, God don't like ugly, and He smites evil." At the time, he thought he best not be ugly or evil, but had he become that man?

He turned to face the detective. "Trey, I have way too many disputes to believe the story of a loving God. To answer your question, am I a good or bad guy? Maybe ask your God. I've had to do horrible things in my life, but none of it was of my choosing. I suppose I could have looked the other way, but the Marines drilled it into me that it was mine to fix. If there is a God, He's responsible for me being the man I am. He and the Marines." He took a gulp rather than a slight touch to the lips of his tumbler of Glenlivet. "Oh, and to be sure, I've been some motherfucker's nightmare; you can take that one to the bank."

Trey stood and patted Babe on the shoulder. "Ya got some soul searching to do, my friend." Trey looked at Max, the older detective. "You leaving, Padna?"

"Nah, gonna have some of the nightly special. Looks like stewed chicken? Tastes good, I bet." He looked at the big guy, "No worries, Babe, I'm not going to browbeat you like some fuckin wife. My partner's sometimes too tight-assed. You are who you are, right? I bet you've seen some nasty shit dealing with dem Talibanese. Sick motherfuckers."

"On that note, y'all," Trey smiled. "I'm outta here and heading home to my beautiful wife. Pregnancy gives her a special glow." He turned and walked out of Louie's Tap.

Max raised his chin and eyebrows as he pointed a finger toward Trinity, then winked with a grin. "Hey, darlin, how 'bout a draft and stewed chicken?"

"Coming your way, Detective."

Babe watched Trinity as she moved to the tap. The sway of her hips and natural sultry ways electrified him, with the spark jumping from his eyes to his heart, igniting a flame below his belt. Since the rape, she'd been a little standoffish and undemonstrative in the bed, all the while claiming she was okay. He felt the difference in her kiss and noticed her usual playful responsiveness turn to stone with his touch. Before, she sizzled with sexual longing, taking every opportunity to climb his body. Trinity was usually the instigator of the over-the-top encounters. His cock was her obsession, not that he ever complained.

Perhaps his girl had the same thing they said he had, PTSD. Maybe she needed help. Just because he wasn't going to be defined by some alphabet diagnosis, maybe her ordeal was a different kettle of fish. If one were to look at the scenarios, the Marines trained him for the issues of combat; no one gets trained for a brutal personal violation. He thought back to when he killed her captor; a quick death was certainly not the ideal outcome. Perhaps slow dismemberment might have felt better, or tying him to a post and watching the alligators slowly consume him. Either way, the fucker would have been terrified and suffered an excruciating demise. A fast death was nothing compared to the pain and agony he put Trinity through.

Max dove into the stewed chicken and rice when placed in front of him. It was as though he hadn't eaten in days. "Shit, they got some good food here. Who woulda thought? I sure wouldn't until I saw you with your nightly dinners, big man." Babe couldn't help but think watching him eat was one of the most unappealing things imaginable, making even the hungriest person lose their appetite. He made an almost grunting sound, a combination of nasal snorts and guttural grunts, defined as disgusting. Max was a nice guy with an astute detective mind; he just wasn't bestowed with the best social graces.

Babe cast his gaze around the perimeter of the bar, a habit he had instilled in him by the Corps. Always be ready. It was one of those nights where thankfully, no one was acting the fool pissing him off. His eyes shifted towards an open door. "Get the fuck out," Babe exclaimed with a smile. His usual pan expression, void of emotion, lit up when a man, maybe five-nine, walked in the door. There was no mistaking the face of his ally, one he'd seen so many times. Babe stood. The man entering smiled with a glint in his eyes as he approached the big guy. They man-hugged, patting the other's back.

"Chop, what brings you to New Orleans?" Babe turned to the detective. "Max, this is Tim Faraday, but we all called him Chop. He's the best helo pilot to take to the sky and by far the gutsiest." He put his arm around Chop's shoulder with a pat. There was an excitement in Babe that Max had never seen. The most he'd ever witnessed was an upturn of his mouth or a slight chuckle. "This man flew without orders or better judgment to grab our scrambling asses from a terrorist compound on more than one occasion. This one time, after taking out the leaders, we mowed most of the foot soldiers down, but a few combatants hid with rocket launchers, trying to light up the copter. This guy," he flicked his thumb at the pilot, "he's got stones of steel."

To look at the man, he seemed a regular Joe. Average stature with hair long enough to be tied up in a knot and sporting a long unkempt beard, the man didn't seem to have an impressive bone in his body.

Babe's military buddy coughed out a laugh, "A lot of hot air. Vicarelli was the shit. You're still one of the strongest motherfuckers I've ever seen. I see you're still working out." Babe tried to include Max in the conversation, but it was evident he was the third wheel and had nothing to add except a few 'no kidding' and 'scary shit' comments.

Babe looked his friend square in the eyes. "So, Chop, what are you doing here? Home's where? San Antonio, if my memory serves me right."

His friend arched an eyebrow. "Still drinking scotch, I see. I'll have one of them." Babe signaled Trinity, ordered his buddy's drink, briefly introduced them, then turned his attention to his pilot friend, who continued to speak. "You remember my wife, Hadley? We moved from San Antone to Pensacola to be closer to her mom. We got a kid now, Jagger. Remember she was pregnant on one of our last ops? He's over a year now."

Still grinning, Babe responded, "Excellent. I remember, in fact, we all thought she was too good-looking for your ass. Where is she? I'm guessing she didn't let you loose to roam the French Quarter on your own." He noticed a sinking look on his friend's face. "Y'all still together, brother?" he waited while Chop gathered his thoughts. Babe told his friend, pointing to Trinity, "That's my lady. I never had one, and well, she's the real deal—smokin' hot, intelligent, funny, and doesn't take shit from anyone; tiny as she is, you wouldn't believe how fast she puts people in their place. I wouldn't cross her. Nope." Babe smiled as he watched her.

Max called Trinity over and paid his bill. "Best damn chicken ever, girl. Better than my momma's cooking, but don't never tell her dat! Take care of my friend here." He patted Babe on the shoulder. Trinity smiled and nodded. "G'night, darlin'. See ya soon," Max raised his chin with a guy nod to Babe and his pilot friend. "You two behave."

Babe watched Max leave, then turned to Chop and asked, "So, you clammed up pretty tight when I asked about Hadley. What gives?"

The guy rubbed his brow with his head held down toward his chest. "I dunno; she's gone. No word, no note, no nothin'. I left for work; she left to drop the kid at daycare. I called her a few times durin' the day like we always do, but no answer. The next thing I know, I get a call from the daycare telling me I needed to pick up my son. I called her work, and they said she hadn't come in or called. It's weird." He looked Babe in the eyes, "Hadley and me been together since high school. We barely argued and even talked about maybe another kid. Something ain't right, Vic. I called the police, but they said they can't do nothing for twenty-four hours at least. The cops said all kinds of things, like maybe she split with another man; it's all bullshit. I'm telling you something's happened to her. I feel it in my bones."

Hearing Chop talk about his missing wife transported Babe back to the incident when Trinity's ex-brother-in-law attacked, raped, and nearly killed her, forming a lump in his throat and a swell of angered fear in his gut. Just remembering that day rushed the dread to the forefront of his mind. His stomach twisted as his heart raced. He'd never forget that horrible pain trapped in his chest. He felt for his friend. "So you came looking for me? Why? How'd you even know where I was or how to find me? I'm not sure how or if I can help, but I'll do whatever I can, brother. You gotta know something." Babe barely wet his lips as he put the glass to his mouth. His mind was rambling, and mid-sip, he looked over and asked again, "How'd you know where to find me?"

The man sat still, staring into his beer. "Remember Vallas?" Babe nodded with a set jaw. "He told me you came to New Orleans; something about maybe going into the VA. That's where I checked first. When you weren't there, I figured you'd try to get some work, and I know it sounds dumb, but I went to the church over by the square and prayed. I asked God to lead me to you, and then I just walked. I landed here. Haven't a clue, but I did. Man, I don't know what you can do if anything, but I needed a broad shoulder to lean on."

Babe ordered another Glenlivet; Trinity squared her eyes and cocked her head. "Babe Vicarelli, you okay, ma man?" He nodded with a half-hearted smile.

He looked at Chop and asked, "Where you staying tonight? Need a place to crash? I don't know what I can do, but give me all y'all's information, including her phone number. I also want the sister's number, husband's name, contact info, and address. Include Hadley's work number and address." He tapped his index finger on the bar top.

Trinity came straight away with his drink. "Okay, so I see that tap, tap, tap of your finger; what's up? You got that look, Babe." His eyes shifted to hers with a pensive stare. "Big guy, I can see your mind racing. Wanna talk?" It was the first time since the day of horror that she felt authentic and not encapsulated in an emotional tomb. He took a long draw on his drink, staring at her over the rim. She flashed a smile that sent an involuntary shiver through his body. One of the patrons banged his mug on the bar; she winked at him. "That's my cue."

Babe turned toward Chop. His stare was more of a glare; something didn't feel right. He and Chop had been through a lot together, and he couldn't fathom him lying about his missing wife. They'd seen too much to lie to each other. *Why me? What the hell can I do?* "You talking straight with me, Faraday? You know nothing and have no idea what could've gone down or where she might have gone?" He took a mouthful of Glenlivet and sucked in through his teeth; he savored the flavor, all the while thinking. *You didn't answer my question.*

Chop was quick to respond. "No, man. Look, I gotta get back to Pensacola for work; I had hoped you might be willing to help."

214

"Yeah, well, write down everything I told you to; I'm hitting the head." What whirled through his mind was that when Trinity went missing, he didn't give a fuck about anything but getting her back. Something felt off, and it bugged him that Chop sought him out. Once again, why?

Returning from the restroom, he asked again, purposefully towering over the man, trying to induce apprehension. "I-I got it all here, everything." Chop's voice stammered.

"One more time, Faraday, why'd you need to find me? No fucking bullshit."

Chop stood and braced himself with a rigid posture. "Because you always seem to figure things out. You see the invisible, hear the silent; you got some extra sense the rest of us slobs don't have, that's why. If you want me the fuck out of here, just say the word. I thought I could count on you." The man looked him straight in the eyes. "I don't know where she is, and I'm worried."

Go to your favorite online retailer for The Identity Lie, Book 2 of the Fit The Crime Series, or my website, corinnearrowood.com. If you like it, please leave a review; they count.

A Special Note

It's important, so here it is again.

The statistics of PTSD are staggering. Many of our Marines and soldiers come home entrenched in the horrors they experienced and the nightmares they cannot escape. If you know one of our heroes that might be suffering from PTSD, contact Wounded Warrior Project, National Center for PTSD, VA Caregiver Support Line at 888-823-7458.

Many Thanks...

To my loving husband, Doug, who stands by me through thick and thin, you're the best. Thanks for the help on rules of law and police procedures, but primarily for listening to my mish-mash of incoherent ideas and stories made up of rambling, nonsensical descriptions. I know I jump from characters and scenes without rhyme or reason—my mind silently fills in the blanks while you try to piece together what I'm saying.

To our children and grandchildren, who are a constant source of inspiration—I love your unbridled enthusiasm and encouragement—thank you for your loving words and kind thoughts. I'm *really* not all that; thanks for loving me.

To Paige Brannon Gunter, my forever editor, gifted with an honest but caring eye for detail, carefully observing plot continuity, and readily making suggestions to enhance the story, you're my go-to girl.

To G. Lee, who flags my dialect and comma splices like there's no tomorrow, and yes, I write like I speak, which is an absolute disaster sometimes.

To K.N. Faulk for pointers in character development—I know you love them all—almost as much as I do.

To Julie Agan for all the information about things only a Marine might know, or should I say, the mom of a Marine. Your help has been outstanding.

To Cyrus Wraith Walker for his innovative designs and his patience with my crazy quirks, lack of technical skills, and indecisiveness. You're the design guru, and I know I ask you to create from scattered ideas.

To our men and women in the armed forces and their families, thank you for your service and sacrifice.

To you, my readers, thank you for spreading the word and supporting me in my writing endeavors. Thank you, thank you, thank you. *As always, I wish you love.*

In lieu of a proper bibliography—

The abundance of Marine YouTube videos, articles, and interviews is fantastic. After many hours and months of research, I learned much. I have always appreciated and felt gratitude for our military services, but thanks to my Marine, Captain Babe Vicarelli, I have been pushed to learn even more. The information on PTSD is vast and ever-increasing. The research was eye-opening and heart-wrenching. Words of thanks can never be enough. I must thank again, Julie Agan, who offered to be a beta reader. As a mother of a Marine, she has been a plethora of information from a different angle than my other sources.

Other Books by the Author

Censored Time Trilogy
A Quarter Past Love (Book I)
Half Past Hate (Book II)
A Strike Past Time (Book III)

Friends Always
A Seat at the Table
PRICE TO PAY
The Presence Between

Be On the Look Out for...
Leave No Doubt

Fit the Crime Series
The Identity Lie (Coming end of 2023)
The Impossible Lie (Coming in 2024)

Visit my website, corinnearrowood.com, and register to win freebies
Reviews are appreciated

About The Author

According to Me

Local girl to the core. There's nowhere on earth like New Orleans! I am still very much in love with my husband of over thirty-five years, handsome hunk, Doug. I'm a Mom, Nana, and great-Nana. Favorite activities include hanging with the hubs, watching grandkids' games and activities, hiking, reading, and traveling. I am addicted to watching The Premier League, particularly Liverpool—The real football—married to a Brit; what can I say? Living my best life writing and playing with my characters and their stories. I'm a Girl Raised In The South (G.R.I.T.) Perhaps the most important thing about me is my faith in God. All of my characters, thus far, have opened a closed heart to an open one filled with Light.

According to the Editors

Born and raised in the enchanting city of New Orleans, the author lends a flavor of authenticity to her books and the characters that come to life in stories of love, lust, betrayal, and murder. Her vivid style of storytelling transports the reader to the very streets of New Orleans with its unique sights, smells, and intoxicating culture.